GINGERBREAD
DANGER

T0361497

Also by Amanda Flower

The Amish Candy Shop Mysteries

The Amish Matchmaker Mysteries

The Katharine Wright Mysteries

Amanda Flower

GINGERBREAD DANGER

Kensington Publishing Corp.
www.kensingtonbooks.com

KENSINGTON BOOKS are published by

Kensington Publishing Corp.
900 Third Avenue
New York, NY 10022

Copyright © 2024 by Amanda Flower

All rights reserved. No part of this book may be reproduced in any form or by any means without the prior written consent of the Publisher, excepting brief quotes used in reviews.

To the extent that the image or images on the cover of this book depict a person or persons, such person or persons are merely models, and are not intended to portray any character or characters featured in the book.

This book is a work of fiction. Names, characters, businesses, organizations, places, events, and incidents either are the product of the author's imagination or are used fictitiously. Any resemblance to actual persons, living or dead, events, or locales is entirely coincidental.

If you purchased this book without a cover you should be aware that this book is stolen property. It was reported as "unsold and destroyed" to the Publisher and neither the Author nor the Publisher has received any payment for this "stripped book."

All Kensington titles, imprints, and distributed lines are available at special quantity discounts for bulk purchases for sales promotion, premiums, fund-raising, educational, or institutional use.

Special book excerpts or customized printings can also be created to fit specific needs. For details, write or phone the office of the Kensington Sales Manager: Attn.: Sales Department. Kensington Publishing Corp., 900 Third Avenue, New York, NY 10022. Phone: 1-800-221-2647.

KENSINGTON and the KENSINGTON COZIES teapot logo Reg US Pat. & TM Off.

First Printing: November 2024
ISBN: 978-1-4967-4375-6

ISBN: 978-1-4967-4376-3 (ebook)

10 9 8 7 6 5 4 3 2 1

Printed in the United States of America

In memory of Reepicheep Thomas Flower-Seymour.
You cannot be replaced.

ACKNOWLEDGMENTS

Thank you as always to my readers who have fallen in love with the Amish village of Harvest and its residents from both the Amish Candy Shop Mysteries and the Amish Matchmaker Mysteries. Bailey, Aiden, and, of course, Jethro, are grateful, too.

I would also like to thank my wonderful agent, Nicole Resciniti, and my awesome editor, Alicia Condon, for their continued support of this series and of me. Thanks to my publicist, Larissa Ackerman, who works tirelessly for all of Kensington's cozy authors.

Gratitude to reader Kimra Bell for her sharp eye during revisions, and love and gratitude to my kind husband, David Seymour, for his unwavering love and support.

Finally, I thank God for allowing me to write for so many years and most of all for the first Christmas that changed the world. Merry Christmas!

CHAPTER ONE

If you have never had to clean taffy off a pig, consider yourself lucky. I wasn't one of the lucky ones.

Jethro, my future mother-in-law's polka-dotted pot-bellied pig, was covered from his snout to the tip of his curly tail in sticky gingerbread taffy. He smelled like an exploded gingerbread house. Not that I had ever smelled such a thing, but I could imagine this would be the scent. The little pig looked up at me with his big brown eyes in a clear call for help and maybe just a hint of blame. If I had not brought him to Swissmen Candyworks, my candy factory tucked away in Ohio's scenic Amish Country, he would not be in this predicament.

In my defense, I hadn't had much of a choice in the matter. My future mother-in-law had foisted the pig on me at the last second. She'd said that the ladies of her church were having a present-wrapping party in the church's Fellowship Hall and Jethro would be in the way. It seemed to me that Juliet always thought Jethro would be in the way when it came to church activities.

While Jethro made his plea, instrumental Christmas music played over the sound system—the holiday was just a week away. "Rockin' Around the Christmas Tree" was on heavy repeat as it was my assistant, Charlotte Little's favorite Christmas song now that she'd left the Amish faith. I wasn't sure what that said about her taste in music in her post-bonnet days.

Swissmen Candyworks had officially opened just before Halloween. The opening date was firm in my mind because I wanted to take full advantage of all the candy-loving holidays that rolled in at the end of the year: Halloween, Thanksgiving, and Christmas. Christmas was the busiest time for the Candyworks and for the candy shop, which I co-owned with my grandmother. Amid everything that I had to do, I certainly didn't have time to wash a pig—or watch a pig, for that matter—but here we were.

My very first concern was that Jethro might be hurt. Molten taffy was nothing to mess around with. The taffy before it is pulled had to reach 254 degrees Fahrenheit. That was hot enough for second- or even first-degree burns if a person, or in this case a pig, wasn't careful.

Thankfully, the taffy he had gotten himself tangled up in was cool enough to work with, but unfortunately, it was still warm enough to be terribly sticky. Not to mention he smelled like the inside of a gingerbread house, and the scent mingled with the aroma of the lavender essential oil that Juliet insisted he needed to have massaged into his hooves each morning to keep him healthy. Have I mentioned that Jethro is spoiled? No one was rubbing essential oils into my feet, that was for certain.

I brushed my ponytail over my shoulder. The last thing I needed was taffy in my curls. "I don't have the slightest clue how you get into these situations, Jethro. It's like you seek out trouble, but only when you're in my charge. Would you do anything like this when you were with Juliet?"

He looked up at me with mournful brown eyes, pleading with me not to be mad. I sighed. There wasn't much I could do to withstand that look. It got me every time. It was also the reason I was pigsitting . . . again. Both he and Juliet had mastered that pitiful expression.

Behind me, I heard what I thought was a mouse squeak, but it was actually a person. Lida Lantz, one of the many new hires in the candy factory, was standing at her stainless-steel worktable with a look of abject terror in her eyes.

"Lida, are you all right?" I asked.

My question spurred her from squeaking to speaking, which I was most grateful for.

"I'm so sorry, Bailey. I just don't know what happened. I was cutting and wrapping taffy. I didn't even know Jethro was in the room. I never would have let him come in here. You said he was only allowed in the gift shop and lobby area. I'm very *gut* at following rules; I can assure you it's true." She took a breath. "I only knew he was there when I heard the crash. I would never let him in the candy packing room."

"Nor should you." I smiled to soften my words. "But Jethro does all sorts of things that he's not allowed to do. He gets away with it because he is so darn cute— and believe me, he knows how to wield his cuteness to his best advantage."

She shook from the top of her prayer cap to her black sneakers. Lida was a sixteen-year-old Amish girl who wore a plain purple dress, white apron, sensible shoes, and a hairnet over her white prayer cap. She was very pretty, with red hair and green eyes, but unfortunately, she also appeared to be in a constant state of nervousness. She vibrated with tension. I hated to think of how Jethro's action might send her over the edge.

She'd begun working at the factory in November and I still hadn't been able to put her at ease, so I tried to give her tasks that didn't require her to deal with the public much.

That morning, I had set her on the task of measuring, cutting, and wrapping taffy. She was currently wrapping peppermint taffy while the gingerbread cooled, but now that most of the gingerbread taffy was on Jethro's back, I doubted we would be putting out that flavor at the Candy Land Experience.

Just thinking about the Candy Land Experience threatened to give me a migraine. In truth, it was a great idea to attract more tourists to Harvest during the holiday season, but just like washing a pig, it wasn't something that I had time to add to my overflowing to-do list.

She tucked a strand of red hair behind her ear. Her nose was bright pink and her eyes shimmered with barely restrained tears. "I'm so sorry this happened. Is he hurt? Please tell me that he's not hurt. I could not live with myself if I hurt the pastor's wife's pig."

I smiled at her, doing my very best to put the young woman at ease. "He's not hurt. He just smells like a gingerbread house. There are much worse things he could—and has—gotten into. Most of those don't smell as nice."

"You're sure?" Tears welled again in her eyes.

"I'm positive. Don't beat yourself up. Jethro is Jethro. There is no other pig in the world that gets into half as much trouble as he does. I should have told you he was in the building and to keep the door shut while you were working in case he wandered in. He has a snout for sweets, and if he smells something tasty, there is no stopping him. He must have slipped out of the lobby when the salesladies weren't looking. I can't blame them. The shop is busy today and they are setting up for the gingerbread house competition. Besides, it's not their job to sell candy *and* keep an eye on my future mother-in-law's pig."

I thought about what my fiancé, Aiden Brody, would think when I told him of Jethro's latest adventure. He was constantly telling me to say no to his mother when it came to pigsitting. That was easy for him to say. He was her son. I was the almost daughter-in-law. There was a big difference.

Lida relaxed a little. "I still feel responsible. He could have been horribly burned if the taffy was just a few degrees hotter."

I nodded. "That is a concern. I will have to put more limitations on Jethro when he visits the candy factory, especially this week."

I took a deep breath as I thought about the week ahead. Between Christmas orders, the factory still finding its stride, the Candy Land Experience, and my parents coming to visit for the holidays, I was about to lose my mind.

Of those events, the one I was most nervous about was the Candy Land Experience, which was the brainchild of community organizer Margot Rawlings. Margot never met a theme party that she didn't like, so in addition to the traditional living nativity that Harvest had on the square every Christmas, she was staging a life-size Candy Land game that families could play day and night. Swissmen Sweets and Swissmen Candyworks would stock it with sweet treats at the candy stations along the game board, but because Margot was organizing it, I was afraid of what else she might want me to do for the event. There was always something more when it came to Margot.

"You're impossible," I said to the pig.

At my feet, Jethro snuffled, as if he didn't like the sound of that.

I shook my finger at him. "Don't you even start. Look at yourself. You're a mess. Now I must give you a bath, and neither one of us is going to enjoy it."

Jethro licked at the taffy on the tip of his snout.

"Do you want me to clean him up?" Lida asked in a timid voice. "I feel so responsible. It's the least I can do."

I couldn't ask her to do that. Washing a pig wasn't the most enjoyable chore in the world, but I was the one who'd brought Jethro to the factory in the first place. It was as much my fault for his current state as Jethro. Besides, this would not be my first pig scrub down, but it was certainly the first involving taffy. I had no idea how I was going to get it out of his hair.

Contrary to popular belief, pigs aren't bald. They have coarse hair all over their bodies. In some breeds, you can see the hair better than others. In the case of Jethro, you had to look very closely, but it stood out more when encrusted in taffy. He looked as if he had thin spikes all over his portly form.

I shook my head. "No, it's my fault he's here. Juliet asked me to keep him with me while she and the church ladies had their gift-wrapping party. He probably would have been better off at the church, but she was afraid he'd run off with the baby Jesus statue from the nativity or something equally scandalous if left to his own devices."

Lida's eyes went wide, and I remembered that the sixteen-year-old had not been working for me for very long. She didn't know my long history with Jethro and his questionable behavior.

And thinking about what I'd said, I was sure the idea of absconding with baby Jesus was shocking to her.

I sighed.

"You did nothing wrong," I repeated for her benefit. "I should have left him at Swissmen Sweets with my *grossmaami*. He knows how the candy shop works and is less likely to get into this kind of trouble. Plus, he's much better behaved for my *grossmaami* than he ever is for me."

She nodded, but her brow was still furrowed in concern. She went back to her task of cutting the pulled taffy into bite-size pieces and wrapping those pieces in wax paper. She seemed hesitant while she worked. She measured each piece of taffy precisely with a ruler. At this rate, she would be lucky to make one hundred pieces in her eight-hour shift. However, I reminded myself her boss was watching her. Me. That would make anyone nervous and take extra care not to make a mistake. She would speed up when she was more comfortable with the task, I was sure.

"I'll take the pig and wash him up. If you could clean the floor and throw away all the taffy that fell on it, that would be a great help."

She set her knife on the table. "Yes, of course."

I smiled at her. "*Danki.*" I picked up Jethro and held him out in front of me so he wouldn't get taffy on my clothes.

He didn't even fight me. I believed he regretted Taffygate already.

Before I left the room, I said, "Oh, I remember why I came here. Do you know where I can find Zeph? I need him to clean the front walk again since it snowed."

She jumped. "Zeph?"

I cocked my head. "Yes, your brother Zeph."

"I—I don't know. I got a ride into the village with a friend. I—I don't know where he is."

I pressed my lips together. "All right. I'm sure he will turn up soon."

She returned her attention to her taffy. "*Ya*, he always does."

CHAPTER TWO

"Now, add the peppermint extract to the fudge and stir." Dressed for Christmas, Charlotte stood in front of her class. She wore a green sweater, white jeans, and her red hair was held back from her face by a wreath-shaped barrette. "Just a few drops are enough. You don't want to overdo it. Too much peppermint can really be a shock to your taste buds."

She walked around the room and nodded as each student carefully dropped peppermint extract into their white fudge mixture. I knew the next step would be adding food coloring and making a swirly design on top of the fudge with a toothpick. I knew this because the fudge she was teaching the seven ladies in the class to make was my old family recipe and our top-seller this time of year.

Although we make all sorts of candies at Swissmen Sweets, and now the Candyworks, too, fudge was the most popular. I believed when people came to visit

Amish Country, eating authentic Amish fudge was always one of the things to do on their vacation. We were happy to sell it to them.

Before Charlotte walked to the next station to advise the student, she looked up and saw me holding out Jethro in front of me as if he was an infant with a stinky diaper. I then realized the distinct gingerbread color of the taffy might lead her to think it was something else entirely.

"Oh! Bailey! Did you come to observe the class?"

I shook my head. "Just passing through. Jethro got into a bit of trouble, as you can see, and I need to clean him up."

"Oh, Jethro!" a women with short black hair cried out as if she was seeing a celebrity on the Hollywood Walk of Fame. "Can we get a picture with him?"

"What is that on him?" another woman asked in a disgusted voice. She was clearly having diaper thoughts.

"Gingerbread taffy. Don't worry, nothing is hurt but his dignity," I said.

Jethro looked back at me as if he were questioning that.

"I want a picture, too," another voice rang out.

I could feel the cell phones begin to point at me. I turned my body to shield Jethro from their snaps.

"Let me get him cleaned up first and we will be happy to do a photo shoot with all of you. This is not the kind of publicity Juliet would want about her pig on social media. As she says, he has an image to uphold."

"Of course he does. He's the most famous pig since Babe," the woman with black hair said. "Don't you agree, Jenny?" She nodded at the woman in the station next to her, Jenny Patterson, a fiftyish woman with short blond hair and cat's-eye glasses that she wore around her neck on a chain.

Of all the women in the class, Jenny was the only one I had met before, and that was because she was the president of the Harvest Garden Club. Jenny had been a regular at the candymaking classes since they started. She never missed a class and always brought a friend or two with her. In fact, this class was made up entirely of members of her garden club. I was grateful for that. The best way to spread the word about the business was word of mouth, and Jenny was doing an excellent job of it.

The Garden Club was sponsoring the Candy Land Experience on the square, so Jenny and I had had countless conversations about the types of candy to offer at the event and where the different candy stations would go.

To keep the game fun and lessen the competitive aspect of it, on certain blocks throughout the life-size board, regardless of whether the player was winning or losing, they would get a piece of candy made right here at the factory. It was a great way to advertise my new business venture and to keep everyone playing in the Christmas spirit.

"What happened to him?" Jenny Patterson asked with anxiety in her voice. "Is he hurt? He has to be at his very best for the live nativity. We can't lose another participant!"

"You lost a participant?" Charlotte asked.

"Yes, the donkey we had lined up went into labor. Can you believe it? Whoever heard of a donkey having a baby in the middle of winter? I blame it on her owner for not scheduling that better."

I decided not to make a comment on the donkey situation. I guessed that between Jenny and Margot, who undoubtedly had had a few choice words to say about the absent donkey, enough had been said on the subject.

"Jethro's fine. He's just had a little run-in with a batch of *cool* gingerbread taffy." I emphasized the word "cool" so that the class members wouldn't be concerned that Jethro had been burned.

"At least he will smell like Christmas," one of the women said.

"He does," I agreed. "And I think I will for the rest of the day, too."

"Bailey, how are you faring with all the robberies happening in Harvest?" the woman with short hair asked. "Are you afraid your shop or even the Candyworks will be next?"

I wrinkled my nose. I didn't ask her what she was talking about. I knew all too well. Over the last month, a number of the Amish businesses and even a few of the most prominent Amish homes had been broken into. Whenever a home or business was hit, everything of value was taken.

"I heard the yarn shop on Apple Street was robbed last night," she said. "Doesn't that strike a little too close to home for you? Your candy shop isn't too far from there."

It *was* too close to home, and what made me even more anxious was knowing that my *maami* lived alone in the apartment over the candy shop. It was the first time she had lived alone in her entire life. My grandfather had lived with her most of her life, and when he passed away, I had moved in. Then, when I moved out, Charlotte lived with her for several years. When Charlotte married Deputy Little during the summer and moved in with him, Maami was left living alone for the very first time. She insisted that she was doing well, but the robberies had me worried.

I was so concerned that I'd asked her to move into my little rental house a few blocks from the candy shop until the perpetrators were caught, but she refused.

The candy shop had been her home for over fifty years; she wasn't going to leave it now. However, with one of the robberies so close, I might have to take more drastic measures to keep her safe.

"I hadn't heard about the yarn shop. Is the owner all right?"

"From what I've heard no one was hurt, just like in all the other break-ins," the woman with dark hair said. "But I can't see that always being the case. One of these times, the culprits are going to pick the wrong house or business and there will be a confrontation that will end very badly."

I shivered at her prediction.

"Why hasn't your fiancé found out who is behind all of this?" Jenny wanted to know. "How hard can it be to find the person who is robbing all these Amish businesses and homes?"

My back stiffened. Aiden was the sheriff of Holmes County. He had been appointed sheriff by the county commissioners when the last sheriff's career ended in disgrace. I had learned rather quickly after his appointment that county citizens came to me with their problems in the hope that I would pass them along to Aiden, and he would ultimately fix them. As much as I wanted to help, being Aiden's carrier pigeon had gotten old really fast.

"Aiden is doing his best," I said. "Believe me, he wants this case to be closed as much as everyone else in the village does. But there are a few special circumstances involved."

"What special circumstances?" Jenny wanted to know. "A robbery is a robbery."

I bit my lip because I knew Aiden wouldn't want me to say any more about it. However, if I were at liberty to speak, I would have pointed out that, indeed, all the robberies had occurred at Amish homes and businesses. None of those places had security systems or cameras, and every place was hit in the middle of the night when no one was there. There were no witnesses, and the criminal or criminals were smart. No physical evidence was left behind. No hair. No fingerprints. No nothing.

I kept my lips sealed. It was time to get on with my task. Jethro was getting very heavy in my outstretched arms. He didn't look particularly comfortable either.

The dark-haired woman narrowed her eyes. "What do you know that you're not telling us? We live in this

village, too. We have a right to know what is happening
to our friends and neighbors."

"Truly, I don't know much at all," I said, hoping she
would let me leave it at that. I turned to Charlotte.
"Have you seen Zeph Lantz? He was supposed to be
here an hour ago. I need him to clear the walk."

"He's out there now. I saw him go by the window
with the shovel," Charlotte said.

I wrinkled my nose. "I must have missed him. I'm
going to get Jethro cleaned up and then drop him off at
Swissmen Sweets before meeting my parents at the
inn." I did my very best to keep my voice neutral as I
said this.

Charlotte cocked her head. She knew just how nervous I was about my parents' visit. It was only the second time they had come to Holmes County since I'd
moved here years ago. I was dreading what they would
say when they saw the factory. They lived in Connecticut in the house where I had grown up, but they
didn't spend much time there. As they were both retired, they traveled the world, going everywhere from
Paris to Bali. They had been to so many countries at
this point, I had lost count.

Now that they had been to so many faraway exotic
places, I could just imagine what they would think
when they returned to Harvest, the village where they
both grew up, met, fell in love, and fled. My father had
grown up Amish and my mother had grown up
English. Dad left the faith for my mother. It was still a
sour spot with my grandmother, but as she had said . . .
if my parents hadn't made that choice, I never would

have been born. She called me the best thing to come from my father's decision.

Charlotte cleared her throat. "As for Jethro, use vegetable oil to clean him up," she suggested. "When my little sister got taffy in her hair, my mother used vegetable oil and it worked like a charm."

"That's good to know. I'd better get to it before it hardens completely."

I took Jethro into the laundry room, which included a stationary tub. This was the best place to give him a vegetable oil bath; it was far too cold outside. The outdoor temperature hovered just below freezing, which was typical for this time of year.

I put Jethro in the tub and told him to stay—whatever good my saying that to the pig would do—and went into the massive supply closet adjacent to the laundry room.

I found a gallon jug of vegetable oil with no trouble at all. Charlotte had organized the closet, and it was a thing of beauty. Everything had a place, and everything was identified with white labels in her perfect penmanship.

I took the vegetable oil, a scrub brush, and a towel back into the laundry room and set to work. I poured vegetable oil on the pig's back and neck—that was where the worst of the sticky taffy was lodged.

Jethro shook his head and oil went flying all over the sink, the tiled wall, and me. I spat some out of my mouth and grabbed a scrub brush. It was time to just dig in and get the job done. Jethro didn't fight me at all while I scrubbed the taffy out of his hair. He knew I meant business.

After the taffy was out, I washed him with antibacterial soap, rinsed him off, and wrapped him in a big white towel.

By the time the bath was over, both Jethro and I were covered from head to toe in water, vegetable oil, and soap. I felt as if I had been basted like a turkey.

He looked up at me and licked the tip of my nose.

"You're welcome," I whispered to the pig. "Don't do that again." Just as I spoke, I saw Zeph walk in front of the window over the sink. He held a shovel over his shoulder as he went. Maybe he was finally shoveling the walk. I could only hope.

I looked a mess, but I carried a sparkling-clean Jethro into the main lobby of the Candyworks. The lobby was one of my favorite rooms in the facility. Even though we were a modern factory, I wanted to give it an Amish, small candy shop feel. It was made to be a much larger replica of the front room of Swissmen Sweets. I used the same colors, the same candy jars for displays, and even had the contractor replicate the old wide plank floor we had in the candy shop. In the factory it was vinyl, not actual wood, but the colors and width of the boards were the same. Half of the lobby was dedicated to bright candy displays and the other half was a waiting area for tour groups and a seating area for customers.

Typically, the center of the room was open, but through the Christmas season there were five tables in the middle of the lobby, with a different elaborate gingerbread house on each. The gingerbread houses were made by members of my staff who had entered a competition for a chance to win a thousand dollars. As I looked around, I knew the competition would be stiff.

Later in the week, two other judges and I would review the gingerbread houses and pick a winner. They were all so well done. I didn't know how we could possibly choose.

I looked at the gingerbread houses and then down at the pig in my arms. I knew this was not a good combination. At the same time, I needed a shower. I smelled like gingerbread and vegetable oil.

Sabrina Troyer, a pretty teenager with lovely hazel eyes and a shy smile, was stocking the gingerbread cookie display in the front window. The gingerbread recipe had been an old family recipe that I had revamped with fresh ginger and crushed cloves. In my humble opinion, the changes made it one of the best gingerbreads anyone had ever tasted, and I wasn't the biggest fan of gingerbread. I was more a chocolate peppermint girl at Christmastime.

The display included gingerbread men, women, and even pigs. All of our pig-shaped sweets flew off the shelves because of Jethro. As of yet, I had not been able to replicate the success of the white and milk chocolate Jethro bars. They sold so well, they were difficult to keep in stock.

"Sabrina, would you mind watching Jethro while I get cleaned up?" I asked.

She set her basket of gingerbread on the wide windowsill. "What happened to you?"

"Jethro got into the taffy."

She took Jethro from my arms. "How did that happen?"

"Long story." I paused. "Have you seen Zeph lately?"

She didn't meet my gaze. "Zeph is outside, I think."

I thanked her and went outdoors, hoping I'd find Zeph clearing the walk, but that wasn't what I found at all.

CHAPTER THREE

Thankfully I'd had the foresight to put two small locker rooms in the factory, one for men and one for women. I also always kept extra clothes in one of the lockers. One never knew when a chocolate bomb would explode around here as we tried to push chocolate and other sugary confections to their limit.

After I got myself cleaned up and collected Jethro from the lobby where I had left him with Sabrina, I headed outside. To my surprise, the walk hadn't been shoveled. Had I imagined Zeph walking by the laundry room window with a shovel on his shoulder? I supposed it was possible. I had a lot on my mind between the factory, the Candy Land Experience, Christmas, and my parents' impending arrival.

I wrinkled my brow. Where was Zeph? I wished I could say that this wasn't the first time he had gone missing when assigned a task. The last few times, I'd reminded him, but I'd let any repercussions slide due to the fact that the factory was still new and all the people working there, including myself, were still trying to figure out how best to run the Candyworks.

But the icy, snow-covered walk that led to the lobby's main door was a hazard and a potential lawsuit if anyone slipped and fell. I couldn't imagine anything worse than a lawsuit for a new business. It could—and probably would—ruin everything that I had worked so hard for.

"Zeph!" I called.

There was no answer. Where could he be?

I groaned. I really didn't want to fire him. It would be the first dismissal since I'd opened the factory, but I knew it was my own fault. I had had reservations about hiring Zeph from the start. He was young—just seventeen—and seemed to be easily distracted. The fact that he hadn't cleared the walk yet was proof of that. Being easily distracted wasn't an unusual trait for a teenager, but it was for an Amish teenager like Zeph.

I had hired him as a favor to his sister Lida. Lida was a model employee. Maybe she was so nervous about doing everything right that she froze with indecision at times, but her brother didn't care at all how or when his duties were completed. I wished the two of them could meet in the middle somewhere when it came to their work ethic.

"Zeph!" I shouted it this time out of desperation. One of the pitfalls of having mostly Amish employees was that I couldn't just text them and ask them where they were, as I would have when I was working at JP Chocolates in New York City years ago.

"What?" came the reply.

I jumped. To be honest, I hadn't expected him to answer me.

"Zeph?"

"Up here!"

I cranked my neck and looked up at the roof of the factory, which at its peak rose thirty feet in the air. Zeph stood on the roof next to a seven-foot-tall red gingerbread man playing piece from Candy Land Experience. The garish figure loomed over me like a hawk looking for an easy meal. I had a feeling that meal just might be Jethro, who was wrapped in a towel and tucked under my arm.

"What are you doing up there? And why do you have that Candy Land piece with you?"

"I'll come down," he called back.

Despite the towel, Jethro shivered in my arms, so I unzipped my parka and tucked him inside. He had a parka of his own, of course, but I had left it at Swissmen Sweets that morning.

Jethro looked up at the playing piece and shuddered. I couldn't say that I blamed him. It really looked like a red demon on a perch. I knew there was no way I was going to let that thing stay up there all the way through Christmas. It would scare all my customers away, and it leaned forward just a little too much, threatening to fall to the ground at any moment. Even though it appeared to be made out of corrugated plastic sheeting and could not be particularly heavy, I couldn't have faux gingerbread men falling on my customer' heads if I wanted the Candyworks to be successful.

Zeph came around the building, grinning from ear to ear. "What do you think? It's pretty great, isn't it? It took me forever to make it stay upright and angle it so it could be seen from the parking lot."

"How big is it?"

"Nine feet. It took a lot of plastic sheeting and a lot of red paint." He showed me his bare hands, which were encrusted with red paint. I dearly hoped that he hadn't moved the playing piece to the roof while the paint was still wet. I didn't need red paint all over my shingles.

"It doesn't look very stable."

"Don't worry about that. It's not going anywhere. I stapled the base to the roof and secured it with so many bungee cords, it would take nothing less than a hurricane to blow it off. I think the fact that it sways in the wind gives it a more lifelike appearance."

Did one want lifelike appearance in a playing piece?

"And why did you put it on the roof?"

His eyes went wide. "Because Margot asked me to do it. I still have to put up the sign that tells everyone to go to the Candy Land Experience on the square. She said you would be fine with it."

I rubbed my eye, which was beginning to twitch. Of course she had.

"How did you get up there?" I asked.

"An extension ladder from the maintenance shed," he said. "Just leaned it against the building and climbed up. It was easy as pie."

I looked up at the roof again. It was encrusted with snow and ice. We'd had a winter storm the week before and the temperature had not yet risen above freezing to melt off the accumulated snow. "I don't think that is a good idea," I said. "The roof is slippery. You could fall."

"I'm as agile as a cat." He grinned from ear to ear. His hazel eyes shone with mischief and his light brown hair peeked out from under his plain black stocking cap. I could see why so many of the young Amish ladies at the factory whispered and blushed when he was near. He was charming.

But I was his boss, and that charm wasn't going to work on me. "I don't want you going back up there alone. It's just too dangerous, and when you do go up there with at least one other person, you have to take the playing piece down."

"Down? Why?" The impish look had disappeared from his face to be replaced with irritation. "I just got it to stand up."

I sighed. "Because I don't want it there. It looks more like a Halloween decoration than Christmas."

"But Margot said—"

"Let me take that up with Margot," I said. Now I felt a headache forming behind my tired eyes.

I should have expected as much when Margot was involved. Even so, she had a lot of nerve to ask one of my employees to put something on my brand-new roof. I would never have done that to her.

"It has to come down," I said. "I know you worked long and hard to put it in place, but it makes me a touch nervous. What if it scares a child? What if it falls on someone entering or exiting the building?"

"Fine." Zeph scowled. "I'll take it down now."

"No! Not right now," I said. "I have to get Jethro to Swissmen Sweets and meet with my parents, who are in town. Perhaps later, when we can have someone help you. Maybe it would be even better to have two people help you. I don't want you going up on the roof again alone. That's too dangerous." I looked down at the un-shoveled walk. "What I need you to do right now is shovel this walk. I expect you to clear the walk every day in the winter, as many times as it snows. We can't have any staff or visitors being hurt."

His cheeks were already red from the cold, but now they turned a deeper shade of red. "Oh, right, I forgot about that. I'll clear it off." He shook his head. "I sincerely apologize. I think I was so excited when Margot asked me to put up the gingerbread man, everything else went out of my head."

"That's very possible," I said with a kind smile. "Margot has a way of convincing people her emergency is everyone's emergency."

"I'll take care of the walk right now, and Beau said he would stop by later after his shift. I bet he can help me on the roof."

Beau Eicher was Zeph's friend, who worked at the Harvest Market, which shared a parking lot with the candy factory. I knew the two young men were close. I had seen them chatting in the parking lot many times since we'd opened, when one or the other was starting or leaving work for the day. Sometimes Lida was with them because she rode in to work with her brother, but when she was, she always stood a little distance away from the boys, as if she didn't want to intrude on their conversation.

"I'm sure you and Beau can do it, but I would prefer there was at least one more person there to hold the ladder. When he arrives, check with Charlotte to see if she can send someone out to help."

He nodded.

"And remember that you report to Charlotte and me, so if someone else, including Margot, asks you to do something, just check with one of us first." I glanced up at the giant game piece again. "It is eye-catching."

"Wait until you see the sign," he said. "It glows."

Terrific. Just like Rudolph's nose.

Much to my relief, Zeph went straight to shoveling the walk. I decided not to give him a hard time about the game piece because Margot had given him the assignment. I knew just how difficult it was to say no to her. She had a way of appealing to a generous person's guilt and sense of duty like no other.

Jethro's head popped out of my parka as I stepped onto the square. We were just a few feet away from the parking lot entrance to Juliet's church. I had a strong urge to drop off the pig and make a run for it, but a promise was a promise. I had told Juliet that I could watch Jethro while she and the ladies wrapped gifts. I had to stand by my word.

Now that I thought about it, Juliet wasn't much different from Margot in her success rate at getting me to undertake annoying tasks. However, her sweet, doe-eyed way of going about it was the polar opposite of Margot's full-frontal assault.

The square looked like . . . well . . . Candy Land. It was a life-size version of the board. Two feet by two feet colorful foam tiles made up the path, and there were huge replicas of candy everywhere I looked. Nine-foot-tall gingerbread men game pieces stood around the square in blue, yellow, and green. The red piece wasn't there. It was on my roof. I hoped that I would be able to convince Margot that that was a very bad idea, and the red piece should join his brethren on the square.

Margot had her trusty bullhorn up to her lips. "No, no, no. The lollipops go to the left of the gazebo, not the right. How many times do I have to say that?"

The two Amish teenagers who were carrying what looked like fiberglass lollipops in red and green shared a look of confusion.

A man I'd never seen before in an expensive-looking wool coat stood beside her and winced as she shouted into the bullhorn. Having been that close to Margot and her bullhorn before, I could feel his pain.

I guessed that he was just shy of sixty. His hair was thin, but he had a full gray beard and mustache. If the clothes hadn't been a dead giveaway, I would have said that he didn't look Amish because of the mustache. The Amish never have mustaches because they are pacifists and historically, mustaches are associated with the military.

He said something to Margot, then shook her hand and hurried down the gazebo steps before disappearing around the back of the structure.

I was so caught up in watching the drama unfold and trying to keep Jethro in my arms that I bumped into a man who was walking around the square. "I'm so sorry," I managed to say.

He ducked his head, but not before I saw an impressive full white beard.

Santa?

"No harm done," the man said and hurried on his way. He wore a red suit, too. Although he was rather thin and not all that tall either. In my childhood, I had always imagined Santa Claus to be a big round fellow. That's what they told us as children.

I shook my head. He was most likely a Santa that Margot had hired for the week leading up to Christmas. It would be a waste of money on the Amish children in the village, but the English children would enjoy sitting on his lap and reciting their lists.

Uriah Schrock, the square's caretaker, stepped in. "Margot, do you mean it goes on the boys' left of the gazebo? They think you mean your left."

Margot threw up her hands. "Well, if they can't understand what I mean, maybe you will have better luck." Her eyes zoomed in on me. "Bailey, where have you been? I expected you would have been here by now to discuss which squares will have candy stations. I have been blowing up your phone. We can't leave these kinds of decisions to the last minute."

I suppressed a sigh. "Margot, I told you that my parents are flying in today and I might be hard to reach. In fact, I'm meeting them at the Village Inn just as soon as I drop Jethro off at Swissmen Sweets. They should be arriving any moment now."

Margot sniffed. "I suppose I forgot that little tidbit. I have had a lot of my mind. Hosting the Candy Land

Experience and the live nativity the same week is more than I bargained for."

I raised my eyebrows. Margot must have been struggling with everything she had to do. I had never heard her admit before that she was having difficulty accomplishing anything. It also gave me pause about complaining to her about the giant game piece on the roof of Swissmen Candyworks. Almost.

"Did you ask Zeph Lantz to put a giant Candy Land game piece on the roof of the Candyworks?"

"I sure did," she said with confidence. "Don't tell me that he didn't do it. I don't need any more problems. I've already lost a donkey because she was giving birth."

"I heard," I said. "And Zeph did put the game piece on my roof. But you should have asked me before telling him to do that." I settled Jethro against my shoulder.

Between the residual gingerbread smell and the vegetable oil, he smelled like a cookie shop.

Margot sniffed and adjusted her winter hat on the short curls atop her head. "I don't have time to ask every shopkeeper permission for everything that needs to be done to bring more shoppers into the village. It all benefits you. You should be grateful. You now have a beacon on the factory to attract more visitors to your new business. I was doing you a favor to pay back the many times that you have helped me on the square."

It was going to take a lot more than that red plastic game piece to pay me back for everything I had done for Margot and the village. In all honesty, she could never afford it.

"I appreciate that," I said. "But I'm just a little concerned because it doesn't look very stable. It could fall from the roof and hurt someone."

"Those game pieces are made out of the finest corrugated plastic."

"What if it's windy? This is December. There is no telling what the weather will be. It looks like a light breeze could send it flying off the building."

"Well, that just tells me Zeph didn't do a great of job of securing the game piece. That's his fault. Not mine. Tell him to get back up there and fix it."

"I understand that you want this event to receive as much attention as possible, but I've already asked him to take it down. We could put it in the parking lot, pointing at the square."

"But then you won't be able to see it from the square. That was the point of putting it on your roof in the first place."

I opened my mouth to tell her what I thought about that suggestion, but she spoke first. "We can discuss this later," she said. "Just as soon as you get your parents settled in. We need to finalize the candy stations in any case."

I sighed, knowing this discussion wasn't over and if Margot had her way, it wouldn't be done until after Christmas, when the Candy Land Experience ended.

Considering the conversation over for now, Margot walked away, waving at the young Amish men. "Haven't you ever played Candy Land before? The piece doesn't go like that! The castle has to be at the end. The point of the game is to be the one to reach the castle first. Don't they teach you anything in Amish school?"

I winced and wondered if anyone would have the nerve to tell Margot that Candy Land wasn't an Amish childhood staple as it was for English children.

My guess was no.

CHAPTER FOUR

As soon as I stepped into Swissmen Sweets, the comforting smell of hot caramel, cinnamon sticks, and peppermint washed over me. The front room was cozy and warm, and several English customers enjoyed warm eggnog and peppermint bark at the three small dinette tables by the front window.

Nutmeg, the shop's resident orange tabby, was curled up in his cat bed under the large window. As soon as Jethro saw him, he began to wriggle in my arms. I set down the pig on the wide-plank floor before he could clock me in the mouth with one of his hooves.

The little pig rushed over to his cat friend, and the pair touched noses before snuggling in the bed together. I was sure as they settled into their nap that Jethro would keep his friend occupied with another outrageous tale about his day. Unfortunately, the taffy incident was just to be expected when it came to Jethro.

"Gerry," one woman said to her companion over

peppermint bark. "Get a picture of that! Have you ever seen a pig and a cat get along so well in your life?"

Gerry started snapping cell phone pictures. Not for the first time, I wondered how many people had pictures of these two together, or how many pictures were taken of the pig and cat with my large white rabbit, Puff, who outweighed them both. At the moment, Puff was in my rental house a few blocks away.

The bunny didn't care much for the cold and she'd burrowed back into bed early that morning when I said I would carry her to Swissmen Sweets. Had I been willing to drive, she would have been game to go, but I preferred to make the short walk into the village whenever I could.

"Bailey dear," Maami said. "We didn't expect to see you until after your parents arrive. Are they here?" She peeked out the window as if she expected to see my parents there.

"They aren't here yet." I removed my phone from the pocket of my parka and checked for text messages from my dad. The last one I saw said they'd landed at Akron-Canton Airport, which was about an hour away from Harvest. "At least, they haven't said they are here. I know they planned to go to the inn before coming to the shop. Mother will want to freshen up after the flight."

Maami nodded. "I can't fault your *maam* for that. I could not imagine how dirty one would feel after being trapped on an airplane."

I glanced out the window at the church. I knew just beyond it was Swissmen Candyworks. A hollow feeling grew in my stomach. If I knew anything at all about

Zephaniah Lantz, it was that he wasn't great at following orders. For my own peace of mind, I had to get back to the factory and make sure he didn't climb up on that roof alone again. I didn't trust him not to do that.

My grandmother's face wrinkled in concern. "Is something wrong?"

I walked over to the counter so that I could speak more quietly with her. I didn't want the customers to overhear. To be honest, I don't know if they would have heard me because they were so enamored with Nutmeg and Jethro. The cat and pig had their own paparazzi.

"I have to get back to the factory before Mom and Dad arrive. At Margot's direction and without consulting me first, Zeph Lantz put a Candy Land game piece on the roof of the Candyworks. I need to help him get it down. I'm afraid it might fall off the roof and hurt someone. I told him not to go up on the roof again alone, but I'm not sure he listened."

Maami placed a hand to her chest. "*Ya*, this is something that you must do. Why would Margot do that without asking you?"

I shook my head. "She said she was trying to attract more people to the Candyworks and the square, but I can't afford the liability if something were to go wrong."

Emily Keim, our candy shop assistant, came into the room through the swinging door that connected the industrial kitchen to the rest of the shop. She carried a tray of nut and caramel bars. Jethro loved nuts and must have caught a whiff of the treats because he jumped out of the cat bed and ran over to her. Emily smiled, broke off a small corner of one of the bars, and fed it to the little pig.

She stood up and wrinkled her nose. "Why does Jethro smell like cooking oil?"

"It's vegetable oil actually, and I had to give him a bath in it because he got covered in gingerbread taffy at the factory. It's a long story."

"It always is with Jethro," Maami said.

"Oh, gingerbread is the other thing I smell," Emily said. "It's much fainter, but it's there."

Maami placed a hand to her chest. "Is he all right? Was he burned?"

"It happened in the packing room thankfully, so the taffy was warm but not boiling hot." I glanced down at the pig, who was licking his lips as if he wanted to make sure he got every last morsel of Emily's nut bar. "He's perfectly fine, but he's a terror for the staff at the Candyworks. The building is just too big to keep track of him. Can I leave him here for a little while?"

Maami shook her head. "With all the new responsibility you have taken on with the Candyworks, you need to make it known to Juliet that you cannot watch her pig every time the whim hits her. We all love Jethro dearly, but he is a handful and not your responsibility."

Jethro gave Emily a pitiful look, and she gave him another small piece of the nut bar. At this rate he would have the entire thing eaten in a matter of minutes.

"When I first came into the room, did I hear you mention Zeph Lantz?" Emily asked.

"Yes," I said, but I didn't ask her if she knew him. Emily and my grandmother were in the same Amish district as Zeph and his sister Lida; they certainly knew who he was even if they didn't know him well. "I have to go back to the factory to make sure he does his work." I paused. "He's only been working for me a week, but it's already been a problem." As soon as I spoke, I felt bad for saying it. It was true that Zeph wasn't the model employee I had dreamed of, but I should just handle the problem instead of complaining to my grandmother and shop assistant.

"You should have asked me before hiring him," Emily said. "Zeph has always been unreliable. I used to help with the children after church so their parents could eat in peace, and he never did as he was told. I don't think he was being purposely rude, but he was easily distracted."

"I'll keep that in mind when I give him assignments in the future, and I'm not going to fire him or anything. It's not his fault that Margot asked him to do something that distracted him from his work."

"*Ya,*" Maami said. "Give the boy a chance. Mistakes are made, but he will learn."

Emily pressed her lips together as if she didn't quite believe that was true. I wanted to learn what Emily really knew about Zeph Lantz. Usually, she wasn't so openly critical of another person. She wasn't even that critical of her own brother, Abel Esh, and Abel was a convicted criminal. There had to be more to the story. However, I thought it was best not to ask her about it in front of my grandmother.

My phone pinged with an incoming text message. **Come back to the factory right now. There's been an accident.**

I stared at the message and felt a lump in my throat. "I have to go."

Maami gripped the sides of her apron. "Bailey, you look as if you have had a great shock. What is wrong? What is going on?"

"I'm not sure, but it sounds bad. I'll let you know as soon as I can." I ran from the candy shop.

My hands shook while I ran across the square back to the Candyworks.

"Where are you going in such a hurry?" Margot shouted at me as I flew by.

I waved at her but did not stop to speak. I had to get to the factory as fast as I could. As I ran, I tried to call Charlotte, but she didn't pick up. That made me worry even more. Was she in the accident? Was she hurt? How badly must she be hurt if she wasn't able to answer the phone?

I had to slow my pace because the sidewalk was slippery from the snow that had melted and now refrozen into a sheet of ice. I wouldn't be able to help anyone if I fell and broke my neck.

Even at a slower pace, I made it to the Candyworks in half the time that it usually took me, but I was completely out of breath and my throat felt as if it was on fire from all the cold air I'd inhaled.

When I saw the factory entrance, I gasped, but it wasn't from the cold.

A small group of people had gathered around the front of the building. They were standing in the very spot where I had been speaking to Zeph an hour or so earlier. My heart twisted in my chest, and I felt as if I couldn't breathe. I didn't want to know what was in the middle of that circle, but I wanted to know, too. Was the not knowing worse than the truth? There was only one way to find out.

I excused myself as I made my way through the crowd, and finally, I had a clear view of the fallen man. As I feared, it was Zeph. He lay face down on the concrete walk, which had been freshly cleared of snow. There was a pool of blood near the top of his head.

My eyes traveled up to the roof, where the giant red Candy Land game piece glowered down at me as if it were pleased with the scene before it. I wasn't sure I would ever be able to play Candy Land again, and I knew for sure that I would never use the red piece.

My eyes fell back on Zeph's unmoving body. He held a sign in his hand that read, "See you in Candy Land!"

I hoped that was where Zeph was now.

CHAPTER FIVE

Before I could even ask Charlotte what had happened, the shrill cries of sirens cut through the air. Flashing lights shone on the bright white snow, and I let out a breath that I hadn't known I'd been holding when I saw the sheriff's SUV peeling into the parking lot. Aiden was here. Everything would be all right now. Well, maybe not all right, but better. I would take better in that moment.

Aiden jumped out of his vehicle. "Bailey!"

My heart warmed at the fact that he looked for me first. He knew how upset I would be by all this. Swissmen Candyworks hadn't even been open three months and this would be the second death on the property. That didn't bode well for the future of the factory.

I waved my glove-covered hand. "I'm here."

He hurried over to me. "Are you all right?"

"Yes. I'm fine."

"What happened?" He glanced at the body as several of his deputies, who had also just arrived, jumped into action and secured the scene. Deputy Little, Charlotte's husband, was among them. I was happy to see him, too. I knew that just as Aiden had come to the factory for me when the call came in, Deputy Little had come for Charlotte.

"I don't know. I wasn't even here when it happened. I was at Swissmen Sweets talking to Maami and Emily."

Charlotte appeared at our side. "He fell off the roof. That's all I know. My candymaking class was taking a break, and I went in search of Zeph to make sure that he'd cleared the walk like Bailey wanted. I was in the lobby when I heard a scream. I found him like this."

"So he screamed when he fell."

She shook her head and her strawberry-blond braid slid from her shoulder. "Maybe, but that's not what I heard. It was definitely a woman who screamed, not a man."

"Did you see this woman?" Aiden asked.

"*Nee*—I mean, no."

Sometimes when Charlotte was nervous, she would lapse into her first language, Pennsylvania Dutch.

"By the time I got to the front of the building, Zeph was the only one there." She turned to me. "I'm sorry that I sent you such a cryptic text message, Bailey. It was all I could write. My class was pouring out of the factory and I was trying to stop the students from seeing him."

"Is that who most of these people are? Members of your candymaking class?" Aiden asked.

She nodded. "That's right. They were making double peppermint fudge that needed to rest before we added the second layer."

He turned to the class members.

"Did anyone see him fall?" Aiden asked the cluster of people standing around the body. They shook their heads and averted their eyes. I didn't know if they did so because they really hadn't seen anything or because they didn't want to get tangled up in the Sheriff's Department's investigation. In any case, it was disheartening that no one stepped forward.

"Someone had to see him fall if there was a scream," Charlotte said.

"Not necessarily," I said. "The woman could have just screamed because she saw the body. It can be shocking if it's not something that you're used to."

Aiden made a face. I knew it was due to the fact that I *was* used to seeing dead bodies and rarely screamed over them anymore.

"I suppose you're right," Charlotte said with a frown. "I thought I was on to something there."

"You were," Aiden said. "I do want to talk to that woman if we can find her."

Charlotte shivered. She wasn't wearing a coat. I was about to tell her to run inside and grab her coat when she said, "I just hope it wasn't his sister, Lida, who saw him. Whenever she finds out, she will be crushed."

I covered my mouth. How had I not thought of Lida? She would be devastated at the news of her brother's death, and it wasn't something that she could find out by accident. The news of the accident must have been traveling like wildfire through the Swiss-men Candyworks and the Amish community, Even without cell phones, the Amish were always the first to know about all the happenings in Holmes County.

"We have to be the first to tell her," I said. "She can't find out by chance."

"And I need to speak to her, too," Aiden said.

"I'll go look for her," Charlotte said and dashed to the door.

"She was wrapping taffy in the candy packing room the last time I saw her," I called after her.

She waved her hand in the air to acknowledge that she'd heard me.

Aiden squeezed my arm before walking over to consult with his deputies and the EMTs who had just arrived.

The paramedics examined the body and checked for a pulse. They listened for breathing. I knew it was just protocol, but it seemed cruel to watch them go through the steps to determine if there was even the slightest chance of saving Zeph. With his neck bent the way it was, it was clear there was no hope.

"Bailey, what should we do? We were in the middle of the candymaking class with Charlotte. We weren't able to finish before this happened."

I turned to find Jenny Patterson staring at me with a questioning look.

I blinked a few times at her question. "The fudge

should be fine if it's cooling. A member of my staff can finish it off and add the second layer for all of you."

"Yes, yes, the fudge will be fine, but we were also set to make truffles," she said in a huffy voice. "I promised my husband truffles. I can't come home empty-handed."

"Under the circumstances, I'm closing the Swissmen Candyworks for the rest of the day. We will give each class member a box of truffles from the shop."

"That won't do. I need to make the truffles myself. That's the whole point of taking a class like this, isn't it? I told everyone that I would be making them myself. You must understand how embarrassing it would be for me to give anyone store-bought truffles."

I stared at her. Was she serious? A young man was dead. Not just a young man, but a teenager, who'd had his whole life in front of him, and she was more upset over truffles? Her actions certainly made me look at Jenny in a whole new light. I hadn't known her well before planning for the Candy Land Experience had begun, but now I realized that I truly didn't know her at all.

Jenny cleared her throat as if she suddenly understood how awful she sounded. "I feel terrible for the boy. I really do, and I understand that you want to close out of respect, but I see no reason for us not to finish our class. The classroom is on the other side of the building."

I bit my lip to give myself time to think before I responded. "Jenny, I'm glad you've enjoyed the class so much, but I can't expect Charlotte or any other member of my staff to teach right now under the circumstances. We're all very upset. Zeph was a coworker, and his sister is also an employee of the Candyworks. She and the rest of her family have to be our priority today."

"Oh." Her eyes widened, as if she'd just made the connection for the first time that Zeph was a person who was loved and would be missed. At times people could be so caught up in their own lives that they were unaware of the suffering around them. It happened to everyone. I was guilty of it myself. Now, I couldn't say that it happened to me when I was standing twenty feet from a dead body . . .

"Yes, I see how that would be difficult." She cleared her throat as if she was unsure whether she should say more. It seemed her need to speak overcame her hesitation. "Will there be any sort of refund since we were only able to make the fudge?"

I clenched my fists to keep my hands warm. I wasn't wearing gloves, and it was getting progressively colder standing outside in the snow. I was also trying very hard to stop myself from snapping at her. "We will refund your money, or you can retake the class at a later date."

"I'd rather retake the class, honestly, but it will have to be before Christmas. There is no reason for me to make truffles after Christmas."

"I'll see what we can do."

She nodded, as if she was finally satisfied with my response. Her gaze traveled over to the body.

The coroner and two EMTs rolled Zeph onto a stretcher. I had to look away.

"I am very sorry for the young man and his sister. I

will keep the whole family in my prayers. Lida in particular. This will break her heart."

I blinked. "You know Lida? I don't remember saying her name."

"Yes, I have heard of her. You must have said her
name."

I frowned.

I really didn't think I'd mentioned her name.

"Oh," Jenny said, looking relieved. "I know who she
is because she helped Charlotte with the candymaking
classes before."

My brow furrowed. That was more likely, but something about her explanation still felt off.

I waved at Sabrina, who had come outside as well.
"Sabrina, can you escort the class members back into
the building to gather up their things and leave? Then
please close up the shop."

The young Amish woman nodded with tears in her
eyes.

Jenny and the rest of the class followed Sabrina into
the shop. Aiden appeared at my side. "That looked like
a tense conversation."

"It was. Jenny Patterson was just being insensitive
considering . . ." I trailed off. I didn't need to tell him
considering what.

Aiden shoved his bare hands into his coat pockets.
"You should go inside, too. The coroner is ruling this
an accident."

I felt a vise tighten in my chest. I hated that my brain
went there, but I wondered if I would be held liable for

Zeph's death. I didn't see how I wouldn't be. He had fallen and died while he was at work. Would it matter that I'd told him not to go up on the roof again alone? The only person who'd heard me say that was Zeph, and there was no asking him about it now.

"What was he doing on the roof?" Aiden asked, breaking into my thoughts.

"He was working on the red gingerbread man up there."

He squinted at the raptorlike game piece. "That doesn't look very safe."

"I know. That's why I asked him to take it down. But I told him to wait until he had help. He said that he would wait until his friend Beau, who works at the Harvest Market, was free to help him." I looked up at the game piece and shuddered. "It doesn't look like he waited for Beau. In fact, considering he is holding that sign, he climbed up on the roof again with the intention of attaching the sign to the game piece. Now, that is an assumption. I don't know if that was what he was really planning to do."

"Why did you ask him to put it up there in the first place?"

"I didn't. Margot asked him to advertise the Candy Land Experience."

"Without checking with you first?"

I nodded. "When she finds out, she will feel just as horrible as we all do. She couldn't possibly know this was going to happen. It was an accident, a terrible accident. No one is to blame."

Aiden looked up at the roof again. "No one is to blame? I'm not sure that is true."

I stared at him. "Do you know something else?"

He shook his head, and I knew that he would tell me when he was ready.

CHAPTER SIX

I watched the quiet ambulance drive away with Zeph's body inside. There was no reason to rush, and that truth broke my heart. Jenny and the other ladies in the class left with the fudge they'd made, boxes of truffles, and the promise that I would be in touch about a makeup date for the class sometime later that week.

Charlotte joined me in the lobby of the factory. We had told the staff the factory was closing for the rest of the day and everyone else had already gone home.

Charlotte looked up at the ceiling, which was twenty feet high. I'd wanted the factory to have an open and airy feel, so two thirds of the building had twenty-foot ceilings like the lobby, and one third was traditional two stories. That portion of the building encompassed the behind-the-scenes part of the factory: the offices, storage, locker rooms, and laundry room.

"I looked all over for Lida," Charlotte said. "But I couldn't find her anywhere. It's odd, too, because she was scheduled to work until five and it's just two now.

I know she hasn't worked for us long, but it's not like her to leave without saying anything at all."

"I can only believe she heard what happened to Zeph and left because she was so upset."

Charlotte nodded. "I'll see what I can find out from some other teenagers in the district. Even though I am older than them and left the Amish way, they are still friendly with me."

"Good idea. I'll ask around, too. She's on the schedule tomorrow, but if she doesn't show up, I won't hold it against her. I just want to know that she's okay. That's the most important thing."

My phone rang. It was my dad, and I winced. I'd completely forgotten about my parents' impending arrival in Harvest. I knew they expected me to be waiting for them on the front steps of the Village Inn when they arrived.

"Hello?"

"Bailey, this has to be wrong. Your mother and I arrived at the inn at the address you gave us and there is no one here. You're not here, and you said that you would be. There is no one to meet us at the desk. This is just unacceptable. We're tired from our long travels and just want to put our feet up. Is that too much to ask?"

"Dad, I'm really sorry. Something came up at the factory and I had to stay a few extra minutes. It's a short walk to the inn from here. I will be there in five minutes."

I ended the call and looked at Charlotte. "I have to . . ."

"Go. I'll lock up."

I thanked her before I dashed out of the building.

Any time my parents came to Harvest it was stressful. My father, in particular, had hated living here and wasn't comfortable with the Amishness of it all. I could only guess that was because he'd rejected this way of life when he was young. My mother wasn't quite as opposed to visiting Holmes County, but because she'd grown up English, her experience was quite a bit different from my father's.

Dad didn't leave the faith because he didn't get along with his parents. He simply could not accept all the church rules. Maami told me once that it broke her heart when my dad left the Amish way, but she'd known he was on that track as early as eight years old.

"He didn't like to be told what to do," she said. "Being Amish is very difficult if you're not a rule follower or you like to question authority. Silas, your father, was both of those."

My parents would be staying in a charming inn just a few hundred yards from the Candyworks. However, I knew it wasn't up to the standards my mother was used to. She and my father had traveled around the world and always stayed in the very best places. The last time they'd visited Harvest, which was over two years ago, they'd stayed at one of the largest and nicest hotels in the county. However, that hotel was not in walking distance of town. My mother wanted to stay closer this time, so she could stroll around the village. I'd hoped she would like my choice in the Village Inn, but it wasn't sounding as if the trip was off to a good start.

When I reached the Village Inn in a few short minutes, I heard my mother before I saw her.

"Maybe we should go back to that hotel we stayed at last time. They had a gym and a sauna. I don't even know if this place has a hair dryer in the room," I overheard her say to my father.

The pair of them stood on the inn's wide front porch with their luggage and scowls on their faces.

I waved. "Mom! Dad!"

Their faces lit up, and some of my anxiety about their visit dissipated. It was good to see them. It had been too long. For so many years it was just the three of us, but when I left for pastry school at eighteen, we grew distant. I knew it was because they were disappointed that I didn't follow their leads and go to college. Even though my father grew up in a candy shop, he never saw making candy as a lucrative career path. I believed by this point I had safely proven him wrong.

I hurried up the stairs, and my mother enveloped me in a massive hug. "Oh, Bailey, I have missed you! You really need to make time to come home to Connecticut more."

"You and Dad are hardly ever home in Connecticut." I returned her hug. "You're always traveling. The number of postcards I get throughout the year from far-off places is astounding."

She laughed. "That is true. We do have the travel bug. Did I tell you that we're going to Fiji for Valentine's Day? February is the perfect time to leave New England for warmer climates." Mom glanced at the inn. "This is quaint. I'm a bit concerned about the lack of staff, though. Didn't you say this place had a full breakfast included every day? I don't see how they can do that when there's no one here."

I withheld comment. It was almost as if my mother had forgotten what it was like to live in the country. True, she had left Holmes County over thirty years ago, but she and my father did live here for the first eighteen years of their lives.

My father gave me a quick hug. "Good to see my girl."

My father was far less into public displays of affection than Mom. Part of that had to do with his own temperament, and part, I suspected, had to do with the fact that he grew up Amish. Rarely would a married Amish couple even hold hands in public.

Dad cleared his throat. "Now, what kind of place have you put us up in? I thought someone would at least help us with our bags."

I frowned. "That isn't like Lillian, the owner, at all. Let's go in and see if we can find her. I'm sure there is a good explanation as to why no one is at the desk. Maybe she went in search of someone to help you with your bags?" Even as I said it, I knew it was a lame excuse. Lillian had known my parents were coming. Every time I saw her in the village, she spoke about it. To her, my parents were like celebrities coming to her little inn. She said they could put her on the map because they were so well traveled. She had read the reviews my mom and dad posted on their travel blog online, which an English friend had printed out for her. She was Amish and wasn't allowed to use a computer. What I didn't tell her was that they could also hurt her business if they penned a scathing review, and here we were, off to a bad start.

I opened the door into the inn. There was a cozy fire

in the hearth and the front desk was clean and organized. The brochures were all in a row in their acrylic
stand. There was nothing to give any indication that
something was wrong.

A small bell sat on the desk next to the closed hotel
ledger. I rang it.

"We already tried that," Dad said.

However, my attempt produced results. A plump
Amish woman in her mid-fifties came into the lobby
from the door behind the desk. Her dark hair was just
starting to turn silver at the roots and her eyes were
bloodshot. She held a plain white handkerchief up to
her nose. "I'm so sorry. Can I help you?"

"Lillian? Are you all right?" I asked.

She looked at me and blinked. She lowered the
handkerchief from her nose. "Bailey?" She blinked,
and then her eyes cleared. "Oh! You must be Bailey's
parents! I'm so sorry. I knew that you would be arriving just about now. My mind has been elsewhere. Have
you been waiting long? I am so embarrassed! This is
not the way to welcome you to Harvest."

"Are you all right?" I asked for a second time. "You
seem upset. What has happened?"

"*Ya*, I am well. I'm just battling a bout of seasonal
allergies." She didn't meet my eyes as she spoke.

Seasonal allergies in December? That didn't seem
right. She was allergic to snow?

She cleared her throat. "Now, let me get you checked
in, Mr. and Mrs. King. We are so happy to have you.
Your daughter Bailey has been a tremendous help to
me in getting my business off the ground. She refers
vacationers to me all the time. There are occasions when

I don't have a vacancy for weeks and weeks. Luckily, I was able to squeeze the two of you in due to a cancellation." She smiled. "Between Christmas and the Candy Land game on the square, everyone wants to come to Harvest this holiday season." She sniffled but seemed to regain her composure.

Now that Lillian had control of herself, she checked my parents into the inn quickly. "I gave you the very best room in the inn. It is here on the first floor. Just down the hallway there. It is room number two." She handed my father the room key, which was an actual key, not a magnetic card like the ones used in most hotels. "Please go down and make yourself comfortable. I will have my son bring your bags, and I will have afternoon tea for you shortly. We have fresh scones with clotted cream and raspberry jam this afternoon as well as tea sandwiches."

"Sounds lovely," my mother said, somewhat pacified after her earlier judgment of the inn.

"Your room has a sitting room, so that is where the tea will be served."

My parents thanked her and started down the hallway. When he realized that I wasn't following them, my father looked over his shoulder. "Bailey, are you coming?"

"I'm going to let you and Mom settle in and freshen up. I have a little bit more work to do at the factory before I'm done for the day. Maami will have dinner for all of us at the candy shop at six. Can you make it?"

He nodded, and the pair of them headed to their room.

It was true that I had work to do—namely giving my

condolences to Zeph's family and calling my attorney and insurance agent for advice about Zeph's accident—but the main reason I didn't follow them was because I was dying to ask Lillian what on earth was going on. I didn't believe for a moment that she had seasonal allergies. It was thirty degrees outside. Every speck of green was under six inches of snow and ice.

I turned back to Lillian and saw a young boy just about ten years old standing next to her by the fireplace.

"Adrien, please take these bags to room two. I will get our guests' tea ready."

Adrien nodded mutely but didn't say a word. I smiled at him as he walked past, but he looked at the ground.

"Bailey, is there something else I could help you with?" Lillian asked. She appeared to be in a little better state now. It was as if tending to her guests had revived her in some way.

I knew Lillian's husband had died in a tractor accident several years ago, and she'd decided to open the inn to make ends meet and provide for her young son. She didn't just host guests there. She also lived there, which was common in many of the Amish businesses in Harvest. The Amish were practical folks at their core. They knew that it didn't make sense to drive to work when you could live under the same roof as your business. I thought it was their Amish farmer mentality at play.

I knew this philosophy was one that Maami firmly believed in. I would never be able to convince her to leave her apartment above the shop. Not only was it practical, it was also the home where she'd lived with my grandfather all their married life. She would believe it was like leaving him behind in some way.

"Lillian, why have you been crying?" I asked.

"Oh!" She put the handkerchief to her eye again. "I need to make your parents their tea." She went through the door behind the counter and disappeared.

Without hesitation, I followed her through the door. It was clear to me Lillian was upset and I wanted to know why.

CHAPTER SEVEN

I found myself in a small kitchen that was clean and orderly. Lillian was in the process of putting scones in the oven to warm and had a tray in the middle of a large table that served as an island of sorts. There wasn't much other counter space. Every nook and cranny was put to use, and by the looks of it, Lillian was quite a gourmet cook. She had a number of pots and pans in different sizes and an impressive spice rack along one wall.

"Bailey!" The baking sheet of scones shook in her hands. "What are you doing in here?"

"I just want to make sure that you're all right. I don't believe it's seasonal allergies that are making you cry."

Tears sprang to her eyes. "I'm sorry that I lied. I couldn't say what was really going on in front of your parents. I don't want them to think staying here is unsafe."

I sucked in a breath. "Unsafe? How?"

She gave a shuddering breath. "I was robbed last night."

"Oh, Lillian, I'm so sorry. Have you called the Sheriff's Department?"

She bit her lip. "I spoke to them this morning. It was such a frightening experience. I gave Deputy Little all the details. He suspects that it's the same culprit who has robbed the other homes and businesses in the village. He promised to come back this afternoon with more information and a statement for me to sign, but he hasn't returned. I have been on pins and needles waiting. I supposed that is why I was so upset when you all came in. I just can't get my mind off what happened. My son was here during the robbery. What if he had been hurt? After losing my husband, I would never survive it if something happen to Adrien."

I didn't add that my parents had been waiting close to thirty minutes to be shown to their room. She didn't need any more stress.

I also knew why Deputy Little hadn't been back. A much more serious event had trumped Lillian's break-in, and that was Zeph's death.

"I know you've already spoken to Deputy Little, but can you tell me what happened? Did you see the person who broke in?"

The kettle whistled, indicating that the water had boiled. She set a plain white teapot and two plain white teacups and saucers on the tray. This was an Amish inn, so there would be no frills or fancy designs on the white porcelain. She went to the stovetop to collect the kettle. "It happened last night and, no, I didn't see the person.

It must have been after I went to bed. I came down the next morning at five as I always do to start making breakfast for the guests. We have a full house due to the holidays and I had much to do. I always stop in my office first. It is where I leave my to-do list from the night before and I scribble down any other reminders for myself on the desk blotter.

"Since my husband died, I don't feel my memory is what it used to be. Now, I have to write everything down to remember it."

I smiled at her. "I'm the same way. I have lists and more lists all over the Candyworks and my home."

My comments seemed to put her a little more at ease.

She nodded. "When I went into the room—it's just a little nook off the pantry actually—I knew something was wrong. Most of the drawers in my desk were open and my to-do lists were scattered across the desktop. I remembered the money that I'd neglected to lock in the safe the night before. I had carelessly left it in my top drawer. It was gone."

"You had cash?" I asked. "Don't most of your guests pay with credit or debit cards?"

"The *Englischers* do." She looked down at her hands. "I had a large Amish party here visiting from Iowa. They paid in bills. Usually what I would do is lock that money in the safe overnight, but I was frazzled because so many people were checking in at the same time. With no real staff, the job of settling the guests is mine. Putting the money away in the safe slipped my mind."

My heart ached for her. Any small business owner

knew what it was like to wear many hats, and it seemed that Lillian was wearing all of them at the Village Inn. It was no wonder she forgot to put the money away. And people in Harvest were not accustomed to worrying about robbery. Except for the last few weeks, I'd never heard of any break-ins or thievery happening in the village.

"You called the Sheriff's Department then?"

She shook her head. "The first thing I did was run upstairs to make sure that Adrien was safe and asleep in his bed. You cannot know the terror that gripped me just imagining for one second that my child had been in danger. Adrien was fine and sound asleep—praise *Gott*. Then I called the sheriff." She cleared her throat. "Deputy Little came quickly. He's such a nice man. I was sad that Charlotte left the Amish way, but I am happy for her that she married such a *gut Englischer*. He asked me so many questions. When was the last time I was in the office, who knew that I had that much money in the office, and did I lock the inn door at night?"

"And what did you tell him?"

"I was in the office just before dinnertime." She thought for a moment. "The Amish family from Iowa, as far as I know, would be the only ones who knew I had the cash, and they'd left. They checked out of the inn and were headed home. They were going by train, I believe." She looked down at her hands again. "They were such a sweet family. There were ten of them. I can't believe they would take the money back. They were some of the very best guests I ever had."

"And the question about locking the inn door at night?" I prompted.

"I do lock the front and back doors every night. It is something I have always done since my husband passed. I just feel much safer that way." She spoke as if she was embarrassed that she locked her doors, but I was happy that she had. Not every Amish household did, and I thought that was too risky. Yes, I knew they believed in God's protection, but I thought being pragmatic could be a way to be protected by God, too.

The Amish had pushed back against the changes in the world since they came to this country hundreds of years ago for religious freedom, but they could not completely hide from the dark side of human nature.

"So after you lock up, no one can come into the building."

She shook her head. "No. All the guests have keys to get in and out of the inn if need be during the night. I don't have any staff other than some Amish girls who clean the rooms for me and turn over the beds. I can't afford to have someone at the desk twenty-four hours a day, and I have to sleep sometime."

I nodded. "Was there any sign of a break in?"

"The deputy didn't find anything. All the doors and windows were locked."

Then it stood to reason that the person who'd stolen the money was already inside the inn as a guest. However, would that make this incident different from the other break-ins in the village?

"How much money was taken?" I asked.

"Over one thousand dollars." She choked on the words. "That money was going to help me open the tea garden that I wanted to add to the inn in the spring. I'm not sure I can do it now. I've been scrimping and saving, but I don't know if it can be done because I lost that money. I have so many regular bills to pay just to keep the inn open. Anything more seems impossible now."

"A tea garden sounds lovely."

"It really did." She was forlorn.

"Don't give up on your idea just yet," I said. "My candy factory is just a few hundred feet away from your front door. Perhaps we can do something together."

She shook her head and began to cry again. "*Nee*, this is *Gott's* way of reminding me that I was becoming too self-reliant. I should be leaning on Him, not trying to make my own way in the world."

"I don't think—"

She stood up. "I am sorry to cut this short, Bailey, but I have much to do."

With that, I knew I had been dismissed.

CHAPTER EIGHT

I left the inn feeling terrible for Lillian. I thought her tea garden would be a great addition to Harvest, and my brain was already considering ways Swissmen Sweets and the factory could partner with her, but if she felt that God was punishing her for being too ambitious, I didn't know if it would ever happen, even if the money that had been stolen from her was recovered. The Amish are taught to do everything in obedience to God. If she felt she was violating that principle, it would be the end of the tea garden before it even began.

On the short walk back to Swissmen Candyworks, my own problems began to rear their heads. I had to find Lida Lantz and make sure she was all right. I had a couple of hours before my parents, Aiden, and I were to have dinner at my grandmother's apartment. I had to find Lida before then. I knew I wouldn't be able to settle my nerves until I spoke to her.

I unlocked the back door to the Candyworks, where

we received deliveries. I couldn't bring myself to go in through the front door just a few feet from where Zeph had hit the pavement. Caution tape marked off the area.

Charlotte, as always, had done a wonderful job of locking up the factory. Unlike some Amish, I always locked my doors. Living alone in New York City all those years, I would have been a fool to leave so much as a window unlocked. When I first moved to Harvest, locking up Swissmen Sweets had been a sticking point between Maami and me. She felt that leaving her door open was a way to provide shelter for someone in trouble, and I thought it was an invitation for trouble. In the end, she began locking up just to appease me, and now that I was periodically involved in murder investigations in the county, it was more important than ever that she lock her doors. I didn't want someone who was arrested because of me showing up on my grandmother's doorstep.

In my office, I opened the tall file cabinet where I kept a file on all my employees. It felt so old-fashioned to have their files on paper, but most of my staff was Amish, so they gave me handwritten applications.

My goal was to type all my employees' information into a database that I could access from my phone, but I hadn't had time to do that yet. I was considering hiring an English member of the community to do some light office work for me so I could get jobs like that done. I hadn't had time to do that yet either. At this point, any new projects would have to be put off until after the Candy Land Experience and Christmas were over. In early January, when people were making New

Year's resolutions to get fit and lose weight, the candy orders would drop significantly and I would have time to put the office in order. The low sales would persist until the very end of January, when Valentine's Day orders started coming in at a breakneck pace.

I rifled through the drawer until I came to the L's. I stopped at Lantz, finding Lida's file and, just behind it, Zephaniah's. My stomach tightened into a hard knot. I removed both files from my drawer.

I opened Lida's file and found she lived on County Road Four on the border of Harvest and Charm. Her handwriting on the application was clear and precise. She'd obviously taken her time filling out the paper. When I opened Zeph's file, I found his handwriting to be hasty and his responses to the questions to be barely considered before he'd scratched down an answer.

This was the first time I was seeing the applications. Lida and many of the staff for the Candyworks had been hired by Charlotte while I was shooting my candy cooking show, *Bailey's Amish Sweets*, in New York City for Gourmet Television.

What surprised me about Lida and Zeph's files was that Zeph had listed a different address on his application from his sister. His address was on Circle Street in Harvest. That was just a few blocks from my little rental house. With my phone, I took a picture of both applications and tucked them into my shoulder bag for safekeeping.

It was very unusual for an Amish teenager to move away from home unless he or she was moving far away for work or was getting married young. Typically, the Amish stayed in their family home. Why had Zeph moved just a few miles away from his parents' home? And when he did, why had Lida stayed behind? These were both questions that I would have to ask Lida in due time.

I left the office and the Candyworks, making sure to lock all the doors after me. I skirted the building and stopped when I saw the impression of the extension ladder in the snow. However, there was no ladder. There were footsteps all around the site where the ladder had fallen, and from what I could tell, it had been fully extended to twenty feet when it hit the snow. I inched closer to the spot. There was no marker there left by the Sheriff's Department telling me to stop.

I inched toward the impression in the snow. Where was the ladder?

It was nearing four o'clock and the sun was beginning to set behind the factory, which faced northeast. The building cast long shadows across the parking lot. One of those shadows was in the shape of a giant Candy Land game piece. The red gingerbread man was still on the roof. I grimaced. Could I take it down? Aiden hadn't told me to leave it there as part of the investigation, and the death had been ruled an accident, so what investigation was there really to make?

For the briefest of seconds, I thought about climbing up on the roof myself to take the gingerbread man down, but even as I had the thought, I dismissed it. No one, not even me, was ever again going on that roof alone. Not to mention, the extension ladder was missing.

The gingerbread man's shadow on the pavement moved violently. Was it the wind? But there was no wind to be felt. The world around me was frozen like the calm before the storm. I hoped for Margot's sake that a winter storm wasn't on the way. If the Candy Land Experience failed, she would be crushed.

The shadow moved again, and I turned and gasped when I saw two figures on the roof. One was the gingerbread man; the other was a person.

"Hey!" I cried.

The shadow shuffled to the edge of the roof.

"Why are you shouting at me?" Aiden asked.

I put a hand to my chest. "Aiden Brody! What are you doing up there?"

"I'm doing my job," he said.

"I don't care what you're doing. Get down from there before you fall just like Zeph."

"I'm not going to fall."

"How did you get up there anyway?" I called. "I can't find the ladder."

"I brought a ladder of my own, and there is a reason you can't find yours."

Before I could ask him what that reason was, he waved. "Coming down."

I snapped a picture of the ladder outline in the snow before it was altogether too dark to see and walked around to the front of the factory. There was an extension ladder leaning against the roof, but it wasn't mine. My extension ladder was aluminum and this one was orange fiberglass. Aiden carefully climbed down the ladder and dusted snow off his coat.

As soon as I saw him, I folded my arms across my chest. "Have you lost your mind? You could have lost your footing the way Zeph did and fallen."

He shook his head. "I don't think that Zeph simply lost his footing."

"Why do you say that?"

"There is no snow or ice on the roof where Zeph must have placed his ladder. I also found a shovel on the roof, so he knew enough to make a clear path while he was up there, and there is even evidence that he put down rock salt, too. He was taking every safety precaution that he could."

"But he fell," I argued.

"I know." He ran his hand through his blond hair. His ears were red from the cold.

I leaned back and looked up. "I can't see the path."

"It comes in from behind the gingerbread man, so you can't see it from the ground, or at least you can't see it from the ground this close to the building. If you were farther away, you might be able to get a peek at it."

"Then how did he fall? Was he startled by something? Did he accidentally step off the cleared path?" I asked.

"No to both questions. He wasn't alone up there. There are footprints all over the place. I assume that he had an altercation with someone."

I shivered. "Someone pushed him off the roof?"

"We don't know that, but he certainly was not up there alone. The second person tried to erase his or her boot prints, but there are two distinct sets of prints up there."

"How did the person try to erase the prints?"

"I found a pine branch on the roof. They ran the branch back and forth over the prints to wipe them away. It's an old trick. The person who did it must have been in a hurry, though, because they didn't do a thorough job. Partials of two boot prints remain. I just called the evidence team to come back and take more pictures."

"If the person tried to erase the boot prints, they may have killed Zeph on purpose."

"Or it was an accident, and they don't want anything to do with it after the fact."

"So what does all this mean?" I asked.

He took a breath. "I can't really call it a homicide at this point, but I'm investigating it as a suspicious death. And I am looking for a person of interest."

Person of interest, not a suspect, I noted. At least, not a suspect just yet.

CHAPTER NINE

I swallowed. "Have you been able to talk to Zeph's family or Lida? Have you found her?"

"I haven't personally spoken to Lida," Aiden said. "Deputy Little went out to their farm to deliver the news, so the family knows. He said they knew before he arrived."

"The Amish grapevine," I said.

He nodded.

"And Lida?" I asked.

"Deputy Little said the family told him she wasn't home."

"Did he believe they were telling the truth?" I asked.

"What reason would they have to lie?" Aiden asked.

I bit my lower lip. Finding Lida was now my primary goal. Second was finding the killer.

Aiden left shortly after that, and I reminded him about dinner with Maami and my parents as he was leaving. He said he would do his best to make it, but I

knew when he was on a big case like this, it wasn't
likely.

I stayed at the factory another thirty minutes while
Aiden's deputies processed the scene. When the deputies left, I knew that I wouldn't have enough time to
drive all the way out to the Lantz farm before dinner to
see if Lida had turned up, so I opted to go to the other
address I'd found in my files, Zeph's home here in the
village proper.

I'd walked to work that morning, so I would have to
walk to the address in Zeph's file.

It was dark now, and the square was empty except
for the Candy Land game pieces. In the twinkle lights
and glow from the lampposts around the village
square, the pieces looked even more menacing than
they had in the daytime. I guessed if Aiden and I had
children someday, I would not be playing the board
game with our kids after this experience.

Circle Street was one block beyond the road my little rental house was on. In this neighborhood, the
houses were a mix of old Victorians that had been there
since the turn of the twentieth century and modest homes
that had been tucked in on small plots in the 1950s and
1960s.

I looked at the address and was surprised to find
that Zeph lived in one of the Victorian homes, and not
just any old house, but a purple one with green gingerbread trim and window boxes filled with Christmas
greenery. It was the least plain house on the street and
the very last place I would expect to find an Amish
young man.

I walked up to the wide porch and rang the doorbell.

I waited a few minutes in the cold, but nothing happened. I knocked on the door.

On the other side, I heard shouting. "I'm coming. I'm coming. I can't gallop anymore."

The door opened a full five minutes after that, and a petite, very elderly woman in a violet pantsuit stood in front of me, clutching the arms of a walker. After seeing the outside of her house and her suit, I guessed that purple was her favorite color. "Who is it?" Her voice was clear and sure.

"I'm so sorry to disturb you. I'm looking for Zeph Lantz. I understand this is where he lives."

"Zeph? He's not here right now. I don't expect him to come back for hours," she replied and made a motion to close the door.

What I didn't want to tell her was that he wasn't coming back at all.

I stuck my foot in the doorway to stop her from closing it. "I'm Bailey King. Zeph works for me at Swissmen Candyworks."

"Oh, yes, that's why you look familiar to me. I love watching you on the telly. You have one of my favorite programs. You represent Harvest and all of Ohio so well. I'm sure your family is proud. You should have said that from the start. Come in. Come in. I've never had a celebrity in my house." She ushered me through the door with the side of her walker. "I'm Beverly Morton, by the way."

I found myself in a Victorian living room that would have put Queen Victoria herself to shame; hers could not have been as opulent. There were frilly doilies and intricately carved glass vases and bowls everywhere.

A doll in Victorian dress sat on a small, doll-size rocking chair next to the fireplace. And the wallpaper was one giant cabbage rose after another. I couldn't look at it for too long without feeling a bit dizzy.

"Sit! Sit! It's not often I get guests who aren't asking for money." She squinted at me as she sat down. "You're not asking for money, are you? Are you here on the behalf of a church or some kind of mission?"

I shook my head. "No, I'm just asking about Zeph." I perched on a dainty-looking chair, praying that it would hold my weight.

"My best guess is that Zeph is at work, but if you came here looking for him, maybe not." She checked the gold lapel watch that hung from the collar of her purple jacket. "It's after closing time now. He's not at the Candyworks?"

"He's not," I said, trying to decide if and when I should tell her about his death. "When I looked up his address in his file, I was surprised to see that he no longer lives at home with his parents. His sister, who is just a year his junior, also works for me, and she's still at home."

She nodded. "Yes, I know it's true most Amish stay home until they marry or some such thing, but my guess is that Zeph has always been different." She waggled her crooked index finger at me. "I'm not saying that he isn't a good Amish young man. He just wants to go about life differently. I'm a free thinker myself and can appreciate that in him. I would have made a terrible Amish woman, I can tell you that."

"I wouldn't have been very good at being Amish either," I said.

"I should say so. You are too business-minded to be an Amish woman." She glanced at my left hand, where the engagement ring from Aiden sat. "Are you married?"

I shook my head. "Engaged."

Beverly nodded. "I thought so. There is an air about you that tells me, *this girl isn't married*. When you marry there will be a different air, I can assure you."

I wasn't sure I liked the sound of that. I didn't want to change when I married Aiden. I shook the thought away. She was a lonely old lady. Maybe that notion was something she made up in her head to make herself feel less alone.

I glanced around the frilly house and tried to imagine Zeph living in such a place. "Where is Zeph's room in your home?"

"He rents out my basement," she said.

"Did he come looking for a room?" I asked.

She shook her head. "No. I offered it to him. I knew him from town. He would do odd jobs for me now and again. One day, he asked if I knew if there was a room for rent in the village, and I said he could stay in the basement if he wanted. I keep the rent low because he does a lot for me around the house."

She lifted her polyester pant leg and showed off a prosthetic leg. "I can't move around as much as I used to." She dropped her pant leg back in place. "He's a very good young man. It must be his Amish upbringing. In my experience, English young people aren't so considerate and polite."

"I'm glad that he's been such a great help to you," I said and wondered who would help this sweet old woman now that Zeph was gone. "Has anyone else been here looking for Zeph?"

She squinted at me. "Looking for Zeph? No, never, you're the first one. In fact, by the way Zeph spoke, no one knew where he was living and he liked it better that way. He told me his community was nosy and he needed his space. I could understand that. I grew up with eight siblings and never got any peace until I moved away from home. They are all gone now. It's hard to believe that I'm the only one left." Her tone was wistful.

I felt for Beverly. She was lonely, and it seemed that Zeph had been good company to her in his way. I didn't know how to tell her the truth about him. I wasn't even sure that I should.

It was also curious to me that Zeph had wanted to keep where he lived a secret, yet he'd written Beverly's address on his job application. Wasn't it more likely people in his district would find out where he lived if he wrote down his new address? Maybe he just didn't want to lie on the application, which I supposed under the circumstances was commendable.

It also made me wonder if he counted his sister Lida in that number of nosy people.

"Did you ever meet anyone from his family?"

"I met his sister once. He was repairing the downspout at the front of the house when she came along. He didn't seem to be all that excited to see her. If I remember correctly, she was telling him about a job. It must have been at your place. Her name was Leslie or something close to that."

"Lida?" I asked.

Beverly nodded. "That sounds about right." She

clapped her hands. "Where are my manners? Would you like something to drink? Coffee? Tea?" She made a move as if she was trying to get up.

I waved for her to settle back in her seat. "That's very kind of you, but I'm fine. Please don't trouble yourself."

"Why are you looking for Zeph?" she asked.

I bit my lip because I couldn't see any way around telling her the truth. I didn't want to lie to this sweet old lady. "I'm not looking for Zeph. I know where he is," I said.

She furrowed her brow. "Then why are you here?"

I took a breath. "There was an accident at the factory today. Zeph fell off the roof."

"Oh my." She covered her mouth. "Is he hurt? Are you here to get him some clothes for the hospital?"

I shook my head. "He—he died."

All the color drained out of Beverly's rosy cheeks and tears appeared in the corners of her eyes. She gave herself a shake, and as quickly as the tears came, they were gone. Her coloring went back to normal. When she collected herself, she managed to say, "I'm so sorry to hear that. He was a good young man. He will be missed." She folded her hands on her lap. "I will not cry," she said with stubborn determination. "I will miss him greatly and remember the good times we had. A person of my age is well acquainted with loss. I have lost my husband, both of my sons, my parents, and all my siblings. I have no more tears to shed."

"I'm so sorry to hear that," I murmured.

"I'm ninety years old. I'm doing well despite my leg." She knocked her cane on the prosthetic leg, and it made a pinging sound. "Everyone says they want to live forever. I believed that before I realized that 'forever' can be quite a lonely place."

My heart ached for her. I didn't know what to say to console her.

Beverly noisily cleared her throat. "The police ruled his death an accident, then?"

"The Sheriff's Department is not sure it was a complete accident."

"Oh? What happened?"

I shook my head. "I can't say anything more, but because Zeph lived here, I thought maybe you would know something about his life. Who were his friends? Did he ever have guests over?"

"Other than his sister stopping by, I don't know anything about any of that. Zeph kept to himself. He barely spoke about anything that was personal."

"So you never saw anyone else, other than Lida?" I asked.

She shook her head. "I barely saw Zeph when he started working. He worked all hours. Mostly late nights. I was always asleep when he got in, and since the basement has its own private entrance, I wasn't aware of his comings and goings."

"He worked late nights?" I asked.

"He said he was on the third shift at the factory."

I frowned. There was no third shift at Swissmen Candyworks. Everyone was finished for the day by six in the evening, sometimes earlier if business was slow. "Where is the entrance to the basement?"

"It's out back down a set of stairs. It's an old cellar-type basement, and you have to go outside to enter it."

She pushed down on her cane and with a few jerks of her body was finally able to stand up. "You can see it for yourself. I'd go down there with you, but I can't make it down the stairs any longer with this bum leg." She tapped her prosthetic again. "I have the spare key to his place in the kitchen."

I stood up and followed her slow progress to the kitchen.

The kitchen was as frilly and over-the-top as the rest of the house, and I was happy to see that Beverly had indulged her taste here as well. It might have been dated, but it was what she liked. At ninety years old she deserved to have what she really wanted, not what was popular at the moment.

She opened an overhead kitchen cupboard. On the back side of the door, there was a line of nails with keys hanging from them. Beverly looked at each key in turn and then plucked one from the center. "Let me show you to the back door."

CHAPTER TEN

Beverly opened the back kitchen door and pointed to the left. I blinked. From where I stood, the entrance to the basement looked like a black hole. I wondered how wise it was for me to go down there alone. If Aiden was right and Zeph had been killed, could the killer be hiding in the basement?

I shook the thoughts from my head. A killer wouldn't come back to the victim's home. Then I remembered that not every killer I had come across was all that bright.

She put the key in my hand. "I'll just let you go down there and take a peek. I need to sit. My missing leg hurts from time to time, especially when I'm upset. Phantom pain, the doctor calls it."

I nodded, stepped out into the cold, and heard the door close behind me. It seemed if I wanted to see where Zeph had been living recently, I was truly on my own.

The steps leading to the basement door were snow-covered and encrusted with ice. They were also impossibly narrow. I tried to imagine Zeph with his size thirteen feet making his way down those stairs. Perhaps he just jumped to the bottom. I removed my phone from the pocket of my parka and turned on the flashlight app. It didn't give as much light as I would have liked, but it was enough to keep me from slipping and breaking my neck.

Finally, after a lot of tentative baby steps, I found myself at the door. Claustrophobia set in. I really did feel as if I was at the bottom of a hole. I noticed a drain at my feet, and that was a relief. I couldn't even imagine what it would be like to be in the stairwell if it was raining and filling with water. I shuddered.

I put the key that Beverly had given me in the lock and turned it. Thankfully, the door opened easily, and I again found myself in the dark.

I brushed my hand against the wall, looking for a light switch. When I found none, I shone my phone on the ceiling and saw a single light bulb with a dangling string. I pulled the string and the bulb's dim light glowed.

Zeph's home was a single room. There was a plaid couch that must also serve as his bed, and his bathroom was separated from the rest of the area with a shower curtain that at the moment was open. My heart hurt. If I had known Zeph had lived in such a place, I would have helped him find another room somewhere in the village. There were studio apartments and boarding-houses that were much better than this.

Beverly may have meant well, but the dank smell of mold made the space barely livable. It was a wonder that Zeph hadn't suffered from a perpetual cold. Also, with her prosthetic leg, how did Beverly know the condition of the basement? When was the last time she had been down here? Had it been in the last decade?

The light bulb didn't illuminate much, but it did allow me to see a table in the corner of the room. I gasped.

Piles of dollar bills and jewelry lay on the old dining table. It was all neatly organized. Next to the piles, there was a notebook that was open to a page with a handwritten heading that said, "Pay Outs."

"'Pay outs'?" Pay outs to whom? And why did Zeph have all this jewelry and money? Where had it come from?

This case had just gotten a lot more interesting; it was time to call Aiden.

Aiden and Deputy Little arrived thirty minutes later. By that time, I was back upstairs with Beverly, enjoying a cup of ginger tea. She told me stories about the time she and her husband moved to California on a whim when they were just married.

"We were only there three months before we came home. If you ask me, nothing beats the heartland of Ohio. We bought this house and I have lived here ever since. That was seventy years ago."

I tried to imagine what it would be like to live in the same place for that long, and I realized that my grandmother was close to it. If my grandfather were alive, they would have been married sixty years this year. She had lived above the candy shop since he'd brought her home as his young bride.

When there was a knock on the door, I told Beverly not to get up, and I let Aiden and the deputy into the house.

Aiden introduced himself and Deputy Little to Beverly, and then turned to me. "When I saw you at Swissmen Candyworks earlier, you didn't tell me that you were going to seek out Zeph's home."

"I assumed that you had already been here."

He shook his head. "We didn't know that he lived here. We were told he was still at home with his parents. When Little went to the parents to tell them the news, they didn't dispute that their son lived with them."

I nodded. The parents' reaction might not have made sense to Aiden, but it did to me. It would be a great embarrassment to the Lantz family if the news got out that Zeph had left the family home. Many would assume he was just one step away from leaving the Amish faith altogether. In many cases, that was true when a younger family member moved out before marriage. It was true for Charlotte. However, I refrained from mentioning that because her husband was standing right in front of me.

Deputy Little stayed back in the living room with Beverly while I walked Aiden through the house to the back door and down those precarious basement steps. At least this time, there was plenty of light from Aiden's high-powered flashlight.

I had left the light on in the basement and stepped aside so that Aiden could have a clear view of the table.

He whistled as he walked over to it. "Wow."

"That's what I thought."

He turned to look at me. "You just found the village thief."

CHAPTER ELEVEN

More deputies were called to Beverly's house, and I stayed as long as I could, until I had to leave for Swissmen Sweets and my parents' welcome dinner. I knew that Maami had been cooking my father's favorite foods all day, and I didn't want to disappoint her by being late. I also didn't want my parents asking me a million questions as to why I blew them off. I would, of course, have to make excuses for Aiden's absence. With this new development in the case, he most definitely wouldn't be able to make the meal.

As I reached Swissmen Sweets, Emily Keim was just leaving from the front door and was about to pull the door closed. When she saw me, she waited. "Bailey, whatever is the matter? You look so pale."

That's when I realized that Maami and Emily, whom I'd seen just before I found Zeph's body on the ground, most likely knew nothing about his death or the repercussions that it could have on our business.

For a split second, I thought about not telling her,

but I quickly dismissed that idea. With Amish gossip surely running wild in the village, she would know soon enough. I wouldn't be surprised if Emily's husband had already heard the news.

"Zeph Lantz died at the factory. That's why I had to rush out of the shop earlier today."

Emily covered her mouth and gasped.

"I've been trying to find out what happened."

She lowered her hand. "Was he murdered?"

I shrugged. "Aiden and his team are still making that determination. It's hard to say."

"Why?"

It wasn't that I thought Emily would share whatever I told her, but I thought it was best to keep the details of Zeph's death quiet for now. It was what Aiden would have wanted me to do.

"I can't say," I said with an apologetic smile.

She nodded. Emily was usually understanding in these types of scenarios. She wasn't one to pressure someone else for information or put pressure on a friend for any reason at all. If I had said the same thing to Charlotte, she would not have stood for it. I couldn't blame my cousin; I was wired the same way.

"I feel so bad for his family," Emily murmured as she retied her bonnet ribbons under her chin. "Zeph was a bit of a troublemaker in the community, but I never thought something like this would happen."

"How was he a troublemaker?" I asked. "You mentioned before that I should have checked with you before hiring him."

She pursed her lips. "I should never have said that. It was unkind. Everyone deserves a chance."

"That's true, but I do need to know why you said it. I have never known you to speak ill of anyone unless there was a very good reason."

She twisted the end of her bonnet ribbon around her finger as if she was debating what to say.

"Please, Emily. It might help me find out what happened to him."

She dropped her hand at her side. "He's been known to have sticky fingers."

"Sticky fingers?"

"He took things. At least he did when he was a small child. It was so embarrassing to his parents." She wouldn't look me in the eye, as if she was embarrassed to even report this habit Zeph had had when he was young.

"What kind of things did he take?" I asked.

She played with the black bonnet ribbons again. She looked very pretty in her wool coat and black bonnet. Emily had bright blue eyes and white-blond hair. She and her husband had two children; her oldest daughter, born out of wedlock, was deaf. She helped her husband manage their Christmas tree farm, cared for his elderly grandmother, and worked for me. All of this went through my head in a split second and reminded me that she needed to go home to her husband and children.

"You can tell me tomorrow. I know you have to go home," I said. "I'm sorry to keep you so long."

She smiled. "I'm not in a big rush to return home. My husband will be busy with Christmas tree sales. As you know, this is our biggest season of the year, and Grandma Leah is making dinner. The girls are with one of my husband's sisters for the night so that he can sell trees without having them underfoot."

"You get the night off?"

"Maybe not the whole night, but an hour or two. I have to say I'm grateful for that. It doesn't happen all that often and certainly not at this time of year." She smiled. "Or ever."

"Well, I don't want to keep you, in any case. You should enjoy what little free time you have."

She gave me her sweet smile again. "You're not keeping me, and to answer your question, I don't know what all he took. I just remember when he was about eleven, Bishop Yoder caught him taking money from the collection plate. By the end of the Sunday services, everyone knew about it. The family was so humiliated that they got up and left the church meal. They didn't come back to church for months. Bishop Yoder finally was able to convince them to return, and Zeph had to write a public apology and read it in front of the congregation during a service."

I grimaced. Of course stealing was wrong, but I could only guess how hard it must have been for Zeph to read that apology in front of the bishop, his parents, and every other member of his district. At the same time, I wasn't surprised at his punishment. The Amish were big on public apologies and not repenting in the dark. If a person really was repentant of their action, they would make it known to everyone in a public forum.

"Did he take money from the collection plate just the one time?" I asked.

"There were whispers of him doing it other times,

but as far as I know, that was the only time he was caught."

"I can understand why Bishop Yoder was upset and why he would have to reprimand Zeph in some way, but doing it in front of the whole congregation seems harsh."

"I don't believe he could have come back into the fold any other way. Ruth was with the bishop when he caught Zeph in the act of stealing, and from what I understand, she insisted on the public apology or she would not allow her husband to invite the Lantz family back to church." She looked this way and that, as if she was afraid Ruth Yoder would come around the corner at any second. "Don't tell anyone I said that."

"Ahh," I said. Ruth Yoder was the bishop's wife, and she most certainly would not let anyone pull a stunt like that without the entire district knowing about it. "I promise not to breathe a word about Ruth. Does she really have the authority to keep a family in the district from attending services? It doesn't seem very Amish to me for the bishop's wife to make such decisions."

Her eyes darted back and forth again. "I think she does because the bishop just wants to keep the peace in his home. Honestly, I think that's how she twists the bishop's arm so he will go along with most of her ideas. Sometimes he puts his foot down, but it's not as often as he used to. He's quite a bit older than she, you know."

I would be tired, too, if I was married to Ruth Yoder. The woman was exhausting.

Emily wound her bonnet ribbon around her finger so tightly this time, the tip of her finger turned snow white. "Please don't repeat anything that I said about the bishop's wife. I don't want any trouble from her."

"I won't say a word," I promised.

She began to shiver and dropped her hand into the fold of her scarf.

"I have kept you out in the cold long enough. It's time for you to go home and enjoy the little bit of free time that you have before your children come home."

"*Danki*, Bailey. I will see you tomorrow, and we will all be praying for Zeph's family."

"Thank you. They need all the prayers they can get."

I watched Emily walk away, but just before I went into the candy shop, I noticed some movement to my left.

Emily's older brother, Abel Esh, stood under the streetlamp smoking a homemade cigarette and watching me. I would not be surprised if he'd listened to my entire conversation with Emily.

Abel was as handsome as his younger sister was beautiful. He had the same white-blond hair and striking blue eyes, and he had the build of someone who'd worked outside most of his life. But his handsomeness was only skin deep. Abel and Emily's older sister, Esther, had had a falling out with Emily when she left the family to marry. Both Abel and Esther would have been happier if Emily had stayed home and continued working indefinitely at Esh Family Pretzels, as it seemed Esther would be doing.

Abel claimed to help Esther in the pretzel shop, but no one in the village believed that. Instead, he was caught up in nefarious activities all over the county, from drug trafficking to bribery. He'd even served time in prison for his misdeeds but was released because of prison overcrowding.

I glared back at him but kept my mouth shut. There was nothing good that I could say to or about Abel Esh.

He blew smoke in my direction and then sauntered away. What on earth could he be up to now? I didn't even want to guess.

When I was sure he was gone, I went into Swissmen Sweets. I closed and locked the candy shop door behind me.

CHAPTER TWELVE

I sighed on the other side of the door and wished that Abel didn't rattle me so much. I supposed because I knew what he was capable of, his presence made me even more nervous. I reminded myself he had every right to be standing on a public square staring at me. It wasn't illegal . . . just creepy.

It wasn't the first time, nor would it be the last, that Abel had glared at me while I came and went from Swissmen Sweets. Tonight, I was feeling especially suspicious because of Zeph Lantz's death.

The lights were off in the front room of Swissmen Sweets, but there was enough light coming in through the windows to make my way.

There was a snuffling at my feet. I looked down to see Jethro looking up at me and licking his snout.

"Did Maami give you a treat?"

He didn't answer, but I knew the truth.

There was a knock on the door behind me, and through the window, I saw my parents standing outside.

I opened the door. "You're right on time." I forced a smile to my face.

"We're always on time," my mother said.

This was true. My mother felt that being late was the rudest thing a person could do. When I worked at JP Chocolates and kept crazy hours, I was late for everything. That had not sat well with her.

I took my parents' coats and hung them on the coat-tree by the door. Then I removed my own coat and added it to the tree.

"You have a pig in the candy shop," Mom said.

"It's Jethro, Aiden's mother's pig. You might remember him from the last time that you were here."

My mother nodded. "Oh, yes, I do recall a pig at the tea we attended for Mother's Day a few years back. I did not expect to see him in the candy shop."

My father had his hands in his pockets and rocked back on his heels as he took everything in. "Every time I come back here, it's like stepping into a time capsule. Nothing changes. It's almost frightening."

My mother chuckled. "Silas, don't be so dramatic. Everything is the same, but that's how the Amish are. They are always the same."

I bit my lip to stop myself from saying something to my mother about making vague generalizations about a whole group of people. I thought it was best to keep my mouth shut. Getting into an argument with my mother was never a good idea, and after the day I'd had, I was in no shape for a war of words.

"I just got here myself. Maami will be upstairs putting the final touches on dinner. She made all your favorites, Dad."

My father rubbed his hands together. "I do miss my mother's home cooking. Your mother is better at take-out."

Mom shrugged. "And proud of it."

I followed my parents upstairs, carrying Jethro with me. The little pig didn't like to walk upstairs when he could be carried. Normally, I would just leave him downstairs if he refused to walk up to my grandmother's apartment, but considering everything that had happened that day, I wanted to keep the little pig close. I wanted to keep everyone I loved close, and for all the trouble he caused, I loved Jethro. He was well aware of it, too.

Maami stepped out of the tiny apartment kitchen when my father reached the top of the stairs. She beamed at her son and daughter-in-law. "I thought I heard two long-missed voices." She hugged my father and then my mother. "How was your journey?"

"It was fine. Everything was easy until we arrived at the inn, but Bailey was able to sort that out," my father said.

Maami looked at me and raised her brows. I shook my head. I would tell her about it later. I didn't want to get into that conversation again with my parents.

"I was just finishing setting the table," Maami said. "The three of you can go sit down and I will go collect supper."

"I'll help you," I said.

Maami nodded, and I followed her into the kitchen. The room was no bigger than a walk-in closet, and it didn't even have a full-size refrigerator or stove. The smaller appliances ran on propane, and if Maami ever had a need to store a lot of food, she used the candy shop kitchen, where there were two industrial-size refrigerators and a freestanding freezer.

She pointed at a tray that held a shepherd's pie, five plates, and silverware. "You can take that out and I will get the water and napkins. What happened when your parents checked into the inn?"

As quickly as I could, I told her about the break-in at the Village Inn, and explained that Aiden wouldn't be able to make it to dinner.

Maami shook her head. "Poor Lillian. She must be beside herself. I'll make her a pie after dinner tonight to take over tomorrow. I know Aiden must be doing all he can to find the people who are committing these terrible crimes, but the community is nervous. At church on Sunday, it was all anyone could talk about. And since the Yoders were robbed, Ruth is livid. If Aiden does find the person behind this, I hope he won't tell Ruth. I would be afraid of what she might do."

My brow went up. I could imagine how Ruth Yoder felt about someone breaking into her home. But Maami couldn't be implying that Ruth would hurt anyone; at least I didn't think that was what she was implying.

"I think it has to be someone from the community to know so much about the places that have been robbed. An *Englischer* would not know which Amish homes and businesses had the most wealth. We all look the same to them."

"It is upsetting, but you can rest assured the break-ins are over. Aiden has found the culprit," I said, hoping to put my grandmother at ease.

"Do you know who is behind the robberies?"

"Yes, but I can't say yet."

She nodded. Anyone else, i.e. Charlotte, would have pried and demanded that I tell them the person's name, but not my grandmother. She just quietly took her tray from the room.

When we were all seated at the table and Maami said the blessing, Dad dug into his food. After his first bite, he looked at my grandmother. "Maam, this is even better than I remember it being. I sure miss your home cooking."

My mother laughed. "That's because he's not getting any home cooking from me. I retired from cooking when Bailey went off to culinary school. Silas has learned to fend for himself."

"She means takeout or eat out," Dad said.

My grandmother's forehead furrowed in confusion. In the Amish world, a wife and mother didn't just decide to stop cooking one day as my mother had. However, Maami was far too sweet and kind to say what she might be thinking about my mother's declaration.

Mom turned to me. "I'm surprised that we didn't wait for Aiden to eat. Your father and I were looking forward to seeing him again. Will he be here soon?"

I had just taken a big bite of pie when she asked the question, and I forced it down my throat with a gulp of water. When I was able to speak, I said, "He can't come tonight, but I'm sure you will be able to see him tomorrow."

"He can't come?" my mother asked with an edge to her voice. "But when we saw you earlier, you said he planned to be here."

"He wanted to be, but a big case opened up and he had to work."

My mother pursed her lips together. "I suppose this is something you will have to get used to, being married to a man in law enforcement. You need to think long and hard before you decide to bring children into that way of life. There will be many times you might feel like a single parent."

I shifted uncomfortably in my seat. This was not how I had wanted the dinner conversation to go.

"Why would she decide not to have children?" Maami asked. "When you marry, it is your duty to have children if you are able. I know not all women are able to bear children, but if they can, they should."

I shifted uncomfortably in my seat. Of course Aiden and I had talked about having children after we married, but we hadn't come to any conclusions yet. Both of our careers were taking off in different directions. At least right now, I couldn't fathom where kids would fit amid our already busy lives. I would never outwardly disagree with my grandmother on such a sensitive topic, but I didn't agree with her on this topic. Not every woman was meant to be a mother, whether they had the physical ability to be one or not.

Maami looked at me. "You do plan to have a baby soon, I hope. It would be so *gut* for you and Aiden to have a child to hold you together when you both are being pulled in so many different directions."

My phone rang, which saved me from having to answer the question. I fished it out of my pocket and saw it was Juliet calling. "Oh, I'm so sorry. I have to take this." I stood up from the table and walked into the hallway. Jethro followed me out of the room. Maybe he wasn't enjoying the baby talk either—if there was a baby, he would no longer be the center of attention in all our lives, especially Juliet's. Knowing how she doted on Jethro, I couldn't imagine how she would be with a grandchild.

Usually, I wouldn't be so rude as to answer my phone at the dinner table, but this was the best means of escape.

"Bailey," Juliet said in my ear. "We're finally done wrapping. Good heavens, it took all day long. There was a great dispute about which color ribbon to use with which wrapping paper. Traditional red or silver, and then Jane Meredith said we should use red and green plaid, which set us back again. Plaid? We aren't a Scottish congregation. Not that there is anything wrong with being Scottish. I love bagpipe music, don't you, especially on St. Patrick's Day."

I didn't bother to tell her St. Patrick's Day was an Irish holiday. I thought she knew, at least that was my hope.

"All that being said, I can pick up Jethro now. You have been a complete dear to keep him for so long. I'm sure he was just a perfect prince for you. He loves you so."

I made some mumbled sound because I was at a loss for words, and finally managed, "Uh, thanks. We're at the candy shop."

"Wonderful. I'm in my car leaving the church. I will be there in one minute."

I ended the call, tucked my phone back into my pocket, and scooped up Jethro. When Juliet said that she would be here in one minute, she really meant it; The church and the candy shop were directly across from each other on the square.

Jethro and I made it to the front door just as Juliet parked her sedan in one of the diagonal spots in front of the shop. I opened the door and a blast of cold hit me in the face. The wind was picking up, and Margot's game pieces were waving wildly on the square. It was a bit disconcerting to see them flapping back and forth. I prayed none of them blew away because Margot would lose her marbles over it. If she was so upset about the red game piece coming down from the candy factory's roof, who knew how she would feel if one of the other game pieces blew away.

"Oh, Bailey, thank you for taking such good care of him," Juliet said. She was bundled up in a pink-and-red polka-dotted parka that came down to her knees, and she wore a matching pink beret on her head.

I handed Jethro over to her. "It was my pleasure. I even gave him a bath."

"You did? You are just the sweetest thing." She peeked into the store, as if she was trying to subtly see who else might be in the building. "I have to say, I was surprised when you said that you were at the candy shop. Are you up late making sweets for the Candy Land Experience tomorrow?"

I shook my head. "No, we are ready here at Swiss-men Sweets for Candy Land. I don't know about the rest of the village."

She chuckled.

"I'm having dinner with my grandmother and my parents."

"Your parents are here?" she asked with a gleam in her eye. "How wonderful. I knew they were coming for Christmas, but I didn't know they would be arriving this early. Can I come in and see them?"

I didn't see how I could talk her out of it.

She entered the shop and shoved Jethro back into my arms. The little pig looked up at me as if to ask what was going on. The short answer was my worst nightmare, which would be Juliet and my mother joining forces against me to plan the wedding. Okay, maybe it wasn't my very worst nightmare, but it was up there with something involving spiders. Shiver.

"I have been dying to talk to your mother about the wedding. I think because you and Aiden have so much going on, it is high time that your mother and I take over the planning. I know she lives far away, but I think we can make it work, and because I'm here, I can be the contact for all the vendors and special meetings."

Vendors? Special meetings?

The only thing I knew for sure about my wedding was that I didn't want it to be long and elaborate; that just wasn't our style. Aiden and I were much simpler. The only place I got elaborate was in creating my candies. That was where I focused all my creativity.

"I don't think that's what we want," I said, but I was talking to the air because she was already halfway up the stairs.

When I reached the top of the stairs, Juliet hurried down the hallway to the sitting room.

"Oh boy," I murmured to Jethro.

He snorted in agreement. At least the pig was on my side on this one.

"I'm so sorry to barge in on all of you when you are having dinner," I heard Juliet say as I stepped into the room. "I just came to collect my pig, but when Bailey said you were here, I could not resist coming up and saying hello. It has been far too long since I saw you last. The reverend and I would love to have you all over for a Christmas dinner while you're here. You're practically family already." She took a breath.

Dad stood up from his chair and held out his hand to shake hers, but Juliet crushed him in a bear hug.

And even though my mother didn't stand, Juliet hugged her while she was seated in her chair.

"I just can't believe in the next year we will all be real family! We have been waiting for this for so long. Bailey and Aiden surely took their time getting engaged, and it seems they are taking just as much time to plan the wedding." Juliet looked at me out of the corner of her eye as if making sure I was paying attention.

I grimaced. Juliet wasn't wasting any time getting to what she believed was the most important topic of the evening.

I opened my mouth to defend myself, but Juliet was faster. "Susan, I would love to take you to lunch tomorrow. We have so much to talk about!"

"Will your pig be coming with us?" my mother asked and glanced at Jethro and me.

"Oh no," Juliet said. "Bailey will watch him while we're at lunch."

Sure I would. I loved it that Juliet had gotten to that level of comfort with me.

Who was I kidding? I loved that little bacon bundle,

and at the moment, I felt he was the only one in the room completely on my side. Even Maami had ideas about what my wedding and married life should be like.

"Lunch would be nice," my mother said tentatively.

"Wonderful!" Juliet cried. "I will pick you up at noon. You're staying at the Village Inn, correct?"

All Mom could do was nod.

"Perfect." Juliet grabbed Jethro from my arms and waltzed out of the room.

After she was gone, my father said, "She seems to be more excited about the wedding than you are, Bailey."

"You have no idea," I replied.

CHAPTER THIRTEEN

That night, I stayed up as late as I could, waiting for Aiden to call. When I didn't hear from him, I called him myself.

"Bailey? What are you doing still up? It's after midnight," he said. Aiden knew that I had to be up at five thirty each morning to make candies at Swissmen Sweets and instruct my staff at Swissmen Candyworks. That was especially true during the Christmas season, and because the candy factory had lost a half day of candy production after Zeph's accident, the following day would be especially hectic.

"I just wanted to hear your voice before I went to sleep," I said.

"I wanted to hear your voice, too," he said.

I could hear the warmth in his voice and I felt better instantly. I was still distraught over Zeph's death, but knowing Aiden was there for me and always would be there for me, I would make it through.

"Any more news about the case?" I asked. I couldn't help myself. I was as nosy as they came.

On the other end of the call, Aiden sighed. "Nothing more than what I have already told you."

"What about the game piece on the factory roof? Can I take it down?" I asked. "It's a bit of an eyesore and is even more disturbing because of what happened to Zeph."

"I don't want you going on that roof," he said. "Now or ever. It's too high and far too steep. Besides, we don't want anyone up there right now until we fully understand the scene. I'll find someone to take it down as soon as it no longer needs to be there for the investigation."

I twisted my mouth. I would have felt better if I could take the game piece down myself because then I knew it would be done in a timely manner, but hearing the worry in Aiden's voice, I decided not to push him. At least, I would give him a few days before I pushed him again.

"How was dinner with Maami and your parents?" Aiden asked.

It wasn't lost on me that he was changing the subject.

"It went fine. Your mom showed up to pick up Jethro. She and my mom made plans to have lunch together. I'm very nervous about that."

"Why? Don't you want our moms to get along?"

"Yes, I do, but I don't trust them. They are up to something, and I think the something involves our wedding. You know both have been very vocal over the fact we haven't made any plans. I would be willing to put money on their staging a wedding intervention."

Aiden laughed. "A wedding intervention? That sounds bad."

"They might even try to trick us into getting married on Christmas Day."

"I wouldn't mind that, Bailey," Aiden said softly. "The sooner I marry you, the better."

I felt as if I had just gotten off the phone with Aiden and fallen asleep when I was jarred awake by my ringing cell phone. I fumbled on the nightstand looking for it and managed to knock it onto the floor. Finally, I contorted my body to reach the phone without actually having to sit up. When I looked at the screen, I expected to see Aiden's face, but instead I saw it was the Swissmen Sweets number. That shook me awake. The only person who would be calling from the candy shop at this time of night was my grandmother. I couldn't think of a single time that my grandmother had called me in the middle of the night. In fact, I could only think of one or two times that she'd called me at all.

I put the phone to my ear. "Maami?"

"*Ya*, Bailey, it's me. I hate to bother you at such an early hour, but there are police outside. The flashing lights woke me up, and when I went to see what was the matter, Deputy Little told me that the cheese shop next door had been broken into. He told me to stay in the candy shop and lock all the doors. I hate to ask this, but—"

Before she could even finish the sentence, I said, "I'll be there in ten minutes. Stay inside like Deputy

Little said and keep your doors locked." I ended the call, jumped out of bed, and threw on some clothes.

I was still pulling on a sweatshirt as I ran down the stairs to the first floor. I felt as if I was on a Tilt-A-Whirl ride as I spun around the room, trying to gather up my coat, hat, scarf, and shoulder bag.

Meanwhile, my giant white rabbit, Puff, watched me from her dog bed by the kitchen. Usually when I came downstairs, Puff went immediately to the kitchen and stared at her food bowl with the same intensity that a great white shark looked at a harbor seal, but it was too early even for her to be motivated to get up.

"I have to go to the candy shop and be with Maami for a little bit. I will come back for you later today and take you to the shop," I explained to the bunny.

It was true she probably had no idea what I was saying, and she certainly didn't know why I was zipping around the house like a toy spinning top.

However, I did get her attention when I filled her bowl with rabbit food and dropped broccoli and cabbage on her plate. The sweet scent of cabbage was enough to motivate her to hop off her bed and into the kitchen.

Seeing that Puff would be all right for a few hours, I ran out the door and to the garage. Normally, I would walk the two blocks to the candy shop, but I had a feeling that I would need my car today.

The drive took all of two minutes, and even before I turned the corner from Apple Street onto Main Street, where the candy shop was, I saw the flashing lights.

All the parking spots in front of the cheese shop were full of Sheriff's Department vehicles, and there was an ambulance, too. I shivered to think of what might have happened.

During the autumn, the cheese shop had changed hands. It had been owned by the same family for years, but when the matriarch passed on, the family decided to sell. Martha Ann Keim, a sweet Amish widow who was in her early fifties, had bought the shop and lived in an apartment above it. In the short time she had been Swissmen Sweets' neighbor, Martha Ann and my grandmother had become fast friends. It was something that I was happy for because I was away from the candy shop so much with Swissmen Candyworks and my cable television show. It was good to know that my grandmother had someone to depend on who was close by.

Maami would be distraught if something had happened to Martha Ann.

I parked across the street from the candy shop and got out.

Glancing at the cars in front of the cheese shop, I didn't see Aiden's department SUV. I frowned. I would have expected him to be the first one on the scene if there was something wrong next door to Swissmen Sweets. He would know how upset I'd be. Why hadn't Aiden called me? He knew that I would worry about a break-in so close to where my grandmother was sleeping.

I stepped out of the car just as Deputy Little came out of the cheese shop. He grimaced when he saw me. That wasn't how I liked to be greeted by Charlotte's husband.

He had his black stocking cap pulled down over his ears. It was cold out and there wasn't a single cloud in the night sky. The temperature had dropped considerably after sunset, and with no cloud cover, it was even more frigid.

I pulled my own stocking cap down over my ears.

"Bailey, I forgot to call you," he said by way of greeting.

"Where's Aiden?" I asked.

"He was here for a short while but was called away."

"Called away by what?"

Deputy Little wrinkled his nose, which told me he either didn't want to respond or was told not to say where Aiden had gone. Fine. I would get that answer when I spoke to Aiden later.

"You were going to call me because of this?" I gestured to all the sheriff vehicles parked in front of my candy shop.

"Yeah," he said in a sheepish voice. "Aiden asked me to call you because he knew you'd want to know."

He had that right, but it still begged the question as to why Aiden hadn't called me himself or even texted. It was true a text might not have woken me up, but had he sent one, I would at least have seen that he'd tried. I didn't like the idea that he gave his deputy the assignment of dealing with me. Why wasn't he there? The question ran through my head, but I had a much more important one first.

"Why is the ambulance here? Was anyone hurt during the break-in? How is Martha Ann?"

"The ambulance is here for Martha Ann. There were actually two—the first one already took her to the hospital."

"Is she okay?" I gasped.

"Martha Ann knocked her head, but she seems okay. They took her to the hospital as a precaution."

"Someone hit her?"

He shook his head. "She says not. She heard noises downstairs and claimed that she bumped her head when she was trying to investigate. She was in such a rush, she didn't put on her glasses and couldn't see where she was going. She managed to knock herself out cold. By the time she came to, whoever was in the shop was long gone. When she saw the state of the place, she used her shop phone to call us."

"What time was that?"

"We got the call at two in the morning," he said.

"And when did Martha Ann hit her head?" I shoved my hands in my pockets. In my haste to leave the house, I had forgotten my gloves.

"Sometime before that."

I made a face at the vagueness of his answer.

"We did ask her," Deputy Little said in a defensive voice. "She doesn't remember the time."

"Does she have memory loss?" I asked worriedly.

"We don't know yet. She probably has at least a slight concussion."

Poor Martha Ann.

"How did you know to come here?" Deputy Little asked.

"My grandmother called me."

"Is she all right? I saw her for a moment when I first arrived, but with Aiden away, I am in charge of the scene. I hope she locked herself in the candy shop like I told her to."

"She did," I said.

I continued to wonder where Aiden was. Because of the nature of his job, I knew there were times when he couldn't tell me exactly what he was doing on any given day or where he planned to go. However, it didn't sit well with me that he wasn't with me in that moment. What could be a bigger case in Holmes County at the moment than this break-in? It had to be related to Zeph's death, didn't it? Because we'd *thought* Zeph was the burglar, but now that there had been another incident after his death, he couldn't be. Could he?

"Can I go into the cheese shop and see what's going on?" I asked.

He grimaced. "You can't. It's a crime scene."

It was a long shot, and I knew there was no point in arguing with him. It seemed that I wouldn't know what had really happened until I had a chance to speak to Martha Ann, and that was assuming she was all right and remembered what had happened.

"What did they take?"

"We don't know everything and won't until Martha Ann is well enough to tell us when she's out of the hospital, but the cash drawer was cleaned out, and from what I can tell, they stole some of the cheese."

"They stole cheese?" I asked. That seemed like an extra low blow to me. Also, what were they going to do with cheese besides eat it? It wasn't as if cheese had a great street value. I stopped myself from saying any of this to Deputy Little.

"Deputy Little! Deputy Little!" Margot Rawlings waved at us while stomping down the sidewalk. It was clear she had left her home in a hurry. She wore a long wool coat over a set of flannel Christmas pajamas.

She had curlers in her hair. All this time, I had thought that her short hair was naturally curly, but now I was learning that she used curlers. I didn't know why, but that was just as disconcerting to me as learning that Zeph might not have worked alone when he robbed those Amish homes and businesses.

She stopped in front of us with her hands on her hips. "What is going on here?"

"Who called you?" the deputy wanted to know.

"I will have you know, Deputy Little, that I have my ear to the ground when things are happening in Harvest. No one has to call me for me to know something is wrong." She looked at the cheese shop. "What happened?"

Deputy Little briefly told Margot about the break-in.

"I'm glad to hear that Martha Ann Keim is all right, but this will not do. This will not do at all! A police presence and crime scene tape does not go with the Christmas spirit." She took a breath. "You're going to have to get this all wrapped up by eight. The camel and the rest of the animals for the live nativity will be arriving then. People from the community will be coming out to watch. We can't give the impression that crime happens here in our beautiful little village."

But crime did happen in Harvest, and it seemed to me that it was occurring more and more often.

"Margot, we'll do our best to wrap up before your event begins, but this is an ever-evolving case. We can't rush it for the sake of tourism," Deputy Little managed to say without a waver in his voice.

I had to say I was impressed by the way he was standing up to Margot. Not many people could.

"You have to," she argued. "All Harvest has to live on is tourism." She poked me in the side. "You tell him that, Bailey."

Had I not been wearing my heavy parka, her poke would really have hurt because even with the parka on, I could feel it.

"I'm not telling him that. Margot, this is serious. This is the seventh Amish business or home to be robbed in a month's time."

"Well, let's downplay it at least. I can't have people afraid to come to Harvest. There has to be a way we can spin it." She held her hand in the air. "We can say it's an inside job. That will actually spark more interest and maybe get even more people to come to the village, especially with all the true-crime fanatics there are in the world."

"An inside job how?" I asked, almost afraid of what her answer might be.

"Crimes against Amish by Amish, so that the English visitors have nothing to worry about."

That was a terrible idea on so many levels, I didn't even know where to start.

Luckily, Deputy Little thought faster than I did. "We cannot assume the culprits are Amish, nor can we assume that Amish businesses and homes will be the only ones that will be hit. It may be that it is easier to target Amish homes and businesses because they don't have security systems and their owners are less on guard than English ones generally are."

Margot glowered at him. "Well, if we can't say it's an inside job, make sure you're out of here before the animals come in or the whole village is in trouble and Christmas will be ruined."

No pressure.

I wanted to ask her how that would put the whole village in trouble, but she marched away. One of her curlers fell to the ground as she went.

I left Deputy Little and unlocked the door to Swissmen Sweets. When I was inside, I found the lights on and my grandmother sitting at one of the small tables at the front of the shop.

She wore her winter coat over her nightdress, and her long white hair was back in a single braid. The only times I'd ever seen my grandmother without her hair in an Amish bun at the nape of her neck were at night. When I stayed with my grandparents when I was a little girl, I would watch in fascination as she removed her hair from its knot and brushed it over and over again until it shone before she braided it for bed. When her hair wasn't braided, it almost reached the floor. I couldn't even guess how heavy it must feel on the back of her head all day. I supposed that was just something Amish women got used to, like so many other things.

"Bailey, I'm so glad you are here. How is Martha Ann?" she asked with anxiety in her voice.

"They took her to the hospital, but Deputy Little believes that she will be all right. She wasn't hurt by the person or persons who broke into the shop. She hit her head trying to see what was going on. It could have been so much worse. Maybe it was a blessing that she wasn't able to confront them."

Maami wrung her hands. "*Ya*, you must be right.

She could have been killed. I hate the idea of Martha Ann lying there hurt while I was next door. I could have done something."

I removed my parka and hung it on the coat-tree by the door. "If you went into the cheese shop when the intruder was there, you would have just gotten hurt too."

"Still . . ." she trailed off.

As much as it terrified me to think of my grandmother running into the cheese shop, I understood her desire to help because I was built the same way. There were many times when I made dubious decisions for the same reason. So far, I had been lucky enough to come out unscathed—at least for the most part—but I couldn't say that all my choices were wise.

"Does Deputy Little know who broke into the cheese shop? Did they catch the person?" Maami asked.

I shook my head.

"Could it be the same person who broke into all those other Amish homes and businesses? It would have to be, wouldn't it? I thought you said Aiden knew who that person was. Was he not able to arrest the person before they struck again? There can't be two of these people doing this, can there?"

I thought of Zeph, and the discovery that I'd made in his basement apartment. "We don't know. It seems to be a very similar crime."

"Do you know more than you're saying?" She studied my face.

I shook my head. Even though I trusted my grandmother implicitly, I didn't want to share what I'd seen in Beverly's basement until it was public knowledge.

There was no telling if it would ever be public knowledge. I cleared my throat. "In any case, with everything that's going on, I'm not comfortable with you staying here by yourself at night. I think you should move to my house for a few days until the Sheriff's Department finds out who is doing all this."

She shook her head. "I can't leave my home. I've lived here for over fifty years. I don't want to sleep anywhere else. I want to be where I shared my life with Jebidiah."

I folded my arms. "Then I guess I'm moving back in until this is all cleared up."

Maami pursed her lips. "I don't think there is anything that I can say to change your mind."

"You're right about that," I agreed.

CHAPTER FOURTEEN

When my cell phone alarm went off at four thirty, I felt as if I had been hit by a bus. I was lucky if I'd gotten one hour of sleep the night before. I reached over to turn on my lamp and my hand hit an oil lantern. That was the moment I remembered I wasn't at home but in the tiny guest bedroom in my grandmother's apartment, where I'd lived when I first moved to Holmes County years ago.

I turned on my phone's flashlight. There wasn't much for me to get ready. I had slept in the clothes I'd worn to the candy shop in the middle of the night.

My phone was almost dead, and I was dead tired. It seemed that both my phone and I had to recharge. I guessed my phone would have better luck with that than I would.

By the time I made it downstairs, I heard voices in the kitchen. Maami and Charlotte were already here, making candies to sell for the day. I pushed the swinging kitchen door open and found Maami at the stove stirring hot caramel and Charlotte at the stainless-steel worktable decorating Jethro chocolate bars with red-colored white chocolate to make Christmas bows around each piggy neck.

"The Jethro bars are so popular. These Christmas ones with the bows are going to fly off the shelves," Charlotte was saying. "We made them at the candy factory to ship out to retailers and the bows doubled our orders." She looked up. "Oh, Bailey, you're up. Cousin Clara was just telling me about your harrowing night. When Luke got home so late last night and told me what happened, I was ready to come here and stay with Cousin Clara. I was so happy to hear that you'd already made the decision to stay."

I rubbed the back of my neck. "It was the right thing to do. I will have to run over to my house this morning, though, and change. I also want to pick up Puff. I can't leave her alone in the house for too long."

"Nutmeg will be happy for the company," Maami said.

"Bailey, that's a good idea, and you do look like you were run over by a tractor," exclaimed Charlotte, who was looking fresh and well-rested.

"I was thinking more of a bus, but a tractor works, too. It's likely more appropriate for where we are."

"Luke was surprised at the break-in," Charlotte said. "I suppose all break-ins are surprising, but he really thought they'd found the person behind the robberies earlier in the day."

Maami looked at me. "Bailey mentioned that, too, but she said nothing more."

"I really can't say anything more."

"It's okay to share things with us," Charlotte said. "We're all family."

I felt that was true, but I didn't know if Aiden would agree.

"All I will say is the person they initially suspected could not have robbed the cheese shop last night. So that person may not have been working alone."

"Or the latest break-in was a copycat," Charlotte piped in.

"The fact that you know the term 'copycat crime' is my fault," I said. "I'm sure Deputy Little is thrilled by that."

"It's not completely your fault, and I can't help picking up some of the terminology, being married to a sheriff's deputy. He's resigned to the fact that I will be close to crime because I'm so close to you."

I frowned. I wasn't sure how I felt about that either. "I'm going to head home now, and then go to the factory to make sure everything is well underway there. We have a lot of time to make up for after closing early yesterday."

"I can go to the factory now," Charlotte offered.

"No, no, I want you to stay here with Maami." I shivered at the idea of my grandmother being alone.

As if she could read my mind, my grandmother said, "Bailey, it's morning now. No one will try anything at this time."

"We can't be too careful," I said. "When the Candy Land Experience and live nativity start later this morning, I'll be more comfortable with you being alone. Not that I like it, but we might not have much choice. Emily has today off. I could call her in to work."

"*Nee*," my grandmother said. "Don't do that. The fact that she's working at all at this time of year is a blessing for us. The Christmas tree farm is so busy, and her husband needs her to be home to help there."

I knew that to be true, too.

I said goodbye to Charlotte and my grandmother and headed to my house. As I walked home, I texted Aiden, **Where were you last night? I thought you would be at the cheese shop.**

My phone rang immediately. "Bailey. I wanted to be in Harvest, but there was another break-in near Berlin. It was in progress. I hoped to catch the thief in the act."

"And?"

"No luck. Whoever it was left before I got there, or had never been there at all. The homeowner said it also could have been a large raccoon trying to open his back door. It was a false alarm. I should have sent a deputy and been at the candy shop with you. I'm sorry." There was real regret in his voice.

"Aiden, it is all right. You thought you were doing the right thing."

"Maybe, but as the sheriff, I should leave some of the investigating up to my deputies. Little and the others are more than capable of handling it. There are times I miss being in the field. I feel like I spend most of my time on my computer or pushing papers back and forth over my desk."

I knew this to be true. Aiden had had a long career in law enforcement, first as a deputy for over ten years, then as an investigator for Ohio's BCI, and even as a private investigator. Going from being on the streets, so to speak, to being the head of a large organization like the Holmes County Sheriff's Department was quite a switch, and it happened at about the same time I'd opened the candy factory. We were both going through big changes in our careers. Was it any wonder that we hadn't spent any time planning our wedding yet?

I told Aiden I'd talk to him later and unlocked the front door to my little rental house.

An hour later, appropriately showered, dressed, and caffeinated, and after dropping Puff off at the candy shop, I walked into Swissmen Candyworks.

As I entered the candy factory, I glanced at Harvest Market, which was also open early. Beau Eicher, Zeph's best friend, sat on a picnic table outside the Market. I knew Lida must be distraught over Zeph's death, but his best friend would be taking it hard, too. I was about to go over and talk to him when he stood up and went back into the Market. I would have to find another time to ask him how he was.

The sales staff was setting up for the day, and the Jethro Christmas bars were front and center. Charlotte was right; they were going to fly off the shelves. I wondered if we should make even more of them. I had tried different chocolate bar shapes of animals and even Amish buggies, but none of them sold like the Jethro bars. As Juliet said, he really was the star of Harvest.

I thanked the ladies for their hard work and went back to my office. Typically, I kept the door locked, especially when Charlotte and I weren't in the factory. We were the only two with access to the room. I trusted my employees, but the office was where I kept all my employee files.

When I'd worked in New York at JP Chocolates, all

the employee files were electronic and stored on a server somewhere, so I didn't even own a filing cabinet. Jean Pierre had put me in charge of hiring and firing because he hated interviewing and conflict. I wasn't fond of either myself, but that experience at JP Chocolates had prepared me for today, when I have so many employees on my staff.

When I'd been in the office the night before, it had been neat and tidy and everything was in its place.

But that wasn't the case right now.

The file cabinet drawers were wide open. Files and papers were littered all over the floor. My desk lamp was knocked over on its side and the bulb was shattered. Shards of glass covered the desktop.

I backed out of the room and went back to the lobby, where the women were setting up for the day. I walked over to the store manager, Maeva Schueller.

"Maeva, has anyone gone into my office this morning?"

She blinked at me. "*Nee*, no one ever goes into your office. We all know that it's off-limits." She spoke as if there was something in my office of real value, but that just wasn't true. I didn't even keep a phone or computer in there. I used my cell for calls and I took my laptop home every night to get work done.

I worked on the computer almost every night. This was especially true now that Aiden was the sheriff. There was very little time to spend with him most nights. He was determined to make Holmes County the safest district in Ohio and put in thousands of extra hours to try to accomplish that goal. Aiden was a workaholic, and it was a trait that I could relate to because I was also guilty of immersing myself in my career. However, there were times our work habits made it hard for us to connect and almost impossible to plan our wedding because every time we spoke of it, we were both completely exhausted.

"I'm not accusing anyone on staff of going in there, but I have to call the police. It looks like someone ransacked the place." I spoke in a hushed tone so that none of the other staff overheard.

She covered her mouth. "Do you think it was the same person who hit Martha Ann over the head in her cheese shop? Isn't that just the most awful thing you have ever heard? Who could hit a woman like that? And a widow, too? The Bible specifically says to care for widows and orphans."

"Martha Ann was hurt, but no one hit her over the head. The Amish grapevine is wrong about that."

Maeva frowned. "It is what I heard."

I wasn't going to argue with her about it right then.

"I have to call Aiden." I paused. "Can you check the safe and all the cash drawers to make sure nothing is missing?"

She swallowed hard and nodded.

Before I called Aiden, I double-checked that I'd closed and locked my office door. I was dying to go in there and search for what might be missing, but I had a feeling I already knew what the intruder was looking for—and it was tucked in the shoulder bag over my arm at the moment.

In my shoulder bag, I had Zeph and Lida Lantz's files.

Was I wrong in thinking that's what the intruder had wanted? The intruder had wanted to know where Zeph Lantz lived. If Zeph did have an accomplice or two in the robberies, and one of them was continuing to break into buildings like the cheese shop, wouldn't that person want to know where Zeph lived, so he could find and resell all the stolen goods Zeph had in his possession? I planned to share my theory with Aiden when he arrived.

I couldn't reach Aiden, but I had a short conversation with the dispatch officer, and she said that they would let Aiden know and send a deputy out right away.

For his sake, I hoped it wasn't Deputy Little they sent, because he had been up late last night with the cheese shop break-in.

After I finished my call, Maeva reported that nothing had been taken from the factory. This confirmed my belief that it was Zeph's file the intruder was after. Or maybe he just got spooked and ran off before he could take anything?

"I thought you would want to know, too, Lida is here today. She's working on taffy again," Maeva said.

I blinked. I was shocked that she was at work.

"I'm going to go talk to her. Call me when the deputy comes. Don't let him in the office without me."

She nodded.

CHAPTER FIFTEEN

I found Lida in the candy wrapping room. She was back at cutting and wrapping taffy. As she worked, large tears slid down her cheeks onto the polished concrete floor.

"Lida?" I asked in a gentle voice.

She jumped, and the box of taffy fell off the table. Taffy pieces scattered all over the room.

"Oh no!" she cried, and the tears came down even faster. "How could I be so clumsy?"

"It is all right," I said. "They are all packed and wrapped. We just have to tuck them back into the box." I knelt on the floor and started to gather up the taffy and put the pieces back in the box.

"I can't do anything right at the moment. I have dropped so many things today. My hands are like useless mitts." She looked at her hands as if that was all the proof she needed to know her statement was true.

"You're doing fine. And everyone has a case of the dropsies now and again. It's nothing to be upset about."

"The dropsies?" She looked up at me. Her eyes and nose were as red as her hair. She was sixteen, but in that moment, she looked no more than six.

"When you drop things over and over again. When I was a little girl, my mother used to call it the dropsies." Mentioning my mother reminded me of the lunch she was going to have with Juliet today. I didn't know how that was going to go. Would they disagree about arrangements or would they have the wedding planned by the dessert course? Either scenario would likely end badly for me.

I had so much going on that I had half a mind to just let them plan the whole thing. It would save me a lot of time. However, my mother had expensive taste and, because Aiden and I planned to pay for the wedding ourselves, I didn't want her making any of the financial decisions.

"I'm surprised you're here today," I said.

She picked up the repacked box of taffy. "I was on the schedule to work."

"I know that, but if you need to take time off, considering . . ."

She wrapped her arm around herself and squeezed her middle, as if she was giving herself a hug. A sob escaped her mouth.

I walked over to her and guided her to a wooden bench. I glanced up at the glass wall that allowed visitors to look into the inner workings of Swissmen Candyworks. I was grateful to see there wasn't a tour walking by at the moment. However, one could arrive at any time. It was best to get Lida behind the scenes as quickly as possible.

"Why don't we go to the break room and chat?" I said.

She nodded numbly and let me pull her to her feet and lead her out of the candy wrapping room.

The break room was just down the hall from my office in the opposite direction from the laundry room. Normally if I had to speak privately to an employee, I would ask them to come to my office, but considering the break-in there, that option was off the table.

The break room was well lit and brightly furnished, with plush rugs and comfortable furniture. There were tables to eat at, but there were also three large sofas where staff could sit and relax while on break. When designing the space, I'd wanted it to be homey and a place where staff would like to hang out during their free time.

I was happy to see that we were the only ones in the room. Lida sat at one of the tables and buried her head in her arms. Her shoulders shook, but she made no sound.

I sat next to her and rubbed her back the way my grandmother would have done if I was ill. We just sat like that for a few minutes.

Finally, she lifted her head and wiped away her tears with the corner of her apron. "I'm so sorry. I'm so sorry. I need to get a better handle on myself. I should get back to work."

"There is no reason to apologize. You have had a terrible shock. Don't worry about the candy right now. Candy can always wait. If it's too difficult to be here, you can go home. You are entitled to bereavement time."

"*Nee, nee,* I want to be at work. I can't be at home right now. My family acts as if Zeph never even existed. How can you do that to your son, your brother? He made mistakes and fell in with the wrong friends, but that doesn't make him disappear from our memories. That's how I see it. My parents and siblings don't agree. They just feel embarrassed and disgraced by his behavior."

"Are you and Zeph the youngest?"

She shook her head. "We have four younger siblings, and . . ." she trailed off.

"And?" I asked.

"We have four younger siblings," she said firmly. "They are all twelve and under. I don't blame them for following my parents' lead when it comes to Zeph and other things. They are young. When I was their age, I never would have questioned our parents."

I wanted to ask her what she meant by "other things," but I didn't have a chance when she said, "They have always singled Zeph out as the troublemaker. It is little wonder he found trouble. There are times I think they brought it on. If you tell someone over and over again that he is bad, does he not become bad because that is what he is taught to believe about himself?"

I thought back to the story that Emily had told me about Zeph stealing from the collection plate. Had that happened before or after he was told that he was the bad child? Had it been the catalyst for the banner his family put on him?

"My father blamed my mother." She paused. "For how Zeph was."

I frowned, certain that she was about to say another name.

"That doesn't seem fair," I said.

"It is the Amish way. The mother of the family is responsible for the children and how they grow up. My father wasn't saying anything that wasn't true. She spoiled them—him." She cleared her throat. "She was much stricter with my younger siblings and with me." She looked up at me. "Please don't make me go home. It's terrible there. No one will talk about Zeph. I don't even know if my parents will have a funeral. Bishop Yoder came over last night, hoping to make arrangements with them, but they wouldn't speak about it. They said Zeph made his choice to leave the family, and that's when their responsibility to him ended."

"But they gave the deputies the impression that he still lived at home. Why would they do that when they were so upset with them?"

She blinked. "You knew that he didn't live at home?"

I nodded. "He wrote his real address on his job application."

"I am surprised that he did."

"Why is that?"

"Because then my parents or the bishop would have known where he was and could have visited him and tried to talk him into coming back home. I know he didn't want to do that. He told me he was never coming home. I didn't agree with his choices, so I helped him get the job here with the hope that being around you and the other kind people here would change him. I have learned that not everyone is as harsh as my parents."

I frowned. I knew from all the years I'd lived in Holmes County that as a whole, the Amish were a very forgiving and understanding group of people when it came to people outside their world making decisions they didn't agree with.

However, when it came to their own flesh and blood, they were much slower to forgive. I supposed it was because they held people in their community to a higher standard. Even so, to deny their son a proper burial seemed a futile and cruel way for Zeph's parents to take a stand.

I tried to keep my face neutral. Generally, I was very accepting of the Amish way of life. Some of my closest friends were Amish and, of course, my grandmother was so dear to me, but the way people used the excuse that something was *just the Amish way of living* didn't sit well with me. It was another reminder to me that, as hard as it was for my grandparents, my father's decision to leave the Amish was ultimately best for both him and, eventually, for me.

"Were your parents upset with Zeph because he moved away from home?" I asked.

"In part, but they also knew he was getting into trouble. It seemed there was nothing either they or the bishop could say to make him stop. In many ways, I thought they were relieved. If he wasn't going to join the church, they would much rather concentrate on the children they could still influence."

"Getting into trouble how?" I asked.

She looked at her feet. "He took things."

I wasn't surprised to hear it after the story Emily had told me. Even so, I knew that it must have been very difficult for Lida to admit.

"You mean he stole."

She wouldn't look at me. "I thought if he got this job and worked here, he wouldn't feel the need to do that anymore. I thought it was a chance for him to start over. It didn't work. My *daed* said it wouldn't work until Zeph repented." She continued to stare at the floor. "I'm afraid that Daed was right. If Zeph didn't repent before he died, does that mean he was condemned?"

I shifted uncomfortably in my seat. This was a question that was way out of my depth to answer. I cleared my throat and said something my grandmother had once said to me. "We can't ever fully know another person's heart. Only God can do that."

She nodded and wiped the tears from her eyes. "You're right. Daed can't know what was in Zeph's heart." She placed a hand on her chest. "I will hold on to that, and the hope I will see him again someday."

"How long had he been taking things?" My question was an abrupt change of topic, but it was necessary to escape the deep conversation that was making me uncomfortable.

"It depends on who you ask."

"I'm asking you."

She sighed and looked down at her hands. Then she sniffed and straightened her shoulders, as if she was giving herself a pep talk. "If you are asking me, he'd been doing it ever since he could walk."

"What do you mean?"

"He always had sticky fingers, as my *daed* called it. Any time something went missing at home, we knew that Zeph had taken it. It was a running joke at home, but in truth, the joke wasn't very funny."

"Did he take things from other people?"

"There have been times . . ."

"Like when he stole from the church collection plate when he was younger."

She gasped. "How do you know about that?"

"I have many friends in your district."

She nodded. "*Ya,* and now, I'm sure every last one of them is remembering all the mistakes he made. He wasn't entirely to blame."

I raised my brow.

"There was one year when we went to public school. My parents were reluctant to send us, but the old schoolhouse for our district was being rebuilt. We either went to public school or were homeschooled. My mother had just had another baby and didn't have the time to homeschool us. My older brothers—*bruder*—and I were the only ones of school age."

I cocked my head. Had I heard her right? Had she said *brothers*? As in there was more than one?

Before I could ask, she went on. "I was in third grade and Zeph was in fourth. He got in trouble countless times for taking little trinkets from the other students and from the classroom. He stole books from the library. Books he could have borrowed for free. One night, the school guidance counselor came to our house to speak to my parents. I listened in while they met in the kitchen. The guidance counselor said that Zeph had a need to take things. She suggested that Zeph ought to talk to someone about it, and maybe be put on medicine. My *daed* was furious and threw her out of the house." She blew out a long breath. "We didn't go back to school after that, and we missed the rest of the school year," she said.

"Did the guidance counselor say that Zeph was compulsively stealing?" I asked.

She shook her head. "I don't know."

She might not know, but that was what the guidance counselor had described to her parents. I tried to imagine how a parent—especially an Amish parent—would receive the news: not well. Also, the guidance counselor's suggestion that Zeph receive therapy and medication for his disorder was going to go absolutely nowhere with an Amish mother and father, especially ones as conservative as the Lantzes were.

My heart hurt even more for Zeph. If he'd had a mental health condition that had led to his taking things, it wasn't his fault. He needed help, as the school counselor had said. He would have benefitted from counseling at the very least, even if his Amish parents weren't willing to consider medication. If he'd had the counseling, he might have been able to get to the root of his problem. He was never going to get a chance to do so now, and that was the saddest part of all.

There was one more subject that I needed to address with Lida, and I knew it would not be easy for her to hear. "Did you know that Zeph was breaking into homes and businesses and stealing from them?"

She looked at her hands for a long moment as if she was afraid to answer. "I knew," she finally whispered. "And that's why he was killed."

CHAPTER SIXTEEN

"Killed?" I asked. "You don't think his death was an accident?"

"I—I don't know," she backpedaled. "All I do know is he found trouble, and I knew someday that trouble would be the end of him." She looked me in the eye. "You have to understand. Despite it all, he was a *gut bruder* to me. He always looked out for me and made sure I had what I needed. When we reached a certain age, our parents kind of forgot about us and concentrated on raising our younger siblings. I was in the middle and forgotten a lot. Zeph, he never forgot me."

"When you said that he found trouble, what do you mean?"

It may have been cruel to focus on that detail, but I couldn't lose this opportunity to better understand what had happened to Zeph.

Lida shook her head and exhaustion settled on her face. It was unlikely that she'd gotten a wink of sleep the night before, and I wondered how many more sleepless nights she had had over Zeph throughout her life. Probably more than she could count. I guessed that I only had two more questions I could ask her before she completely shut down.

She made a face. "It wasn't always his fault he found trouble. Others influenced him. They led him in the wrong direction."

"What do you mean by that? Are you saying that Zeph was working with someone else?"

"He never told me that." The way she phrased her response made me think she knew very well that Zeph was working with someone else.

"If you really believe your brother was murdered, the sheriff has to know who influenced him to rob all those Amish homes and businesses."

With tears in her eyes, she shook her head. I would get no more information out of her today.

My phone rang. Margot Rawlings's face popped up on my screen. It was a picture of her standing at the top of the gazebo steps, holding her bullhorn in one hand and her clipboard in the other. She was shouting into the bullhorn. It was the most *Margot* picture I'd ever taken, and the perfect choice for my phone contact list.

I already knew why she was calling. The Candy Land Experience was set to open at ten, and even though that was over an hour from now, she was wondering why the candy had not been delivered yet. Margot was the type who hated lateness and saw being on time as being late. She thought an hour or two early was on time, so I knew why she was calling and knew that I would get an earful about it.

However, seeing Margot's call gave me an idea. If

Lida insisted on working that day, what better place for her to be than on the village square, where there would be so much activity it was bound to keep her mind off Zeph?

"What do you say to working at the Candy Land Experience today? If you are looking for distraction, that just might be the thing."

"But what about the taffy?" She rubbed her eyes.

"I can find someone else to finish cutting and wrapping. We need someone from the factory to replenish the different candy stations while the games are going on, and you can stay warm in Swissmen Sweets when you aren't filling stations."

I knew my grandmother's kind and gentle touch was just what Lida needed at a time like this. Maami never judged, even when she didn't agree with someone's choices. I knew that better than anyone.

I let Margot's call go to voicemail; she wasn't going to like that one bit. I stood up. "Take a minute to get yourself together and meet me in the lobby. We will walk over to the square together."

She nodded.

As I was leaving the room, she called my name. "Bailey?"

I turned to face her.

"*Danki*," she said. "*Danki* for caring enough to ask about Zeph. Not many people do."

I nodded and left the room just as my phone rang again.

Walking back to the lobby, I answered the call.

"Where is my candy?" Margot said in my ear.

"We're just getting it together," I replied. "Lida and I will be there in a few minutes."

"Lida? You're making the poor girl work the day after her brother's death?" Margot was aghast.

"Margot, I would never do that. Lida just needs a break from her family. As you can imagine, things are very heavy at home right now, so she would like to work. I thought replenishing the candy would be a good distraction for her that doesn't take too much effort. Believe me when I say that she didn't have to work today, but I'm also not going to chase her away when she is in distress."

"Very good. Very good," Margot said. "We'll keep her distracted. Don't you worry about that."

I wasn't. I just hoped that Margot didn't distract Lida too much, or think of another assignment to give her, like the one she'd given Zeph, putting the game piece on the roof of the factory.

Thankfully, the candy sellers had all the candy packed and ready to take to the square. All Lida and I had to do was load it on two wagons and walk out the door.

As Lida and I made our way to the square, she looked back and forth as if she was afraid that someone was going to jump out of the bushes and scare her. I almost asked her if she was all right, but that seemed like a pointless question, considering what she'd been through. I wanted to put the candy out as quickly as possible and get her to Maami, who would take care of her. I couldn't think of anyone better to help her heal.

Not that healing would come quickly. Grief took

such a heavy toll on a person—even people with the strongest faith.

Where there was deep love, there was the potential for profound loss. Funny, when I thought of that, my mind instantly went to Aiden.

"There you are!" Margot said as she hurried down the gazebo steps. "Do you know where the candy is going?"

I nodded.

"Good, because the camel is almost here and I have to be ready." She turned to Lida, and for a brief moment, her face softened. She took Lida's mitten-covered hand in both of hers. "I am so terribly sorry about what happened to Zeph. I feel responsible. I was the one who told him to go on the factory roof and put the game piece up there. I wasn't thinking about how icy it must be. I hope you can forgive me."

Lida blinked rapidly as if she were fighting back tears. "It wasn't your fault."

Margot's face cleared. "Thank you. Please give your parents my condolences as well." She took a breath and turned to me. "We expect a large turnout today. Kids are out of school for winter break and their parents are looking for ways to keep them occupied. I don't want any of the candy stations falling below half-filled at any time." She said this in her direct, no-nonsense way.

It almost gave me whiplash to watch Margot speaking so sincerely to Lida one moment and barking orders the next.

"This has to be a hit, Bailey. Don't you forget that," Margot warned, and with one last nod at the two of us, she marched away.

Lida's eyes were huge. "She's very bossy." After she said that, she clapped a hand over her mouth.

I laughed. "She *is* bossy, and she would be the first to admit it, so don't feel bad for saying so."

She lowered her hand, but her cheeks were still bright red.

"Let's get the candy stations filled and then you can go to Swissmen Sweets and help my grandmother while you wait to refill the stations. Does that sound like a good idea?"

"*Ya*, miss." She cleared her throat. "I just have to say, it's so very kind of you to let me have this important job today. I won't let you down, and I will be sure to keep the stations full like Margot asked." She paused. "And I wanted to say, I know there were times when you were frustrated by Zeph, but you were always kind to him. You always gave him a second and third chance. I can't tell you how much that meant to me. I'm grateful that my *bruder* was able to see some kindness before he passed."

Tears came to my eyes at her sincere words. The truth was Zeph drove me crazy and there were countless times I thought about firing him.

Lida was the reason I could never bring myself to do it. Thinking of Lida and how sweet and dedicated to her work she was, I would never fire her brother. And truth be told, I did believe in second, third, and even fourth and fifth chances. I wouldn't be where I was today if I hadn't gotten extra chances myself. When I was a chocolatier starting out in New York, I made so many mistakes with recipes and with customers, but Jean Pierre never gave up on me. And now that I was in a position to give others the same chances he'd given me, I wasn't going to waste the opportunity.

There were six candy stations to fill across the game board. Each one of them was on a wooden pedestal. The containers holding the candy varied; some were treasure boxes, others were baskets, and still others were Christmas boxes. In the first container we put peppermints, and from there we filled the containers with hard candy, chocolate kisses, peanut brittle, butterscotch bits, and the some of the gingerbread taffy that Lida had cut and wrapped.

The very last station was in the gazebo, which had been transformed to look like the castle at the end of the Candy Land board game. The gazebo had been completely covered in shimmering plastic wrapping and larger-than-life pieces of candy were all over it. The roof even got a makeover so that it looked like the top of an ice cream sundae, complete with cascading chocolate in the form of brown streamers and a cherry on the top made of a red balloon.

I had seen Margot's creations on the square before. They were always eye-catching, but I had never seen anything like the Candy Land Experience. She had really gone all out on this one.

By the time we got to the last station, the game was beginning, and there were at least two dozen people waiting at the starting line. Lida seemed to enjoy the task of arranging and displaying the candy. I wondered if perhaps I had put her in the wrong position at the factory. She might have been happier working in the front of the house, selling candy, than in the back making it. She seemed to have a natural eye for an attractive display. I would speak to the lobby manager at my first chance to see if there was a spot for Lida in the front of the factory.

She set the last piece of gingerbread taffy in the treasure box by the castle as the game started. There were cheers and laughter coming from both the children and adults. The Candy Land Experience was a success. Not that I ever doubted it would be with Margot at the helm. She wouldn't allow it to be anything but successful.

Lida pulled the wagon away from the game board and we made our way to the candy shop. She smiled when a child held up a giant game card and it showed a picture of a peppermint. He was going straight to the first candy station.

"I'll come out every fifteen minutes to check the stations," Lida said in a serious tone.

I didn't think she would have to come out that often, but I didn't correct her because she seemed so much happier with her new assignment.

We were about to cross Main Street and head to Swissmen Sweets when she stopped abruptly at the edge of the road and gasped.

"Lida? What's wrong?" I asked.

She stared at me, the whites of her eyes as prominent as the snow around us. "Nothing's wrong. I—I just was surprised by the camel."

I followed her line of sight. Sure enough, Melchior the camel was being led out of a horse trailer. Maybe "led" was the wrong choice of words, as he dug his back hooves into the trailer floor and would not budge from the ramp. The two large Amish men who pulled at his lead weren't having any luck moving him.

"Melchior? Haven't you been to the live nativity before?" I asked. "He's here every year, and I see his attitude hasn't changed one bit."

"*Ya*, I just didn't expect the camel to be here right now at the Candy Land Experience. I'm concerned that he will eat the candy." She wouldn't look me in the eye.

I frowned. There was something more to her discomfort than Melchior.

"I would be more concerned about Jethro eating the candy than Melchior," I said.

She nodded, but her eyes were still troubled, and I knew it had nothing to do with the camel.

CHAPTER SEVENTEEN

When we stepped into the candy shop, it was busy. Both my grandmother and Charlotte were working the counter, trying to fill order after order.

"They need help." Lida removed her coat and hung it on the hall tree, ready to jump into the fray.

"I need to head back to the factory. Will you be all right here?" I asked.

She nodded. "I'm glad that the shop is busy. I want to be busy."

"Bailey!"

I turned and saw Jenny Patterson from the Garden Club sitting at a table with three other women.

Lida joined my grandmother and cousin behind the counter. By the grateful looks on Maami and Charlotte's faces, they were happy for the help.

"Bailey," Jenny said in a sharper tone. "Have you made a decision as to when we can repeat that class?"

I sighed and walked over to the table.

Jenny didn't bother with any niceties as she adjusted

her cat's-eye glasses on the bridge of her nose and said, "Now, what do you plan to do about our class?"

As a business owner, I knew I had to answer her. I smiled at each lady in turn. "The last twenty-four hours have been a bit overwhelming. I haven't really had the time to think about it."

Jenny opened her mouth to protest, but one of her companions put a hand on her arm. "Jenny, Bailey has been very kind to give us a free lesson, but we can't expect her to have a plan in less than twenty-four hours when she has so much happening."

Jenny scowled at the piece of fudge on her plate. "I suppose that's true."

"It is true, and Clara was very kind to let us sit and warm up here in the candy shop while we wait to go into Candy Land."

"Yes, that was very kind." Jenny gave me a sheepish smile.

"Bailey, can I talk to you for a moment in private?" Jenny's friend said.

I blinked. "Yes, of course."

I recognized the woman as a member of the Garden Club and one of the ladies who had been taking the candymaking class the day Zeph died, but I'd never met her formally. What could this private conversation be about?

She grabbed her coat off the back of her chair and headed for the door. My brow went up; it seemed that she wanted a very private conversation if she was willing to take it out into the cold.

I said my goodbyes to Jenny and the others and went out the door.

The woman, who I guessed was anywhere from fifty-five to sixty-five, stood under the gas streetlamp in front of Swissmen Sweets. She watched as the two Amish men continued to coax Melchior to get off the trailer. What they needed were carrots. I knew from past experience with Melchior that he loved carrots.

The Candy Land Experience was a big success. A little girl stood in the gazebo jumping up and down. She had just beaten her entire family at the game and was overjoyed. It seemed that this harebrained idea of a life-size Candy Land was a hit. If there was one thing I knew about Margot, it was that she would be patting herself on the back.

"I'm Nadine. I'm the secretary of the Garden Club."

I nodded. "It's nice to see you again."

"I'm sorry to bother you on such a busy day," she began. "But I just wanted to check if the police have decided what happened to Zeph. Was it an accident, as they thought?"

I blinked. This was the last question I'd expected to get from a Garden Club member.

"Did you know Zeph?"

She pursed her lips. "Not well, but I am neighbors with his landlord. I live just across the street from her. I knew that she was renting a room to Zeph. I saw him coming and going at all hours of the day and night."

"You saw him at night, too?"

"I don't sleep very well. I have a genetic condition that makes me get up every hour because my legs pain me so much. It's a nervous system issue. Night is the worst. I stay up and read, for the most part."

"When you saw Zeph come home late at night, was he always alone?"

"What are you implying?" she asked, aghast.

"I'm not implying anything at all. I just wondered if he always walked home or if someone dropped him off. From what I know, he didn't have a horse and buggy to get around in."

"He didn't, but he had one of those electronic scooters. The one he had was so loud, I could hear him coming halfway down the street."

I nodded. E-bikes and e-scooters were becoming increasingly popular in the Amish communities as ways to get from place to place. They were quicker than walking and didn't involve the hassle of keeping a horse, and they were more reliable than having to wait at the mercy of an Amish driver. Until moving to Harvest, I hadn't known about Amish drivers. They were Englishers who drove the Amish to their appointments or shopping. I found it amusing that the Amish had been using "Ubers" long before any app for ride-sharing was created.

I hadn't known that Zeph had a scooter, but that wasn't saying much. So many of my employees at the factory had e-bikes and e-scooters that I didn't know who owned which of the many transports parked at the bike racks that I had installed outside the factory's front door.

"When he was coming in, he always seemed to have a lot of stuff with him."

"What do you mean when you say that?"

She cleared her throat. "He would have a backpack on his back and a backpack on his chest, and they looked heavy. I told Beverly that she might want to have a talk with him to see what he was up to, but she insisted that he was a fine young man. She believed I was just being a nosy neighbor."

I knew what a nosy neighbor was like; I had one in my next-door neighbor, Penny. She was always there to report on the happenings on the street and she made a special note of the times that Aiden was at my home later than when she deemed appropriate. Usually after those visits, she would question me at length. I could understand why Beverly was frustrated over Nadine spying on her home. However, at the same time, why wouldn't she want to ask Zeph about the large backpacks?

Nadine cleared her throat. "I saw the police going in and out of his basement apartment yesterday. It looked to me as if they were taking out bins of things. What was all that about?"

I wasn't going to tell her that Aiden and I believed Zeph was the burglar. At least we had until the cheese shop had also been robbed.

"Because I think he is the one who committed all those break-ins in the Amish community." She shook her head. "I've thought that for a while now."

"Why didn't you go to the sheriff?"

I tried to keep my voice from sounding accusatory, but I didn't do very well. I would much rather that Zeph was alive and in jail than dead. I believed Lida would feel the same way. Had Nadine gone to the police, Zeph might still be alive . . .

"Well, I am not one to talk about others. I told Beverly my concerns, but she seemed to think I was an old gossip." She sniffed. "That doesn't seem right at all, seeing how she is at least twenty years older than I am." She shook her head. "And what if I was wrong? I didn't want to be accusing an innocent man. I wanted Beverly to go down to the basement and check, but she refused. I decided it was her problem and left it at that. Now, I can tell by the look on your face that you believe I did the wrong thing, but it can't be helped. I made the best choice I could with the information I had."

"Why are you telling me all this?" I asked.

She blinked. "Well, I have to assume that you're looking into Zeph's death. That is what you do, isn't it? Other than making candy, you're like some sort of town detective, and I have heard rumblings that he was murdered."

If Nadine had heard that Zeph was murdered, it wouldn't be long before the rest of Holmes County heard it as well. Having this news spread through Amish Country was the last thing Aiden would want.

I thanked Nadine for the information, and she walked back to the candy shop. I had no doubt in my mind that she would discuss our conversation with Jenny and the rest of the ladies from the Garden Club. By the end of the first day of the Candy Land Experience, everyone would know that Zeph had broken into Amish homes and businesses and had been killed.

I walked back to the factory, hoping that I'd done the right thing for Lida. Maybe it was a bad idea to have her work at all. Before I'd left, I'd told her if she decided it was too much and wanted to go home, all she had to do was go into Swissmen Sweets and tell my grandmother.

At the same time, I couldn't shake the idea that Lida had seen and was afraid of something at the Candy Land Experience. What could it have been? Or *who* could it have been? The square had already been crowded with game pieces and nativity animals, including Melchior the camel. There was a lot of commotion.

I wished I had paid better attention to what she had been looking at when we crossed the street. I wished a lot of things . . . and my greatest wish was that I had forbidden Zeph from ever climbing up on that roof.

CHAPTER EIGHTEEN

I went back to my office and did my best to put it in order. Aiden and his team had come and gone, and I was left to clean up the mess. The act of organizing files and straightening books and papers soothed me. From what I could tell, nothing was missing, but then again, I didn't have every file in my cabinet memorized. I was far more reliant on my computer to get work done.

I was so grateful that I had kept the laptop with me the night before. I didn't know what I would have done if that had been stolen.

When my office was livable again, I opened the laptop and logged onto the software to view the cameras. My one regret now was not having a camera in my office. There was one in the hallway outside the office, but apparently the culprit had come in through the office window. It was very likely he or she didn't even go into any other part of the building.

I knew Aiden and his deputies would have already

looked at this footage, but maybe there was something they'd missed. I had to check and see.

I flipped through the recent clips on the screen and stopped at one taken at three in the morning. There was a dark, indistinct figure in the frame. The person was dressed all in black and stood out in the snowy night. The image came from camera five, which was at the back of the building. It wasn't far from where I'd found the ladder on the ground and showed two thirds of the back side of the building.

The figure walked through the snow to my office window. From what I could tell, the window opened easily, and the person climbed inside. That was the end of the clip. There wasn't another clip from that camera until the person climbed back out ten minutes later. From what I could tell, there was nothing in his hands. That didn't mean that he didn't have something in his coat pockets, though.

What he took, if anything, I still didn't know. I hadn't yet moved fully into the office. There wasn't much in there other than the filing cabinet and the desk. The two files I thought the intruder would be most interested in, Zeph's and Lida's, were at my home.

I watched the video again and again, looking for anything to identify the intruder. There was nothing. I knew that Aiden must have watched the video dozens of times, too.

There was a chance that this break-in was unrelated to Zeph's death. The intruder may have broken in simply to steal from the Candyworks. Perhaps they got spooked before they could make off with anything.

There wouldn't have been much they could have

taken other than items from the lobby shop, like the little gifts and bags of candy we sell there and maybe candymaking equipment. Some of the equipment was expensive and would be hard to replace, but it would also be almost impossible for one person to move the most expensive and heaviest equipment.

As for any money, it was put in the safe every night either by Charlotte or me. I was too much of a big city girl not to lock it away even though we were in the middle of Amish Country, where supposedly nothing ever happened.

I'd learned years ago that a lot of bad things can happen here in Amish Country, just like every other part of the world.

I closed my laptop and got up. It was time to do my real job, which wasn't playing detective but making and selling candy.

I spent the rest of the day working at the Candyworks and running back and forth from Swissmen Sweets to replenish the candy that Lida was using to refill the game stations. In so many ways, it was a normal workday for me, but in the back of my head all I could think about was Zeph and what had happened to him. Could it really have been murder?

It was hard to think it wasn't when the second set of footprints on the roof was blurred with a pine branch.

Close to midday, I walked over to the square to see how Lida was doing. I found her topping off one of the candy stations with peppermints.

The game board was busy—there were at least five families playing the game on the board at the same time. Children laughed and rolled the football-size dice that Uriah had made from foam just for the game. It was only the first day and some of the dice were looking a bit the worse for wear, but the children didn't seem to mind when they stopped at the candy stations and loaded their pockets with sweets.

I didn't see Lida on the game board, so I assumed that she was in Swissmen Sweets with Charlotte and my grandmother. I was about to head there when a frantic cry rang through the air. "Jethro! Jethro! Where are you?"

The pig was missing . . . again.

It came as no surprise that it was Juliet who was shouting for her pig. She wore a long gray-and-white polka-dotted wool coat over black slacks and paired the outfit with fashionable boots. Her hair was piled on the top of her head in an elaborate braided knot set off by pink polka-dotted earmuffs. Juliet loved polka dots. What was unclear was whether she loved them because of Jethro or whether she'd picked Jethro as her comfort animal because she loved polka dots.

Juliet was not in the right outfit to be on a pig chase with those high-heeled boots. I knew that would leave the pig-finding to me.

"Jethro!" she cried again. Her voice grew increasingly more desperate.

I discarded my plan to go to the candy shop and hurried over to her. "Juliet, what's happened?"

"Oh Bailey! You're just the person I need to see. It's Jethro. He's missing. He was with me at the church for my woman's Bible study and then he ran off."

"What made him run off?" I asked. Jethro was one to wander off from time to time, but he never went much further than his next snack or place to take a nap.

"One of the ladies bumped into him with her walker. He was sleeping by the door and she accidentally struck him. I knew that he was sleeping there before class began and I should have moved him. I couldn't bring myself to do it because he looked so comfortable. He was scared awake and fled. He shot right out of the church door and down the steps. Minerva—that's the woman who bumped him—feels horrible." She took a breath. "I came outside alone because I thought I would find him easily, but I have looked all over the churchyard and even peeked in the cemetery. He's nowhere to be seen. Now I'm really getting worried." She grabbed my hands and squeezed them tight with her icy fingers. "I don't know what I would do without him."

"Juliet, take a moment to catch your breath. There is no reason to panic. Jethro is around here somewhere, hiding until he feels better. He knows the village as well as any of us do. He will be able to find his way back to the church. He might be even making his way there now. Why don't you go back to the church and I will keep looking for him?"

"I—I can't." She cleared her throat. "I don't mean that. I can go back to the church, of course, but our meeting is over, and I'm meeting your mother for lunch in a few minutes at the café. I don't want to be late."

It was a good thing that Juliet wanted to be on time for my mother. Susan King did not abide tardiness.

"You go to the café and I will continue to look for Jethro. I'm sure Uriah and some of the others here will help me. When I find him, I'll bring him to the café and join you for coffee."

"Oh, no. You can't do that."

I furrowed my brow. I would have thought my pig-finding record spoke for itself. "I can't find him? I've found him dozens of times before."

"No, you can't come to the café. When you find him, just text me and take him to the candy shop so he can recover with his friends Puff and Nutmeg."

I pulled my knit gloves from the pocket of my parka and put them on my cold hands. "Why can't I come to the café?"

"You're too busy," she said in a rush. "You don't have time to sit down with your mother and me this close to Christmas. You have too much to do at the factory."

This was true. I did have a lot to do that day: manage the candy factory, monitor the candy at the Candy Land Experience, and solve a possible murder. However, I also had to learn what my mother and Juliet were conspiring about in regard to my wedding. Considering the fact that Juliet didn't want me to come to the café, I guessed it was because of those wedding plans.

Juliet looked this way and that. I didn't know if she was scanning the grounds for Jethro or searching for a way to get out of this conversation with me.

"Was someone looking for a pig?" Uriah called from the stable.

Juliet and I walked across the square to where Uriah

stood. We stopped in our tracks. Melchior was settled on a fresh patch of straw. His legs were bent toward his body, and right up against his stomach was a little black-and-white potbellied pig.

Jethro, the toaster-size pig, was sleeping contentedly next to his new friend.

If the large camel and the small pig made an odd pair, they didn't know that. And Jethro's two closest friends were a rabbit and a tabby cat, so I didn't know why I was surprised that he would befriend a camel, too. They were curled up together in the stable just beside the empty manger.

"I would not be surprised if the first Christmas had a scene just like that," Uriah said.

It would not have surprised me either.

"Oh, my heavens! Jethro, there you are. Oh, Bailey, I should have known that he would come to the manger scene. He is such an integral part of it during the Christmas parade." She took a step toward the stables and stopped when Melchior opened one eye. "Bailey, can you be a dear and get Jethro for me?"

I was going to be spat on by the camel. I just knew it.

"Jethro," I said in a soothing voice. "It's time to get up and go home. Come on, buddy."

The pig slowly opened his eyes. By the way he behaved, I would have thought he'd been asleep for hours, not just the few minutes since he raced out of the church. Jethro looked at me groggily and gave a great yawn.

I took a step closer, and Melchior blew hot air out of

his nose that in the cold appeared as puffs of smoke. I yelped and stepped back.

"I'll get him," Uriah said.

I could not have been more grateful when he said that. Uriah stepped into the stable, patted Melchior on the shoulder, and picked up the pig.

Melchior sighed as his friend was carried away. The camel laid his head on his hooves. I couldn't help but feel a little sorry for him. He just wanted someone to hang out with him in the manger scene.

Uriah handed Jethro over to Juliet, and she hugged the little pig tightly to her chest. "Don't ever run off like that again."

It was a good thing Jethro didn't have the capacity to make such a promise because heaven knew he would never be able to keep it.

"Thank you, Uriah and Bailey." Juliet tapped a napkin to her face to blot her tears. "You found him just when I needed him most, and now I won't be late for my appointment."

"You mean lunch with my mother," I said.

She blushed. "Yes, that is what I mean."

"I'm done here on the square for now," I said. "I will go with you."

Juliet's face paled and she swallowed hard. "You don't want to be spending your day with us. Don't be ridiculous. Your mother and I will have a nice visit . . . alone."

I frowned. Juliet really didn't want me to go to the café.

"I'll at least stop in and say hello. I haven't spent

much time with my parents since they arrived and I feel bad about that. Both Aiden and I have been so busy."

She held Jethro a little more tightly to her chest, and the little pig's eyes bugged out.

"Maybe Jethro would like to walk on his leash," I suggested.

Juliet nodded. She removed Jethro's blue-and-white polka-dotted leash from her coat pocket and snapped it on his collar before setting him on the ground.

The little bacon bundle looked up at me gratefully. He was happy not being squeezed within an inch of his life by his mistress.

Juliet nervously glanced at me every few feet as we made the short walk to the café.

Through the large picture windows at the front of the café, I could see the place was packed. The inside was decorated for the holidays, and there was just as much red and green inside the café as could be found on the square. I guessed that Lois Henry had something to do with that. Lois's granddaughter, Darcy Woodin, owned the café and did all the cooking and baking. She was extremely talented. Lois helped out in the café whenever she could. She was the hostess, waited tables, and I guessed put herself in charge of the holiday décor.

"Looks like the café is busy," I said. "Are you sure this will be a good place for my mother and you to talk and get to know each other? You might not even be able to hear each other."

Juliet didn't say anything in reply, but she did appear to be nervous. Her posture was as straight as if someone had taped a yardstick to her back. Juliet was a fine Southern lady and she always exhibited poise and good posture. But I had never seen her this tense before.

I put my hand on the door handle. "Are you going to tell me what is going on?"

She wouldn't meet my eyes. "There is nothing going on, Bailey. Why would you ask me that?"

"You look like you might faint at a moment's notice."

Her face fell. "Your mother asked me not to tell you." Tears gathered in her eyes. "It's been so hard for me. I know you and Aiden aren't married yet, but I already view you as my daughter, and—"

Before she could tell me what secret my mother had asked her to keep, I was jerked forward as the café door was opened from inside. I stumbled into a short man with a full gray beard and round glasses. He beamed from ear to ear. "This must be the bride!"

CHAPTER NINETEEN

I stared at the man. He looked strangely familiar, but he wasn't from Harvest. His clothes were far too expensive, and his boots shone as if he had just stepped away from a shoeshine stand. No one shined their shoes in the village, especially in winter with all the snow, ice, and salt on the ground. It would be a completely futile act.

"Excuse me?" I asked.

"You must be the bride. I'm Hampton Longly, and I am beyond thrilled to be planning your wedding!"

"Planning my wedding?" I felt as if I was slow on the uptake. I had never hired a wedding planner, nor had it ever crossed my mind to do so. I had worked with so many of them when I was a chocolatier at JP Chocolates in New York, and the experience had left a bad taste in my mouth. Bridezillas and groomzillas were bad, but they didn't hold a candle to wedding plannerzillas. Those were the absolute worst.

He clapped a hand on the side of his cheek. "Good

gracious, did I ruin the surprise?" He looked over his shoulder. "You haven't told her yet?"

My mother stood just a few feet behind him, and my delayed thought process kicked into gear as all the clues fell into place. Of course my mother had hired the wedding planner, and this was also why Juliet hadn't wanted me to join them in the café.

"What's done is done," my mother said in a matter-of-fact way. "Let's go back to our table and talk about the wedding. Now that everything is out in the open, it's a good time to start planning this event. We don't have much time. Bailey and Aiden promised to marry next year, and we are at the end of December."

Just because we were getting married next year, it didn't mean the wedding would happen in the next couple of months. However, I bit my tongue to stop myself from correcting my mother. I had a lot I wanted to say to her, but it would be best done privately.

Hampton Longly held the door open so Juliet and I could step inside. Jethro followed behind us on his leash. He kept looking longingly over his shoulder at the square. Most likely thinking about taking a long nap with his camel friend, Melchior.

"Brought the pig," Hampton cried. "Wonderful! I was hoping you would. As I was told, he will be a big part of the ceremony and the entertainment during the reception, it's good to meet him in person and see what we are working with. He's much smaller in real life. That's not a bad thing. It means he's more portable."

Entertainment at the reception? Who said anything like that? Out of respect for my Amish friends who would be in attendance, there would be no loud rock music or dancing. I wasn't planning anything more than some canned instrumental music in the background. However, I didn't believe that was my mother's idea of entertainment, and I was afraid to ask what Jethro's role would be in all of it.

In the café, the chatter died down as soon as we were inside. I recognized faces, and most of the diners were local. All were curious about the two people in our party they didn't know: my mother and Hampton Longly, the wedding planner.

Lois Henry, who would stand out in any crowd with her spiky purple-red hair, bright makeup, and chunky jewelry, stepped out from behind the counter with a carafe of coffee in her hand. "I have a table ready for you in the back corner. It's the closest thing to privacy I can give you." She lowered her voice. "But we all know that every last person in here today will be hanging on your slightest word." Her Christmas bell earrings shook as she spoke.

Hampton laughed. "I welcome a little gossip. The more you're being talked about, the more you're being noticed. In my business, that's a good thing." He smiled at me. "I would think the same for you and your career on television."

I wouldn't call my cooking show a career. I taped ten to twelve episodes a year. All in a two-week stay in New York. My real career was as a candymaker. The television show would come and go. The candymaking was forever.

The table in the back corner was small, and Lois did her best to make sure we were comfortable in the cramped space.

Lois fussed over the table. "If this doesn't work for you, I can give you all your food to go and you can eat it in the church or another place."

Juliet looked as if she was going to agree that that was a good idea, but my mother spoke up first. "No, we will stay here. Packing everything up will just take more time, and we don't have any time to waste. Most brides getting married next year are well into their planning, if not completely set. Bailey hasn't done a single thing yet."

Hampton smiled. "That's why you hired me. By the end of this meal, everything will be settled."

"What would you all like?" Lois asked. "I can give you more time to look at the menus, but if you are in a rush, I can take your order now."

"Those cranberry orange waffles sound divine," Hampton said.

Juliet ordered a grilled cheese with fries and my mother asked for fresh fruit and yogurt.

When it was my turn to order, I said, "I'll just have a coffee with cream and sugar."

I knew I wouldn't be able to eat until I learned exactly what my mother had planned. Mom was a planner, and I was, too, when it came to my job. In my personal life, not so much. I suspected the lack of wedding planning had brought my mother to the breaking point. Even so, she shouldn't have hired a wedding planner without consulting me first. I tried to swallow the irritation that was boiling up inside me.

Lois filled coffee mugs and left the table to place our order with Darcy.

Hampton folded his hands on the tabletop. "I can

guarantee you that I will give your daughter a wedding worthy of the star she is. This will be good press, too, for the business. I can ask for features in several outlets. We might even do an exclusive with her in her wedding dress." He glanced down at Jethro at Juliet's feet. "And the pig, of course. Let's not forget to measure him for a tux." He looked to me. "Have you bought your dress yet?"

"No," I said.

"Good. I need to be there when you try on dresses to make sure that we find the right one to fit our theme."

I was not taking Hampton Longly wedding dress shopping with me. I was already nervous about the idea of looking for a dress. Some girls dream about their wedding days their whole lives. I wasn't one of those girls. I'd never even thought about what I might want in a dress. I was hoping the old adage was true: "When you know, you know." It had proven true for Aiden. The first time I had met my future husband, I thought he was special. I had been right, more than right. I hoped that instinct would work for me in regard to the dress as well.

"I think that's a lovely idea," my mother said with a smile. "I would like someone with taste at the fitting. I don't know that I can be there. Bailey's father and I have dozens of trips planned for the New Year. We have to take that into consideration when we pick a date. Should we get out our calendars and coordinate now? There is no telling when Silas and I will have a chance to add another cruise to our travels."

Hampton clapped. "Yes, picking a wedding date is a must. That is the most important piece! From there we can go with colors and décor. We can't even pick what the bridal party is wearing without a date. You can't have a maid of honor wearing pastels in October." He shuddered, as if he could not think of anything worse.

He turned to me. "Are you going to be a summer bride? Fall? I think fall is nice for a wedding, and it will give us much more time to plan. Everything worth having will already be booked for the summer."

"I can't pick a wedding date without Aiden. I don't know his schedule, and I don't know my filming schedule for next year. In fact, I haven't even heard if my show has been picked up for another season."

Bailey's Amish Sweets had been on Gourmet Television for the last three years. That was a much longer run than I'd ever expected. At the start of each new filming season, I am always expecting it to be canceled.

Hampton waved away my concern. "Oh, my dear, the groom has little or no say in these sorts of things, and every bride is entitled to choose her wedding date. Your producer will have to adapt."

He had never met my producer. Clearly.

"I don't think—"

"A fall wedding would be best," my mom said. "It's before the weather gets too awful here, and it will give us more time to plan. Maybe at the very end of September? It would be more likely we can have some events outside then, and Silas and I don't leave for Nepal until October first."

Hampton wrote diligently in his notebook, and then looked at his phone. "Good, good. We will shoot for the last Saturday in September. You do want a Saturday, don't you? It's becoming more and more popular for weddings to be on Friday evenings, or even Sundays now. If you want to follow the trend, you might want to pick one of those days."

"Yes, it has to be a Saturday," Mom said. "My husband's Amish family would never come to a non-Amish Sunday wedding, and as for Friday, most of the Amish go home at dusk. Evening is for family time in the community."

He nodded. "How interesting. In the short time that I have been here, I have learned so much about the people. It's quite fascinating. I, personally, could never be Amish. How do they even feed themselves without a microwave? And no cell phones?" He shuddered again, more dramatically this time. "I would not be able to do my job."

I didn't want to break it to him, but "wedding planner" wasn't a job in the Amish community.

"Now, Bailey, I hate to bring up a delicate subject," Hampton said. "But I heard that there was an accident at your factory." He paused. "Is there any concern about how this will impact your wedding?"

"What do you mean?" I asked.

He cleared his throat. "If you have to defend yourself in a wrongful death case, it may impact the wedding budget."

My face flushed. Yes, any business owner in my position would be worried about being sued, but he seemed more concerned over whether or not I could afford the lavish wedding he had planned than the fact that one of my employees had died.

I ground my teeth. "I don't know what Zeph's death has to do with my wedding, and I don't understand why you would bring it up."

Hampton's face flushed. "I just have to look at the wedding from every angle, and that includes speed bumps."

"Zeph's death is not a speed bump."

He flushed. "Good. Good. That's good to know."

"Bailey, Hampton is just trying to help you with the wedding. You shouldn't be so rude to him," my mother said.

I stared at her. How could they be so callous? I glanced at Juliet. She was staring down at her hands. Obviously, she wasn't comfortable with this conversation either.

My thoughts wandered off to Zeph. He was so young, and now he would never get married. He would never have children. He would never again crack a joke or hug his sister.

"Bailey!" my mother said rather firmly and in such a way that I knew it wasn't the first time she had called my name to try to get my attention.

I blinked. "What?"

"What do you want for flowers?" she asked.

Lois appeared at the side of the table, saving me from having to answer the question. She set the food in front of us.

She placed a grilled cheese in front of me. I was about to tell her that I hadn't ordered it when she patted my arm. "You are going to need this," she whispered.

The flower question was tabled for the time being

when Juliet spoke up. "I think the wedding should be held in the church. The reverend would be happy to officiate."

"We aren't religious people," my mother said. "Outside in a tent would be better. It's more neutral ground."

I shook the cobwebs from my head. "Mother, can I speak to you for a moment?"

My mother looked up from her list. "Bailey, we are in the middle of a meeting."

"It won't take long."

She sighed and gave Hampton a wan smile. "You will have to excuse us for a minute."

"Take your time," Hampton said graciously. "This will give me time to measure the pig for a tux."

Just five years ago, I would have found a sentence like that peculiar even living in New York City. Now it didn't even faze me.

There wasn't really any spot to talk privately inside the café.

"Do you mind if we go outside?" I asked.

My mother gave an all-suffering sigh but grabbed her coat from the back of her chair and followed me out.

When we were outside, my mother shrugged on her coat and folded her arms in front of herself. "Bailey, what is this about? Hampton is a very busy man, and I don't want to waste his time or your father's money."

"I didn't ask you to spend any time or money at all on my wedding. I told you Aiden and I would take care of it."

"And you haven't even thought about it."

"I've thought about it," I said. "But we are both very busy."

"Oh really. How much have you thought about it? What can you tell me about your plans?"

"We want to get married in Harvest."

"And?" She raised her eyebrow as she waited for a response.

I didn't make any reply because I had no more to say.

"This is exactly why I hired Hampton. He's the very best wedding planner in Ohio. It took me months to find him. He came all the way from Columbus just to meet with us today. We have to give him the respect he deserves. I can't be here all the time to handle planning the wedding."

"Mother, you should have asked me first. That was the least you could have done. You went behind my back and hired Hampton and you expect me to just go along with it."

Her eyes narrowed. "And what would you have said?"

"That I don't want a wedding planner."

"That's why I didn't ask you," she said triumphantly. "Consider this your father's and my wedding gift to you."

I opened my mouth to argue.

"Bailey." Unexpected tears came to her eyes. "You are our only daughter, our only child. We want to give you the wedding of your dreams."

I knew it wasn't the wedding of my dreams that she wanted. She wanted the wedding of *her* dreams. My father had run away from his Amish community to marry my mother, so the two of them had eloped. My mother always regretted it. She would really have liked to have a big wedding if things had been different.

The door to the café opened and Hampton appeared. "Susan, Bailey, please hurry back. Juliet and I are looking at hot-air balloon options. Wouldn't it be wonderful to float away in a hot-air balloon after the ceremony?" He grinned from ear to ear. "It gives me chills!"

"I don't think that's something my fiancé will want to do," I said.

"Oh, honey," Hampton said with a wave of his hand. "That's for me to decide."

When he said that, I realized where I had seen him before. It had been on the square with Margot. I had thought he was just a tourist, but that wasn't the case.

That meant he was here not just for today but had arrived at least a day ago. Why would he tell my mother that he was just in for this meeting? What was he doing in Harvest early?

"I think a hot-air balloon sounds lovely, Hampton," my mother said. "But we will have to really zero in on the date now because something like that would be extremely weather dependent." She walked past him back into the café.

"You're completely right," he said, following her inside.

I stood on the sidewalk in the snow for a long moment and wondered how I'd ended up here.

CHAPTER TWENTY

I did not follow my mother back into the café. Instead, I poked my head in the door and asked Hampton if he had a moment to speak to me alone.

He glanced over his shoulder as if he was looking for my mother as some sort of lifeline to pull him back into the café, but she was already on the opposite side of the café.

He stepped outside and let the door close behind him. "Miss Bailey, I know that you were surprised that your mother hired me to plan your wedding, but I can assure you that you are in very good hands. I will give you the wedding of your dreams."

"You're in Harvest just for the wedding planning?" I asked.

He blinked at me. "Why else would I be here? I can assure you I don't have any other clients in your little village. The Amish aren't calling me to plan their weddings." He laughed at his own joke.

I wasn't laughing. "Then what were you doing on the square yesterday?"

"On the square?" he asked.

I pointed at the square. "I remember seeing you there. You tend to stand out in Harvest."

He smiled. "I always want to stand out, so thank you for that compliment."

When he saw I wasn't smiling, his tone became more serious. "I didn't tell your mother this, but I have been here for about three days, researching all that Harvest has to offer. I want to know the viable options for your wedding. I spoke to venue owners, caterers, and salons in the county. It's important to me that I use local vendors whenever possible for a wedding. It keeps costs down and helps the community."

I wrinkled my brow and was partially placated by what he'd said. I thought it was important to use local vendors, too. Even so, I couldn't stop myself from saying, "But you said you *just* arrived. As in you got here today."

"Pish. 'Just' is a relative term. What I meant to say was I *just* arrived a few days ago. It makes no difference. I didn't charge your parents for that time. It was my own research. This is such a picturesque place; I might encourage more of my brides to get married here. It could be a great, off-the-beaten-path location for a big wedding." He removed his phone from his pocket and spoke into it. "Look into Amish Country weddings as a package to sell." When he finished the voice note, he looked at me. "Was there anything else?" His eyes were bright behind his glasses.

I frowned. "I guess not." Something about the way

he spoke to me set me off balance, but I couldn't put my finger on why. I was comfortable speaking to rich Upper East Side mothers and television producers. One would think that I wouldn't be flummoxed by a wedding planner.

"Can you tell Juliet and my mother that I had to go back to work?"

"No problem at all. That might be better, really. Your mother and I can put a proposal together for you to review. I understand you're very busy, and I think this will make the process so much easier for you." He smiled. "Remember, you're my number one client right now. I want you to have the best wedding anyone could ever imagine."

Hampton went back into the café, and I watched him go with what I knew had to be a perplexed look on my face.

Shaking my head, I headed back to the square in search of Lida. I needed to get back to the factory, but I also wanted to finish my original mission for coming to the square in the first place, and that was to make sure Lida was okay.

I spotted her at the third candy station. She was facing a woman and nodding over and over again. It wasn't until I was closer that I saw it was Jenny Patterson she was speaking to.

"I think you are better off now, dear. He was trouble. Everyone knew that, even your parents," Jenny said.

Tears gathered in Lida's eyes, but she didn't let them fall.

Jenny couldn't possibly be talking about Zeph, could she?

I increased my pace and hurried over to them. "Lida, I just wanted to check whether you needed more candy from the factory."

She looked up at me and blinked away her tears. "*Nee*, I think we will have enough for the rest of the day. The last batch you brought was more than enough."

Jenny turned. "Bailey King, you're just the person I have been looking for. The ladies in the Garden Club and I are eager to hear when we will have our makeup class. As you know, Christmas will be here before you know it."

I pressed my lips together to keep myself from saying something I might regret. I didn't know for certain that Jenny was speaking to Lida about Zeph, but I didn't know what else it could be either. If she had told his sister she was better off without him . . . that was just cruel.

As I didn't know the extent of the conversation, I decided to ask Lida about it later. I felt she would be more upset if I made a big deal about it right in front of Jenny.

And we'd already broached the Garden Club's "rescheduling." I recognized that life went on, but the callousness of the women in the club was very off-putting. Jenny tapped her foot and looked at me expectantly, and I realized it'd be better to get this class over with.

"Would tomorrow at two in the afternoon work for all of you?" I asked. "It's the best time we have. Charlotte's not available, but I will teach the class."

Jenny put her hand to her chest. "We will be getting our lesson from *you*? That is such an honor. Charlotte is a gifted candymaker, but to be taught by Bailey King—that is a chance not to be missed! Two tomorrow afternoon will be fine." She clapped her hands together. "I can't wait to tell the other ladies. They will be beside themselves!" With that, she hurried away from the candy station.

Lida and I watched her go.

"Lida, what were you and Jenny speaking about?"

She looked at me. "Just candy. She wanted to know about the class. I didn't have an answer for her, so I was very glad when you happened by."

I cocked my head. "It was only about the class?"

She frowned. "*Ya.*"

She seemed so calm and certain, I wondered if I'd misunderstood what I had heard Jenny say just before I arrived. Yes, that must have been it.

But I suspected I was wrong.

CHAPTER TWENTY-ONE

On weekdays in the winter, both the factory and the shop closed at four. Right after closing, I knew it was time for me to visit Zeph's parents and offer my condolences. Lida said that I wouldn't be welcome on the Lantz farm, and that was most likely true. Even so, I had to try. I was Zeph's boss and he'd died on my property. I had to visit them.

After locking up the factory for the night, I walked back to the square. From what I could tell, the Candy Land Experience was a hit. There was a line of people waiting to play because only so many people could be on the board at once. Lida hurried from station to station refilling candy. Even though all the shops around the square were closing, the board game was going strong, and with the streetlamps and Christmas lights illuminating the square, it looked as if it would go well into the night. In any case, I guessed by suppertime the game would be far less crowded. Harvest was an early-to-bed kind of community, so I couldn't believe the game would be in heavy use after eight in the evening.

Hopefully, the candy wouldn't run out before then.

Margot walked over to join me. "The best part about this game is that it needs no supervision. Yes, we are giving out candy, but everyone knows how to play. It's not as if we have to explain anything."

"Lida has been refilling the candy." I held up the bag of candy I'd brought with me. "I have been refreshing her supply every few hours."

"She's done a stellar job. No sooner does someone take one piece of candy than she is out with a new one to take its place. If you're not careful, I will steal her from you to work on the square for Uriah and me. I could use a few more reliable people keeping this place up."

"What a nice compliment for Lida," I said, unsure of how else to reply. I hefted the giant bag of candy. "This is the last refill she will make as it's the end of the day."

Margot opened her mouth to argue, but I spoke before she could.

"There is enough candy here to last another hour or two. I have some errands to run. When I get back, I'll refill the candy again for any latecomers to the square."

Margot nodded, as if that was all she needed to know. "Good, and you can keep refilling it throughout the evening."

It was a statement, not a question.

I opened my mouth to protest, but Margot's next words stopped me. "I heard that you're staying at the candy shop at night now. I hope this doesn't mean there is trouble between you and Aiden."

I frowned. "Aiden and I are fine. You must have heard about the break-in at the cheese shop last night. I don't feel safe with my grandmother sleeping over the candy shop alone. She doesn't want to leave her home, so it made sense for me to stay with her."

Margot adjusted the beret on her curls. "That is a sweet thing for you to do, and I have to say that I do like the idea of your being on the square twenty-four seven. You can keep an eye on things at night. Melchior can be a bit of a diva at times, and I have some concerns about teenagers ransacking the display. Yes," she said, considering. "That's just what we need. I expect a full report in the morning. If you can set an alarm and check on the square every hour, that would be my preference."

I stopped myself from rolling my eyes. Leave it to Margot to make use of me in the midst of a stressful situation. "I can't guarantee that I will be able to watch the square all night long."

"You'll have help. Uriah will be here."

"You're making Uriah stay up all night?"

"The square grounds are his responsibility, and he can sleep. I'm just asking him to make rounds every ninety minutes. I don't think that's too much. Reverend Brook gave him a key to the church. He can sleep in there."

"On a pew?" I asked.

"Don't be silly. There is a couch in the counseling room." She waved away my concern. "Don't worry about it. I worked it all out with Uriah and Reverend

Brook. I'm only telling you so you won't be spooked if you see someone walking around the square at night. It will be Uriah."

I knew Uriah would agree to do it out of the kindness of his heart, but it was a big ask even for Margot. As for me, I would not be checking on the square every hour but decided not to tell Margot as much.

"One more thing." Margot held up a finger.

I raised my brow.

"As we agreed yesterday, let's keep this whole burglary business hush-hush. We don't want visitors to start thinking that Harvest isn't a safe place." With that, she walked away.

I shook my head and went in search of Lida. Her shift was long over. It was possible that she'd already found a ride home. However, I saw her refilling the candy stations. She took great care to lay the candy canes in the basket in a decorative circle and seemed to take some solace in making the design.

Two little boys in snowsuits came up to Lida. "Candy canes!" they cried in unison.

She smiled at the small boys, who could not have been more than four years old. "We made these at the candy factory."

"A factory of candy?" one little boy asked in awe. He looked back to an adult who must be his father. "I want to go to the factory."

The man stepped forward. "Maybe another time. The two of you have had so much sugar today, you might not sleep for a week! Your mother will never forgive me for this."

"I'll sleep," the second little boy said with confidence. "Candy doesn't keep me up."

His father looked unconvinced.

"Can I give them each a candy cane?" Lida asked the father.

He nodded. "At this point you can't make them any more hyper. We have hit the max."

The boys cheered as Lida handed them the candy canes.

Shaking his head, the father rolled the playing dice in his hand. "Pink square."

With candy canes in hand, the two boys ran down the game board's path to the pink square that was six places away.

"You're very good with children," I said, walking up to her.

Lida jumped. "Oh, Bailey."

"I'm sorry if I scared you."

She shook her head. "It's not your fault. I feel like I'm walking underwater right now." She looked around as if she were searching for something in particular.

What it was, I didn't know.

"Everything seems to make me jump today."

Grief. It was a feeling I knew well. When my *gross-daadi* passed away, I felt the same way. There was a ringing in my ears that wouldn't go away for weeks. It was as if I was tuned in to every electric hum around me. Many times, I was in the middle of a task at the candy shop and forgot what I was doing. I burned countless pots of caramel because my thoughts floated in another place and time. I was in the candy shop. I was present. But at the same time, I wasn't. My soul felt as if it was somewhere lost in space.

I didn't voice any of that to Lida. She would pass through grief in her own way. Everyone did. And contrary to what some say, there was no time limit or expiration date on grief when you lost someone you loved. I learned that when my grandfather passed. It was a lesson I hoped I would not have to learn again for a very long time.

She rearranged the candy canes in the basket, filling in the two small gaps left behind by the candies she'd given the boys. Each piece of candy we gave away at the Candy Land Experience had a sticker about Swissmen Candyworks, with our location, phone number, and website. We were giving away a great deal of candy, but I hoped it would pay off in the long run and create repeat customers. Even if they had traveled to Holmes County from far away and wouldn't come back any time soon, they could always shop online. It said that on the sticker, too.

"I wanted to ask if I could take you home," I said. "Your shift is over."

Lida frowned. "You don't have to do that. I can get a ride with . . ." She trailed off, and tears sprang to her eyes. We both knew she had almost said Zeph's name.

She cleared her throat. "I could use a ride, *ya*. An *Englisch* neighbor who was running errands brought me to the village today. My parents didn't want me to go to work this morning, so I doubt they would be willing to pick me up in the buggy."

"My car is parked behind the factory."

"*Danki*," she said as she placed three more candy canes artfully in the basket. Noticing again Lida's eye for pattern and design, I planned to ask her if she would like to work on the displays in the candy factory's lobby. The lobby manager said she had the space for her and would be happy for the help.

I decided to wait until Lida was in a better headspace to bring it up, though. I had a feeling she would turn down the idea right now because she wouldn't feel she deserved it after her brother's death.

I popped into Swissmen Sweets to tell my grandmother and Charlotte where I was headed. Charlotte said she had to stay at the candy shop to work on a few more things and promised to remain until I got back. I knew there wasn't anything pressing enough to keep her in the shop so long and that she was staying because both of us were nervous about Maami being alone in the shop after dark, even with all the windows locked and the doors bolted closed.

Lida and I walked to the Candyworks in silence. We both had a lot on our minds. At the moment, I was going over and over again in my head what I could say to her family about the loss of Zeph that wouldn't sound cliché. Nothing came to mind.

If they believed that Zeph had fallen away from the church, saying anything about his being "in a better place" or had been "taken too early" would just be offensive. As Amish parents, they might believe their son had been condemned because of his actions while he was alive. That was the most heartbreaking part.

And to be honest, I couldn't see the trite phrases

being helpful to any parent who'd lost a child, no matter what that parent's beliefs were.

As I turned my car onto Lida's road, she removed her mittens and twisted them in her pale hands. "It's just up there. The second house on the right. There is a solar-powered lamppost at the end of the driveway. You can just drop me there. There is no reason for you to turn into the driveway."

"I'd like to come in and talk to your parents." I glanced at her before refocusing on the country road in front of me.

"*Nee, nee,* you shouldn't do that. They wouldn't like it at all. The only *Englischers* who have ever been to my house are our neighbors, and my *daed* barely tolerates them. And the police, I suppose, when they came to tell my family about Zeph. Daed does not like the fact that Zeph and I were working for an *Englischer* business."

"Yes, the candy shop and factory are mine and I'm English, but they are also my *grossmaami*'s, and she is Amish."

"It doesn't matter. You're the face of Swissmen Sweets and the candy factory. Because of that, they believe it to be too *Englisch.*"

I'd never thought it would come to the point that I would be considered the face of Swissmen Sweets. In my mind, it would always be my grandparents' shop. However, that others believed it was a side effect of *Bailey's Amish Sweets.*

The car reached the end of the driveway, and I was torn as to what to do. It was dark and cold. The Lantz family had just lost their only son; a son that they must have heard by now appeared to be involved with the break-ins in the Harvest Amish community. It was a lot to digest.

"You're right," I said, turning in my seat to face her. "I'll speak to your parents another time. It has only been one day, and it's just too soon."

She unbuckled her seat belt and put her hand on the door handle as if she was about to open the door. "*Danki*, Bailey."

"*Willkomen*," I replied in Pennsylvania Dutch with a smile.

"I'll be at work tomorrow," she said more confidently than she'd spoken all day. "Would it be all right if I was in charge of replenishing the candies on the square again?"

I smiled. "It would be more than all right, and I wanted to tell you that Margot said you're doing a wonderful job."

I could make out just the hint of a smile on her face in the dim lamppost light coming through the windshield.

"Do you need a ride to work tomorrow? I can pick you up, or send Charlotte," I offered.

"*Nee*, I'll ask my neighbor to drive me again. She is very kind for an *E*—" She stopped herself from speaking.

She had been about to say that "she was very kind for an *Englischer*." I did not take offense.

In Holmes County, the English and the Amish communities were intertwined and dependent on each other, but still, there was some mistrust on both sides. The more conservative the Amish, the greater the mistrust. Considering what the Lantz family had been through in the last twenty-four hours, their distrust of the English community would be understandably high.

Lida opened her car door and immediately, a flashlight beam caught us both in the eyes. I had to hold up a hand to block the light as I heard an angry-sounding man shout at Lida in Pennsylvania Dutch.

CHAPTER TWENTY-TWO

I still had my hand over my eyes. "Can you please lower your light?"

A moment later, the glaring light was gone, and spots danced in front of my eyes. When the spots cleared, I saw Lida through the open passenger door standing with a middle-aged Amish man whom I could only assume was her father.

"Lida, get in the house," her father said in English.

She didn't even look at me as she ducked her head and ran toward the large gray farmhouse. Shadows moved across the light coming out of the home's many windows. I knew the rest of the family was watching.

Mr. Lantz slammed the car's passenger door shut with so much force the vehicle shook. He turned and stomped back to the large farmhouse.

I jumped out of my car. "Mr. Lantz!"

He kept walking.

"Mr. Lantz." I jogged a few steps forward. "I wanted to give my condolences on the loss of your son."

He stopped, turned around, and said in the most menacing voice I had ever heard, "I don't have a son. I only have daughters."

It might have been a mistake, but I forged ahead anyway. "Zeph was a free spirit."

He glared at me. "You say that like it is a compliment. It is not in the Amish world. It is the worst possible thing a young person can be. It led to his death."

"I—I—"

"Enough," he snapped. "I know very well he died while working for you. You should thank *Gott* that we are Amish and do not believe in punishing others for their transgressions. If it had been an *Englisch* child, would you not be sued and dragged into court?"

I couldn't think of anything to say in reply because what he said was true. Technically, the Lantz family had the right to sue me over their son's death. In America, a lawsuit could be filed for almost any reason at all. However, the Amish rarely used the justice system to settle their grievances.

"I have nothing to say to you. He worked for you and the conditions were unsafe. Now, he is dead. What do you have to say about that?" he asked.

Was it possible Mr. Lantz didn't know that Zeph might have been murdered? If so, I couldn't be the one to tell him. That was Aiden's place. I couldn't tell Mr. Lantz that Zeph was a burglar either. The only thing I could say was that I was sorry. I had already delivered that message. Mr. Lantz was right. It was time for me to leave.

"I am sincerely sorry," I said.

"Your apologies mean nothing. How can we continue to allow our daughter to work for you? In fact, I am telling her tonight that she can't go back to the candy factory tomorrow or ever again!"

I felt a pang in my chest. It was true that I'd told Zeph not to go on the roof again in the ice and snow. I hadn't been the one up on the roof with him—assuming Aiden was right about what had happened.

However, none of that seemed to matter. Zeph fell— whether by accident or not—and it had happened while I was responsible for him. That was something I would have to live with for the rest of my own life. I didn't know yet how I could.

"Mark." A voice came out of the dark. "It is time for me to leave. I have prayed with your wife and daughters." The speaker came into the light of the lamppost, and I wasn't surprised to see Bishop Yoder. As the leader of the Amish district, he was the one who set the rules for the community and who visited families when they were in pain.

The bishop and I had a cordial relationship. I found him to be a compassionate and thoughtful leader. When my *grossdaadi* passed away, he was kind to my grandmother. In the last few years, I had seen him make exceptions to the district's strict rules when necessary for the safety of its members. For one, he now allowed widows who lived alone to have a telephone attached to their homes. It was still outside, but it was a great improvement over a shed phone that might be a hundred feet if not fields away from the widow's front door.

The only complaint I truly had about the bishop wasn't even about him but about his wife, Ruth Yoder, who always had a reprimand or two for me. She believed I made Harvest "English" and corrupted the youth of the community with my television show and the many visitors it brought to the village.

Her vision for Harvest was in stark contrast to Margot Rawlings's vision. Ruth wanted the village and the Amish community to remain small and separate from the rest of the county. Margot wanted it to be the star of Holmes County.

Bishop Yoder nodded at me. "Mark, go see to your wife and children. As a husband and father, you will be greatly needed. They require your guidance and comfort. I will make sure that Bailey leaves the farm."

Mark Lantz glared at me, but then he nodded to his bishop's request. Before leaving, he shot me one last venomous scowl and then marched away.

"Bailey, come with me. You can walk me to my buggy," Bishop Yoder said in his melodious voice.

I could just imagine listening to him on a Sunday morning and wanting to melt into one of the hard folding chairs that the district used and wishing to take a nap. When I was a young child and visited my grandparents in the summer, I attended their church services on Sunday. I lost count of how many times I'd fallen asleep. My *daadi* used to tweak my ear to wake me up. It got to the point that I had trained myself to fall asleep with my hands over my ears.

Bishop Yoder cocked his head to one side. The twist of his neck was more off-kilter than I had ever seen it before. Not for the first time, I wondered just how old the bishop was. I knew he was much older than Ruth, and she was in her late sixties. Ruth and Bishop Yoder had married after his first wife passed away. His white beard hung down past the second button on his winter coat. His eyes held understanding, as if he could read every emotion that traveled across my face. He had been the district's bishop for a very long time. There was a good chance he had consoled people in every state of turmoil, even those who felt responsible for another person's death.

"Can you walk me to my buggy, Bailey?" he asked for the second time.

I nodded.

The bishop and I walked in silence, and when we reached his buggy, I recognized it as the one that Ruth generally drove into town. It was one of the shiniest and most expensive buggies in the county. It had battery-operated headlights and taillights. Battery-operated light was permitted in the district, but very few district members used it. That included my grandmother, who was much more comfortable with the candle and oil lamp lighting that she always used. It didn't matter how many times I begged her to make the switch for fire safety. She would tell me again and again, it was what my grandfather had used in their home, so it would be what she used as well.

When we reached the buggy, the bishop made a clicking sound with his tongue to wake up his slumbering horse. The horse shook his head as if to dispel any cobwebs.

"*Gut gual. Gut gual*," the bishop whispered in a kind voice.

The animal stopped shaking and rested its head on

the bishop's shoulder. He scratched the animal's nose. "Why are you here, Bailey?"

I cleared my throat. "Lida Lantz works at the Candyworks for me, and I gave her a ride home."

"Is that the only reason?" He patted the horse on its cheek one final time before walking to the buggy and setting his large Bible on the bench seat inside.

"It was the main reason."

"You were not welcome." He delivered this like the statement of fact it was.

"I wasn't," I admitted and wrapped my arms around myself to fight the cold. Despite my thick coat, boots, and hat, I was freezing. "And now Mark Lantz has forbidden Lida to work for me. I understand his reasoning, but I think what she needs right now is to keep busy. From what I can tell, it is the best way to deal with her grief. She said so herself."

The bishop removed the heavy horse blanket from the animal's back. "That may be true, but she must obey her father. He is the head of their home, and I see nothing wrong with his wanting to keep the family close at this difficult time when they have lost a son."

"Mark Lantz told me that he only had daughters."

The bishop carefully folded the blanket and set it in the back seat of the buggy. "He told me the same as well. However, Zeph was his son, and he knows that. He was upset over the way Zeph behaved. He and I had conversations about it often. It is always a man's wish that his son will follow in his footsteps, to carry on the family name in goodness and respect for our community. Zephaniah was Mark's last hope. He was greatly disappointed when Zeph turned his back on the family to live on his own."

"But he didn't leave the Amish faith," I argued. "He still dressed Amish. He still saw himself as an Amish man."

"He didn't leave, but he didn't commit either. At times, a child's not making a clear choice is more painful for a parent to watch than the child abandoning our way of life completely."

"Lida said that there would be no funeral for her brother."

"That was why I was here tonight. No matter what Zephaniah may have done or not done, his family deserves the closure a funeral service will provide. Funerals are for the living, not the dead. Nothing more can be done to bring Zeph to the Father now."

I wondered if the bishop knew that we suspected Zeph was behind the robberies in the Amish community. If that was true, he would have to know it was Zeph who'd broken into his home.

"I reminded Mark that the honoring of a person's life is as important for the living as it is for the dead. It is even more important for the living, so they can let go and move on."

"Did his father agree?"

"In the end, *ya,* but he only wants the immediate family there. He does not want the funeral open to the whole community. How they will be able to keep people from coming, I do not know. In our community, when another member is in turmoil and pain, we come out to show we care. Many in the district will simply ignore Mark Lantz's request for privacy."

I knew this was true. When my grandfather died years ago, my *grossmaami* very much wanted to be alone with her grief, but the community just would not allow it. Visitor after visitor made their way through the small candy shop. Casseroles, breads, and pies were given by the dozens. It was overwhelming, but the most overwhelming part was the outpouring of love for my grandfather and support for my grandmother.

"I'm surprised that you are the only one from the district who is here. Usually when tragedy strikes, everyone comes out." I shoved my hands deep in my coat pockets. The act did little to warm them.

"I asked district members to give the family a few days. I've known Mark since he was a child. He's stubborn and proud. He will not welcome the community." He reached up and scratched his horse behind the ear. "After the funeral, I hope he will be more open to sympathy. He might not like the intrusion, but the company is something his wife and daughters need to recover."

I thought of Lida, and I agreed that she needed support. She had seemed the happiest refilling candy at the Candy Land Experience. The constant activity kept her mind off losing her brother.

"The service will be in a few days. At times like these, the sooner there can be closure, the better." He walked to the buggy door.

I knew my conversation with him would end soon. "I'm glad you were able to talk them into it, Bishop Yoder. Lida was devastated at the idea her brother would not have a service."

"Lida is a *gut* young lady. She has followed the edicts of the district, but her weakness had always been Zephaniah. She loved and idolized her brother. Maybe because he was jovial and the most outgoing of her family. She would do anything for him. I was afraid that anything was just a little too much."

I frowned and watched as the bishop climbed into his buggy and guided the horse away from the tree. In the snow, the farmhouse looked bright and cheery. I could see a fire roaring in the fireplace and children seated in front of it playing some sort of game. To anyone driving by, they would look like a carefree Amish family enjoying a winter's evening together, but I knew better. There was pain there, pain that hadn't just started when Zeph was killed, pain that went back for years.

CHAPTER TWENTY-THREE

The next morning, I awoke with a raging headache because I had gotten one of the worst night's sleeps of my life. Sleeping in the double bed in my grandmother's guest room, I woke up every hour, listening for sounds of someone trying to break into the candy shop. Every creak and crack of the old brick building as it settled put me on edge. Usually, I would listen to music or leave on the television to help myself relax, but there was no television to watch, and I didn't want to wake my grandmother by listening to music on my phone.

Other than the creaks and cracks of the building, I heard nothing. There was no familiar electric hum either. The utter silence was eerie.

I'd tried to call Aiden, but he didn't answer. I had so many things to talk to him about: Zeph, Lida, the wedding. I longed for us to be married, if for no other reason than to find ourselves in the same place each night. Aiden was my friend and confidant, my strength when the weight of the world threatened to crush me. I missed him terribly.

Around two in the morning, I tiptoed to my grandmother's bedroom door and listened. Still nothing. I prayed that Aiden caught the person or persons behind the robberies soon because my heart couldn't take being so worried about my grandmother's safety.

When my alarm went off at five and it was time to actually get up, I felt as if I'd sunk into a pit. It took four attempts to open my eyes. Puff, who had moved to the candy shop with me, wiggled her ears. I could only see her because she was bright white and there was just enough light coming in through the slim space between the curtains to make out the rabbit's rotund shape. She resembled the bottom third of a snowman, but I wasn't going to tell her that.

I stumbled out of bed. I needed coffee, and I needed it badly.

The steps leading to the first floor were too steep for Puff to safely hop down, so I carried her. I grimaced when I picked up the bunny. To me, it felt as if she had gained a couple of pounds since the summer. The vet would not be pleased.

Nutmeg, our orange tabby, waited for his rotund friend at the bottom of the stairs. I set Puff next to the cat. The two touched noses and then hopped/walked over to Nutmeg's bed under the large picture window for a daylong nap. Their plan was very appealing, and I had to admit I was jealous.

I went through the swinging door into the industrial kitchen and found my grandmother sitting at the high stainless-steel table going through her recipe box of candies.

Maami knew all her recipes by heart, but she still relied on her box of recipes to remind her of what she'd made before and to help her choose which special candies she was going to make that day or week. She made something special every day at Swissmen Sweets, and whatever she chose was sure to be the first candy to sell out.

There were certain candies that we made at the shop every day, like fudge, truffles, and the milk and white chocolate Jethro bars, but in addition to those candies, we added a special each day. It was a nice surprise for the local customers to have the variety, and it helped us to hone our skills.

At the candy factory, it was different. The majority of candies made there were standing orders or online orders. There wasn't quite as much creativity about what to make as there was at Swissmen Sweets, and I knew that was what my grandmother loved the most about being a candymaker.

She looked up and smiled at me. "Do you know, before I married your *grossdaadi*, I didn't even have a candy thermometer? I had never made a piece of candy in my life. In my old district, such treats were viewed as frivolous and wasteful." She shook her head. "Your *grossdaadi* taught me candy was something to enjoy and share—in moderation, of course. Moderation is always the key to anything." She flipped through a few more recipe cards. "And now not a day goes by when I don't think about and make candy. It was a gift he gave me. Just one of the many. There are far too many to count."

"It was a gift he gave me, too," I said as I remembered my summers in Ohio and learning to make chocolates and other candies from my *daadi*. It had been those summers that had spurred my interest in candymaking, especially chocolate, and pursuing a career as a chocolatier in New York City. I could never have known his gift and my choice would lead to so many wonderful things, like my career in television, Swissmen Candyworks, and meeting my future husband. None of it would have happened without my grandfather or without chocolate.

Maami would not agree with me that those things were just a circumstance of fate and chance. In her belief, they were predestined to happen. She told me more than once that her God picked Aiden to be my husband long before either one of us were born. I liked to think she was right.

"We have made so many recipes these last few weeks with peppermint. I needed to go to the recipe box for inspiration. I'm looking for another Christmas recipe that is not peppermint." She plucked a card from the box. "Yes, here we go! Gingerbread fudge!"

"Gingerbread fudge?" I asked. "I've never heard of that and certainly have never made it."

"It's delicious if you like gingerbread, which many people do not. However, I might just be able to convince them with this recipe. It's all about getting just enough spice without letting it overwhelm the candy. With the gingerbread men a feature in the Candy Land

Experience, this will be just the treat to fill one of the baskets on the game board."

My face must have given away what I thought about that.

"You don't like that idea?" she asked as she began refiling her recipes. "I'm sure I could find another recipe that would work just as well."

"No, no, it's the right recipe for the occasion. It's just that I have a personal aversion to it. It's not your fault."

"You don't like gingerbread?"

"It's not that. But every time I think about gingerbread, I think of the game piece on the roof of the Candyworks."

Her hands froze over her recipe box. "Oh, my. It is because of Zeph?" She started to tuck the recipe card back in her box. "I should have been more sensitive to the fact that gingerbread might be upsetting to you."

I sat down on the stool next to hers. "No, make it. Please. I know it will be a hit with the people playing the game."

"If you're sure?" She pulled the card back out of the box.

"I am," I said and took the recipe card from her hand, placing it on the table.

"Is the gingerbread man still on the roof of the factory?"

I sighed. "Yes. Aiden promised me that they would have it removed as soon as possible. Until then, they don't want to make any changes to the scene."

She frowned. "Why is that a concern? Zeph slipped

on the snow and ice, did he not? That was an accident, a horrible one, of course, but we will do all we can to help the family."

I twisted my mouth.

My grandmother placed a wrinkled hand to her cheek. "Oh, Bailey! Another murder?"

"You make it sound like it happens all the time."

"Doesn't it?" she asked.

She had a point.

"I think the fudge is a perfect idea, and we can use one of our small Christmas tree molds and shape the pieces with that. I'd much rather they look like Christmas trees than actual gingerbread men under the circumstances."

"If you are sure . . ." She trailed off.

"I am, and we still don't know how Zeph died exactly. Well, I will correct that. We know that he died from the fall, but we don't know if it was an accident or something more sinister." I walked over to the percolator on the stove, where my grandmother had a fresh pot of coffee ready to drink. In her business, the district allowed her to use electricity. She could technically use an electric coffee maker in the candy shop, but she still chose to make it on the stovetop, and I would be the first to admit it had a different, more authentic taste when brewed that way.

She shook her head. "My heart goes out to the Lantz family. Now they've lost both of their sons."

I choked on my coffee. "Both of their sons?" I squawked. "I thought Zeph was the only son. Lida never mentioned another brother."

"She wouldn't," Maami said as she slowly pushed herself off the stool and moved over to the spice wall.

There was every spice a person could imagine on that wall, organized on wooden shelves made by my grandfather. Each spice was in a glass jar and labeled in my grandfather's hand. There might be better uses for the wall. When we got a new freezer, we'd had to do lots of finagling in the kitchen to make enough space for it. It would have fit perfectly against that wall, but I couldn't even bring myself to suggest it. I knew how much Maami loved her spice wall, and it reminded her of my grandfather. I had made plenty of changes to the business since I'd moved to Ohio. That was one I refused to make.

She selected nutmeg, ginger, allspice, cloves, and cinnamon. One thing was guaranteed—the gingerbread fudge would be packed with flavor.

She set the jars on the worktable. "Their eldest son is still living, but he left the Amish way. From what I have heard, he lives in Millersburg. I don't know much more than that."

I let out a breath. "So he's alive. They didn't truly lose him."

"He is as *gut* as lost," she said. "He left the church after baptism, so he is shunned by the community."

I made a face.

"I know you don't approve of the Amish practice of shunning. There are aspects that I don't like about it either, but when a member makes a promise to follow the Amish way, to be a servant to *Gott,* and then turns his back on his vow, there has to be a punishment befitting the betrayal."

I bit my lower lip to keep myself from saying anything that might upset my grandmother. She knew where I stood on this issue. We had discussed it many times before. We have agreed to disagree.

"What is his brother's name?" I asked.

"Malachi," she said and then cocked her head. "Are you going to track him down?"

"You bet. I think Aiden and his deputies believe, as I did, that Zeph was the only son in the family. I doubt anyone in the family mentioned Malachi, especially if he was shunned."

Most Amish were born at home, so there was no public record of many Amish children until they were adults and began working. At that point, the adults had to pay income tax like everyone else in the country.

"Well, don't spend too much time on it. Remember, your parents are here for just a short while and they want to visit with Aiden and you before they go back home." She paused. "Your mother is very eager to plan the wedding."

"I know. She hired a wedding planner." I grimaced into my coffee.

Maami's blue eyes went wide as she measured spices into a glass bowl. "I did not know that. Your mother and Juliet were both here last evening, and they couldn't speak enough about the wedding. They did not tell me about the wedding planner."

"Probably because I'm not happy about it." I sighed and started removing candy molds from one of the high cabinets. "Obviously I don't want anyone to lose work or a client. We are a small business, too, but they should have asked me."

"They didn't ask you?"

"No." I set the Christmas tree molds on the table.

Red cinnamon candy pearls would be just the added touch that would make my grandmother's gingerbread fudge pop. I went to the cupboard in search of them.

Maami removed a large block of butter from the refrigerator and set it on a cutting board on the worktable. The fudge that we made at the candy shop and the factory would never be called a low-calorie food.

"Bailey," Maami said, "you need to take control of the wedding. You know that I have said very little about it, but if you don't start, your mother and Juliet will run away with it."

I made a face just as I found the candy pearls. "Maybe it would be easier to let them do the planning."

"It might be for now, but can you promise me that you won't be disappointed with their plans or resentful because the wedding is more about them than it is about you and Aiden?"

I bit my lip and didn't say a word because I couldn't make that promise. The truth was I liked planning. I liked lists and organizing events, but when it came to the wedding, I kept wondering, why rush it?

Did this mean I had cold feet?

I stewed on this question for a moment while my grandmother cut the butter into cubes. I didn't have cold feet when it came to Aiden. I knew he was my person, and I had known it for years, even when distance challenged our relationship. I wanted to be married. The aspect I was nervous about was the wedding and the expectations set by our families and the entire village of Harvest.

Maami must have sensed my anxiety because she walked over to me and patted my cheek. "In the end, what matters most is you will be married to a man you love and who loves you. The wedding is one day. Do not fret on it so."

Yes, that was what mattered most.

CHAPTER TWENTY-FOUR

I very much wanted to talk to Lida about her oldest brother, Malachi, and planned to do that when I got to the factory later that morning. Then, I remembered that she wasn't coming in to work at the Candyworks that day or ever again because her father forbade it. There had to be another way to reach her.

A little before nine, I walked across the square. The Candy Land Experience opened at ten, but there were already people milling around the square, sipping coffee and hot cocoa they'd purchased at the café and looking at the elaborate decorations.

Melchior and the animals in the live nativity were also drawing a crowd.

A little English boy held up his glazed doughnut to the camel, which ate it in one bite. The boy giggled, and Uriah appeared from the other side of the manger scene. "Please don't feed the camel. We're afraid that he won't be allowed to come back next Christmas if we send him home too chunky."

The boy giggled at the mental image of a chunky camel and his parents guided him away.

I waved to Uriah, and he shook his head. "So many people have given Melchior treats that I'm afraid his owner will ban him from the square next Christmas."

He pointed at the sign: "Don't feed the camel!"

"I guess that's not working." He removed his black felt hat, ran his hand through his white hair, and slapped the hat back on his head.

The camel held his head over Uriah's shoulder. "Oh, you. How can I stay mad at you for long when you are as cuddly as a kitten?"

The camel showed his teeth, as if that was his plan all along.

Uriah patted the top of the camel's nose. "After working with Melchior, I have asked my wife, Millie, if she could have a camel on the farm."

I smiled. "And how did that go over?"

"She said we could hardly handle her two goats, Phillip and Peter. How in the world would she manage a camel?" He shook his head, as if he felt that Millie was shortsighted. "And then she asked what we would use him for. Isn't it obvious that camels are good for transportation?"

I barked a laugh. The idea of Uriah in his Amish dress going down the road on the back of a camel was far too much to envision.

Melchior seemed to take offense at my laughter and spat in the snow an inch from my boot. I had to believe that the aim had been intentional. It was a warning shot, like a pirate shooting over the bow. Next time, it would be a direct hit. I took two big steps back from the camel, hoping that was out of range.

"Don't get your hump up in a twist," Uriah said. "Bailey didn't mean to laugh. She thinks you'd be a great addition to any farm."

The camel walked away, back into the stable. He lay in the fresh stray between a donkey and two sheep. The sheep had to scoot over to make room for him because it was clear Melchior was at the very top of the pecking order in the nativity.

He closed his eyes as if he was settling in for a nap. His long eyelashes fluttered, fanning at the end in wisps. The sheep and the donkey were snoozing, too. I wondered if there were rabbits at the first Christmas because Puff sleeps most of the time. She'd fit right in with this crowd. However, she wouldn't want to be out in the weather. She hated being cold even more than she hated for her snow-white coat to have one speck of dirt on it. She was a diva through and through.

I changed the subject. "Lida Lantz, who was refilling the candies yesterday, won't be here today."

"Oh, why not? I had a very nice time with Lida. She is a hardworking girl. Whenever the candies were just half-full, she was already there adding more. I liked chatting with her, too. She's been through a lot for one so young."

I nodded. "I'll take over for today, and if I get called away, I'll ask one of the candy sellers from the factory to fill in."

I knew one of the young staff who would like to take on the assignment.

He nodded. "How is Lida doing?" he asked. "It was clear to me that she didn't want to speak about her brother's death. It was all too fresh. Is she not coming to work today because she's too upset? I understand if that's her reason."

"Yes." I nodded. I didn't feel that it was my place to say she wasn't working for me any longer because her father wouldn't allow it.

Uriah tugged on his long gray beard. "It's awful. I have always liked Zeph. He helped me on the square for a little extra money from time to time. He always had an odd job or two. His work wasn't fixed to one place. I was happy to learn that he had gotten a position at Candyworks. I just knew if he settled down, he would go far. He had it in him to go far. It's such a shame that he never got the chance."

I agreed. Zeph had only been seventeen when he died. He'd had his whole life in front of him. That was the hard part about the loss.

I bit my lip as I considered how to phrase my next question. I didn't want to give too much away, but at the same time I thought Uriah was a good judge of character. I was curious as to how much he really knew about Zeph Lantz and his activities.

"The family is having a private funeral for him. I don't know when yet," I said.

"A private funeral?" Uriah exclaimed. "That will never do."

"It's his father's wish," I said. "Bishop Yoder told me of it himself."

He shook his head. "I can't say that I agree with the choice. Zeph wasn't shunned by the community. He was still in *rumspringa* and as yet had not made his choice about staying in the church. He should have a proper burial."

I was relieved to hear Uriah felt the same way I did on this topic.

"Whether Mark Lantz likes it or not, the community will come out to support his family." Uriah folded his arms.

"Do you know Mark?" I drew out the mittens my grandmother had given me that morning. I still had not been back to my house to collect my gloves. When I pulled the mittens onto my cold hands, they felt and looked like navy-blue flippers. I didn't know how I was to do much of anything with them on.

"He's from the district, so *ya*, I know him. However, I knew his father, Jeremiah Lantz, much better. He was an old friend of mine. Sadly, he passed as a young man. I was living in Indiana at the time, and I always regretted not coming back for the funeral." He shook his head. "But I had a young family of my own back then. I simply could not leave."

"How old was Mark when his father passed?"

"I would say about eight years old."

"How awful," I murmured. "Can I ask how he died?"

"Jeremiah wasn't the most devoted Amish man in the world. Even though he was baptized, he dabbled in the *Englisch* life now and again. He liked to drive cars and things like that. The church elders spoke to him about it many times and he was on and off probation with the church more times than I could count."

"Probation?" I had thought I had lived in Holmes

County long enough to know about every aspect of Amish life. I had never before heard the term "probation" in reference to the Amish.

"It can happen if a member breaks one of the district's minor rules. I'm not talking about leaving the church or turning one's back on *Gott*. A common example is when a young man lets his hair grow too long. If he corrects the problem—cuts his hair—and confesses his transgression in front of the church, he will be reinstated. During a probation period he is not allowed to participate in normal district activities, like attending services or social events."

"Because he didn't get a haircut?" I yelped.

"That is just one small example. You have to remember, before someone is placed on probation, the church elders and the bishop would have spoken to him or her several times about what they're doing. Probation happens when the member ignores those warnings."

Uriah must have read my face because he said, "This is just the first step to keep members of the district on the straight and narrow. Correcting their missteps in these small instances keeps them from making larger mistakes, like leaving the district. I know it's difficult for an *Englischer* to understand."

It was very difficult. Perhaps that kind of discipline worked with some members of the church, but it couldn't work with all of them. I thought of my cousin Charlotte, who had grown up in a particularly rigid district. She wasn't even allowed to play a musical instrument there. I would never call Charlotte rebellious, but she'd rebelled and left. She eventually joined Maami's district, but I believed she'd already pulled away from the Amish way of life. She eventually left altogether so that she could marry Deputy Little.

If her district hadn't held on to her so tightly, would she still be living there with her parents and siblings? I wondered. Would she be married to a man from the district now and have children? Would she be as happy in that life as she was with Deputy Little? I didn't have the answers to any of those questions.

"While Jeremiah was on probation," Uriah went on, "he got into a car accident and was killed."

"How awful. Was anyone else hurt?"

Uriah shook his head. "No, thankfully he was alone. From what the sheriff's deputies told his wife, he lost control of the car on a rainy night and ran off the road into a tree. It was just a tragic accident."

"But I suppose the church leaders didn't see it that way," I said.

He leaned on the handle of his shovel. "This was during the time when Bishop Yoder's father was the bishop. He was a very different man from his son. He was much stricter. Also, he liked to use people's mistakes as examples to scare other members into following the rules. Granted, I was in Indiana at the time, but from what I heard the following Sunday after Jeremiah's death, the bishop preached on it and said that Jeremiah had been punished by *Gott* for his disobedience."

"How awful," I whispered.

"What made it even more awful was that the Lantz family was at the service. Mark was young and heard every last word of it. From that day forward, he was the perfect Amish child. He never slipped out of line. He never made a mistake. He did everything he was told to do and expected to do. He was determined to be a perfect Amish man."

"So having a son who was more like his father than himself must have been difficult."

"Very difficult," Uriah agreed.

"My grandmother just told me that Zeph and Lida had another brother named Malachi."

He nodded. "But I wouldn't say anything about that son to Mark. He was furious when Malachi left the Amish way. Even if Malachi changed his mind and came back, I don't know that his father would forgive him."

Melchior grunted from his spot among the other manger scene animals. A camel grunt was quite an interesting sound.

Uriah raised his brow. "That's his way of telling me that he is ready for breakfast. I'm starting to learn his quirks. By the time the Candy Land Experience is over, I might be able to anticipate his next move. I've only been spat on twice. I've learned to dodge him."

I grimaced and took another step away from Melchior. Being spat on didn't sound at all like a pleasant experience to me.

CHAPTER TWENTY-FIVE

I thanked Uriah for the information and went about the task of filling the candy stations around the game board. I wanted everything in place before the game began; it promised to be another busy day at Swissmen Sweets and Swissmen Candyworks. As I moved from station to station with my baskets of candy, it felt surreal to be walking in a life-size board game. I had to admit Margot had pulled it off—with the giant pieces of candy all around me, I felt as if I was in the middle of Candy Land.

I dropped licorice, taffy, peppermints, and gumdrops at each of the stations. My grandmother's gingerbread fudge wasn't ready yet. It was still cooling in the candy shop, but by the afternoon, one of my young factory workers could use it to refill one of the stations. I knew that it would be a hit with customers. So many visitors told us they came to our candy shop because they could find homemade candy there that they couldn't find anywhere else. I would guess that gingerbread fudge was on that list.

Because the game board was so large and I wanted to take as much care displaying the candies as Lida had the day before, it took me close to an hour to finish to my own satisfaction.

Walking to the factory, I expected to see the red game piece still glowering down at me from the factory roof. However, I was relieved to find it was gone. Aiden must have asked a deputy to finally take it down. I wrinkled my brow. I was surprised that he hadn't told me, though.

I shook my head. It wasn't worth worrying about. I had plenty of more pressing problems. I was just happy to see the game piece gone, and I hoped that I would never see it again.

When I arrived at the factory, visitors were already lined up to go on the first candymaking tour, set for ten thirty. They ranged from children to older adults. I was grateful that the factory was getting so much attention, and I knew that was thanks in part to Margot's Candy Land Experience. But considering what had happened to Zeph, the cost was not worth it.

That morning, there was no evidence at all that there had been such a terrible accident right outside the front door of Swissmen Candyworks. Everything had been cleared away. It made me uncomfortable how quickly every sign of Zeph's death had been erased even though I had wanted it all gone.

Maeva walked over to me with a bright smile on her face. When she saw my expression, her face fell. "Bailey, are you all right?"

I forced a smile to my own face. "Yes, I'm just pre-occupied."

"Okay," she said, as if she didn't quite believe me.

Honestly, I wouldn't have quite believed my answer either.

"We have had a record number of people sign up for the tour," Maeva said. "We're booked for every tour, with more people wanting to be placed on a waiting list. As soon as people started going to the Candy Land Experience on the square, they started coming here. It's been great advertising, but I'm afraid we will be overrun."

My eyes went wide. "I didn't know the impact would be that immediate. Call in two extra guides and see if we can add at least two tours every day for the rest of the week. The Candy Land Experience will end Saturday. When that happens, there will be a lot fewer people in Harvest."

She nodded. "I will make some phone calls now. I'm sure the staff will be happy to make a little extra money this close to Christmas."

I nodded. "Anything else I need to know about?"

"Lida Lantz didn't report to work today. This was supposed to be her first day as a candy seller in the lobby."

"That's my fault. I should have told one of you—she won't be coming in at least for a few days." I couldn't bring myself to say just yet that Lida was never coming back to the factory. Maybe I was still hoping that her father would change his mind.

"I understand. In some ways, I wasn't surprised that she didn't show up. I was more surprised that she came to work yesterday. Losing a sibling is a terrible blow," she said, as if she spoke from experience. "It's so sad what happened to her brother. He was a *gut* young man."

I raised my brow. This was the first time I had heard anyone at all call Zeph "a good young man." The consensus was that he was in a lot of trouble all the time.

"Did you know him well?"

She shook her head. "*Nee*, but when my husband was hurt at work last year, we were in real trouble making payments on our farm. Zeph just showed up one day and gave us enough money to pay our mortgage for two months. He told us it was from his district."

"You're not in the same district as the Lantz family?"

She shook her head. "*Nee*. I was so grateful that I sought out Bishop Yoder to thank him." She paused, as if she was considering what she should say next.

"And?"

"He said the money wasn't from the district. It must have been a gift from *Gott*."

"Maeva!" one of the candy sellers called. "Your tour is ready to leave."

She waved at the other woman. "If you see Lida, please tell her I'm sorry and thought a lot of her *bruder*."

"I will," I said and watched her join her tour on the other side of the large room.

My head spun with this new information. Where had Zeph got the money to help Maeva's family? Had he stolen it? Considering that Uriah had just told me Zeph only worked odd jobs here and there until I hired him a short time ago, it seemed to be the only explanation.

If he'd stolen the money, why would he give it away? Had I had an Amish Robin Hood on my hands?

All I knew was that Maeva had spoken to Bishop Yoder about it, so I needed to speak to him again.

CHAPTER TWENTY-SIX

Everything was going smoothly at the factory and I had a few hours free before I had to teach the makeup class for Jenny and the rest of the Harvest Garden Club. Planning to make a visit to Bishop Yoder, I walked to my car, which I had left parked behind the factory.

It had snowed again the night before, so there was a thin layer of white covering all the car windows. I couldn't see inside.

I unlocked the door and reached in with the intention of turning on the ignition so I could get the defroster going. Then I reached into the back seat for my window scraper and let out a bloodcurdling scream.

An answering scream sounded by the dumpsters that we shared with Harvest Market.

I jumped back from the car.

Beau Eicher stood beside the dumpster holding a black trash bag and staring at me as if I was the Ghost of Christmas Past. He dropped the bag on the blacktop. "Are you okay?"

I pressed a hand to my chest. "I think so."

Beau was a tall lanky teenager with a crooked smile and countless freckles. I didn't know him well, but I had seen him hanging out with Zeph in the parking lot more than once because the boys were close friends. Seeing Beau reminded me of the day Zeph died; Zeph had said that he would wait for Beau to help him remove the game piece from the factory roof.

I managed to catch my breath. "There's something in my car."

He walked over to me. "What is it?" He peered through the car's back window and jumped back. "Is that a dead guy?"

"No." I shook my head. "It's the red game piece from Candy Land that was on the factory roof."

"Oh." He paled. "Why would you put that in your car?"

"I didn't put it there," I said. "Someone else must have done it to scare me."

He took two big steps back. "If you're okay, I should get back to work. Ansel doesn't like it when I take too long to get rid of the trash. He thinks I'm goofing off."

"Zeph said he was going to ask you for help taking the game piece off the roof."

"Zeph is dead." His voice caught, as if he could barely get the words out. "I know a lot of people are relieved, but I'm not. He was my friend."

"I know. He talked about you often."

Tears came to Beau's eyes, and he blinked them

away. "I should get back to work." He walked back to the dumpster, picked up the trash bag, and flung it inside. "Zeph used to ask me for help, but not for a long while. There were other people helping him lately." He continued to blink away tears and turned on his heel. "I have to get back to work."

"Beau, when was the last time you saw Zeph?" I asked.

He turned around. "The morning he died. He told me to stay away from him, so I did." He glanced back at my car. "Maybe whatever is in your car is a warning."

I swallowed. "A warning?"

He nodded. "That's what I would think." He turned and walked back to the Market.

Was it a warning or just a sick joke?

With a deep breath, I poked my head into the car again. This time I was ready for what I saw: the giant red corrugated plastic game piece, bent to look as if it was sitting in the back seat of my car.

And there was a message, though not a written one.

It was even more frightening than words. A rope was tied around the game piece's neck so tightly that the plastic buckled.

I jumped back from the car a second time with my phone in my hand.

"Bailey, you are actually where I need you to be for once," Margot said as she marched across the parking lot, carrying two orange traffic cones. She dropped the cones in front of me, and they teetered back and forth before settling on the pavement. "Those are a lot heavier than they look. There are more in the back of my pickup. You and Uriah can set them up for the parade. What I have learned over the years about the Christmas parade is that it needs to be contained and organized before it starts. If not, sheep and wisemen wander off and it's a great big mess. You can use the cones to mark the spots where the marchers should wait until the parade begins."

I vaguely remembered Margot mentioning a few weeks ago that the parking lot shared by the Candyworks and the Market would be used as the Christmas parade staging area on Friday night. I had not known that I was in charge of it. Then again, there were many things that I didn't know I was doing when Margot handed out directives.

"Margot, I can't do that right now. I have to call Aiden. There's been an incident."

"An incident?" She looked around. "Don't tell me you found another dead body. We will have to have an intervention for you if that keeps up."

"I didn't find a dead body. But the red Candy Land game piece is in my car."

She looked into my car. "Why would you go and bend my game piece like that?" She straightened up with a scowl on her face. "That wasn't easy to make, and I don't have any of the red plastic left to make another one."

"I didn't do it. Someone else put it in the back of my car."

She looked in the car again. "Well, that's strange. Do you think the rope around its neck was used to get it down from the roof?"

"No, it's a warning." I paused. "For me."

I called Aiden.

Aiden, Deputy Little, and two other deputies were behind the candy factory searching my car and the surrounding area within the hour. Across the parking lot, Uriah set up the traffic cones for the parade waiting area. It looked as if he was cordoning off a crime scene of his own. Margot had long since returned to the square to oversee the final preparations for the parade.

Aiden scowled as the two deputies tried to remove the game piece from my back seat.

"My land!" one of the deputies cried. "How'd they even get this thing back here? We are going to need a crowbar to get it out."

"Be careful," Aiden said. "Don't tear it. It's evidence."

The deputy nodded. He and his partner got back to work trying to remove the game piece from my car.

"What are you going to do with it?" I asked.

"We will take it to the station and look for any evidence like hairs or fingerprints, anything that might tell us who put it there," Aiden said.

"Can you get fingerprints from it?" I asked.

"We hope to, but there is no guarantee. People are much more likely to be wearing gloves or mittens this time of year," Aiden admitted. "Now, tell me, why would someone leave this message for you?"

"They were making a point about Zeph, of course," I said.

"Who was?"

"I don't know. If I knew that, I would probably have hand-delivered the killer to you by now."

He sighed because he knew it was likely the truth. I

was relentless about finding answers, and I had delivered a killer to Aiden more than once. He knew it wasn't an idle comment.

"It might have been a harmless prank," I suggested.

"I don't think so," he said. "I would have been more inclined to think that if the game piece was simply stuffed into your car, but the rope around the neck wasn't a subtle message."

As much as I hated to, I had to agree with him on that point.

"How many people know that you have been asking questions about Zeph's death?"

I shrugged. "I don't know. I don't feel like I have spoken to too many people about it, but I think it's safe to say that many people in the village would assume that I was looking into it. You know, based on my reputation."

Aiden groaned.

He waited.

"There is another Lantz son."

"What do you mean?"

I went on to tell him about Malachi Lantz, who'd left the Amish faith and was shunned. "He's still in the county. Maami thought he was in Millersburg, but that's all I have to go on."

"Okay, but what is the connection here? If he left the church, he might not even know that Zeph is dead."

My eyes went wide. I hadn't thought about that possibility, but if he was completely estranged from the Amish community, he might not know that Zeph had died. "It's worth looking into," I said a bit defensively. "Especially because it appears that Zeph was on the cusp of leaving the Amish way. He moved out of his family home. That is a no-no if you plan to stay Amish. If he was going to stay in the faith, he would have lived in his family's home until he was married."

Aiden nodded. "Yes, it is worth looking into. I will have Deputy Little track him down and have a conversation with him."

"Or I could do it," I suggested.

"No." Aiden's voice was firm. "I don't want you anywhere close to this investigation."

"But—"

"Bailey, do I have to remind you that there was a plastic cutout of a game piece in your car with a rope around its neck? Your investigation is over."

We would see about that. I still believed that my personal ties to the Amish gave me the best chance of putting an end to the questions about Zeph's death once and for all.

CHAPTER TWENTY-SEVEN

I made no promises to Aiden that I would stop asking questions about Zeph. He would have been shocked if I had.

I still had an hour before my class with Jenny and the Garden Club. The timing would be tight, but I decided to risk it and drive out to the Yoder farm to speak with Bishop Yoder again. Had he owned a cell phone, I simply would have called him to ask my questions, but communication wasn't simple when it came to the Amish community.

The Yoder farm was on several hundred acres and was one of the largest in the county. The family raised dairy cows, sheep, horses, turkeys, and chickens. This time of year, with a thick layer of snow across the wide fields and pastures, it looked like a clean white blanket. The animals were inside their various barns and pens on such a cold day. When I turned down the Yoders' long driveway, I was surprised to see five or six Amish buggies parked in front of the house. All the horses had blankets on their backs and feed bags around their necks, as if their owners expected the animals would be out in the cold for a long while.

I almost turned my car around. I didn't want to interrupt some sort of church meeting, and I had only forty-five minutes before I had to turn around and head back to the candy factory. I did not want to keep Jenny waiting. She was already in a foul mood that her first class was interrupted.

Just then, the front door opened and a short elderly Amish woman in a navy dress and white prayer cap stood there. "Well, are you coming in or not? Staying out there dithering isn't going to get your questions answered."

I smiled. Uriah's wife, Millie, was just the person I needed to see. I got out of the car and walked to the wide porch.

As I usually did when I was at the Yoder home—which wasn't often—I noted the odd shape of the farmhouse. The Yoders had lived on the property for at least five generations. Each generation had added to the house as the family grew, but it seemed there was no overall plan. Maami told me that when Ruth married the bishop, she had a large room put on the front of the house so that church meetings could be held at the Yoder home no matter the weather. If she had it her way, the district would meet at her home every Sunday they had church. However, that was contrary to Amish tradition, which dictated that each household should take a turn at hosting the church service. That practice was designed to build a close community bond among the church members.

To disguise how oddly the front room jutted out from the building, Ruth had added a wide wraparound front porch.

Millie enveloped me in a hug as soon as I reached the door.

"Uriah has told me about what is happening in the village, and I knew you needed a hug," she said as she pulled away.

"I did," I agreed.

She smiled. Her white hair was perfectly tethered at the nape of her neck in an Amish bun. Her dress and apron were clean and pressed, and her prayer cap sat squarely on the top of her white hair. Her clothing was a far cry from Lois Henry's. Whenever I went into the Sunbeam Café, I never knew what Lois would look like, other than that her clothes and hair would be bright. For as Plain and devout as Millie appeared, Lois was the complete opposite—preferring bright hair, makeup, clothes, and jewelry.

Despite their very different appearances, Millie and Lois were the best of friends.

"You came at the right time—we are in the middle of a Double Stitch meeting," Millie explained.

I stepped into the house after her and she helped me out of my parka. Four other Amish women were in the house, including Ruth Yoder, with her steel-gray hair and perpetual scowl. The rest of the women smiled in welcome at me.

Although we had a Christmas tree in Swissmen Sweets and several at the Candyworks, the decorations were for the tourists that flooded Holmes County during the Christmas season. The Amish didn't decorate their homes with Christmas trees. The only nod to the upcoming holiday was pine boughs across the fireplace and a large pine cone wreath on the front door. The Amish were truly Plain people, and Ruth had very few knickknacks or pieces of art up in her house at all. I suspected that was the case because she felt she needed to show how best to be the perfect Amish housekeeper and wife.

"I don't want to intrude." I looked around the room. "I was looking for the bishop. Is he home?"

Ruth sniffed from the oak rocker where she sat. She had a stack of quilting squares on her lap, which she folded into quarters and cut. The fabric was black and cream. "He is not home. He is at the private burial for Zephaniah Lantz today."

"Oh!" I said in surprise. I knew that Mark Lantz had agreed to the funeral, but I hadn't realized that it would be so soon. I hadn't even known that the Sheriff Department had released the body back to the family.

"If you ask me, it's a disgrace that the family is excluding the rest of the community. I told my husband that I should at least be there to represent the mothers in the district and show our support. He told me *nee*." She sniffed. "He is my husband and I must do his bidding, but if he thinks he is getting a roast when he comes home, he is sadly mistaken."

Raellen Raber, who was an Amish mother of nine and the youngest member of the group, laughed.

Ruth shot her a withering look, and Raellen swallowed her fit of giggles.

Millie pointed to an open seat on a sofa. "Have a seat, Bailey. I'll get you a piece of pie."

I couldn't say no to pie. It would be rude.

"What did you want to talk to the bishop about?" Leah Bontrager asked. Leah was about Millie and Ruth's age and had a businesslike demeanor about her.

"I actually wanted to speak to him about Zeph." I perched on the sofa. The fabric was soft chenille, and I was so tired from lack of sleep over the last couple of days, I was tempted to lean my head back and take a short nap.

However, with Ruth watching me, that was out of the question. I guessed that she was anti naps because she would see them as time wasters.

"You're investigating his death, aren't you?" Ruth asked. "I don't understand why you can't leave well enough alone."

"I don't know it's 'well enough,'" I said.

Millie returned from the kitchen with a large piece of pumpkin pie and a mug of coffee with cream and sugar, just the way I liked it. She set them on the small side table by my seat and then sat on the other end of the sofa, where she had been piecing together a lap quilt. "Is that because it looks like murder?"

The other women in the room gasped.

"Millie, how can you say that?" Ruth asked. "He fell off a roof."

"That's not what I heard from Uriah." She began threading her needle.

Iris Young, the last member of the group and a new mother who worked part-time at the café waiting tables, placed a hand on her chest. "Another murder in Harvest?"

"It's not a murder," Ruth said.

"It looks like it," Millie replied, unfazed by Ruth's tone. "Someone pushed Zeph off the roof."

The women gasped again.

"Did you hear that from Uriah, too?" I asked.

She looked at me and nodded. "Deputy Little told him."

At least I wasn't the one to slip and share details about a case this time.

"That is the dumbest way to kill someone I have ever heard," Raellen said.

Ruth scowled. "Do you often think about ways to kill someone?"

Raellen's face turned bright red. "No, I didn't say that."

"Let's get back to the matter at hand," Leah said. "Bailey, what did you want to ask the bishop?"

I looked around the room at all the women and realized that every last one of them knew of Zeph's tendency to steal. He'd had to confess it in front of the church, so speaking of it wasn't going to come as a surprise to these women.

I cleared my throat. "There is a woman who works at my factory named Maeva. She told me that years ago Zeph gave her money to help her family when her husband was ill. She was so grateful to him for doing that. She's not a member of your district, but she made a point of telling Bishop Yoder what Zeph had done. She thanked the bishop."

"Where did he get the money?" Iris asked.

Ruth glowered at her. "He stole it. What Bailey is trying not so successfully to tell us is that Zephaniah stole from others to give to a person in need."

Raellen, who was known to be a gossip, said, "Why don't I know about this? I have never heard this before."

"It was an open secret. Maeva wasn't the only one he did that for," Leah said. "I know at least a half-dozen families who got piles of money from Zeph to help them in their time of need. It's why we tolerated his behavior for so long."

"What behavior?" I asked.

"The stealing," she said, looking me in the eye. "He never stopped."

"The district knew he was stealing and didn't do anything about it?" I asked, confused. It was true that I didn't grow up Amish, but this seemed to go against everything they taught.

"No one knew for certain that was what he was doing," Ruth said and gave Leah an irritated look. "But when he had so much money to give families in trouble, we had suspicions."

"No one asked him?"

Ruth pressed her lips together. "The bishop spoke to him several times, but when he stopped coming to church . . ." She shrugged.

"Did Bishop Yoder speak to his parents?"

"*Ya*," Ruth said. "He made sure they knew he wanted to help Zeph, not hurt him. Zeph Lantz was one of my husband's projects."

"Projects?" I asked.

She eyed me. "There have been a number of young Amish men over the years who have floundered. They don't know if they want to join the church or leave the community. They get into trouble. In Zeph's case, the way he attracted attention was having all that money to give away."

"Where did the bishop think the money was coming from?" I asked.

Ruth frowned and looked down at her fabric.

"Don't stop telling her the truth," Leah interjected.

When Ruth didn't say anything, Leah spoke up again, "We all thought he stole it. There was no other explanation as to how he could have all that money to give away."

"Like Robin Hood?" I mused.

"Who?" Raellen asked.

All the Amish women looked at me, confused.

"How long did this go on?" I asked.

"For years," Millie said. "At least that is what I heard when I moved home to Ohio from Michigan a few years back."

Leah nodded. "He was known to take things as a child. I think he had always stolen. As you can imagine, his father was furious over it."

"What was the bishop going to do?" Ruth wanted to know. "Zeph put himself out of reach when he stopped coming to Sunday services and district events, and there are many pressing concerns in the community."

"He could have spoken to a deputy," I said. "Stealing is a crime."

She glared at me. "Do you really think Bishop Yoder

would have wanted to turn over one of our own to the police?"

"Aiden would have been compassionate," I said in defense of my fiancé.

"This was going on long before Aiden was sheriff." Ruth smoothed her quilt square on her lap and dropped her scissors into the sewing basket by her feet. "How kind do you think the previous sheriff would have been to Zeph?"

Not very, I realized. Now I couldn't blame Bishop Yoder for not bringing the stealing to the Sheriff Department's attention.

"It likely would have ended fine, but Zeph got greedy," Leah said. "No one knew where he got the money. Then the robberies began in our district. That was a mistake."

"You all think that he was the one who was stealing from the district?" I asked.

"Who else could it have been?" Raellen said.

Ruth nodded. "When things of value go missing, Zephaniah Lantz was the first person to come to mind."

Then I thought back to the money and jewelry I'd seen in Zeph's basement apartment. What should have jumped out at me from the start was the jewelry. The Amish don't wear jewelry. They don't even wear wedding bands. Zeph wasn't just stealing from the Amish, and by the look of all the loot that was in his apartment, he had been stealing for a very long time.

Aiden must realize that not all the thievery had happened in the Amish community. However, he had said nothing to me about it. Considering the game piece with the rope around its neck, I had to wonder if this case was much bigger than I'd thought. Everyone seemed to think Zeph had worked alone and stole from the rich to give to the poor just like Robin Hood, though my Amish friends knew nothing about the legend.

"Why would he suddenly change and steal from the Amish in his home district?" I asked.

"Now, we don't know that he was the one doing that," said Iris, who had remained quiet for most of the conversation. "We can't just make that assumption because of his past."

Ruth glowered at her. "All I know is the person who broke into our home and stole from us knew where we kept the church's money. It had to be a member of the district to know that."

"The church's money was stolen?" I asked.

She nodded. "So your idea that Zeph was stealing from those who have too much and giving to those with little is wrong. That money was saved to give to members struggling with medical bills or damage to their homes."

I did know that. The Amish didn't purchase any sort of insurance. They relied on their community to help them when times were difficult. Her district had given my grandmother money to help pay the hospital bills after my grandfather died. It hadn't covered everything, but it helped. Thankfully my parents and I could make up the difference for my grandmother. Otherwise, she might have had to sell the candy shop.

If Zeph was an Amish Robin Hood, as I thought, why steal from the church? Why steal from members of his district at all? He either didn't do it or he had a very good reason. However, I had no idea what that reason could be.

"The reasons for doing wrong do not matter. It is still a sin. Sin leads to more sin," Ruth said ominously.

In this case, the sin might just have led to Zephaniah Lantz's death.

CHAPTER TWENTY-EIGHT

I made my way back to the factory just as the candy-making class was about to start. I had called the factory before I left and asked Maeva and some of the others in the lobby to get everything ready for the class so that I could just run in and start teaching.

Perhaps it had been a bad idea to cut it so close, but the information I'd learned from Ruth Yoder and the rest of her quilting circle had been worth it.

Assuming that Zeph had been breaking in and stealing from people in his own community, why had he changed his pattern? Before he had stolen and given money to Amish families in need. Now, he was stealing from Amish families. That didn't make sense.

And there was another problem: the cheese shop. The cheese shop had been broken into after Zeph died. As Charlotte had said, he had either been working with someone or it was a copycat crime.

I walked into the back door of the factory and caught my breath in my office before I made my way to the classroom. Everything in the office was back in place after my own break-in.

I didn't have any concrete proof of it, but I was convinced whoever had broken into the office had been in search of Zeph's address. That made me think it was his partner in crime, so to speak. Or, at the very least, it was someone who knew that he must have money and stolen goods stashed in his home.

I grabbed a bottle of water from the minifridge in the corner of the office and headed to the classroom.

Maeva stood in front of the class. "*Ya, ya,* I heard from Bailey. She is on her way here."

"I don't know why she is late. She knew we were coming," Jenny complained. "Honestly, this is no way to manage a business."

"Oh, Bailey!" Maeva cried. There was utter relief on her face. "Everything is ready like you asked. I should get back to the lobby. There is just one girl there now. The other staff member is at her lunch." She bolted out of the room, obviously eager to get away. That didn't bode well for me.

I stood in front of the classroom of eight women. They were each at a cooking station with a burner and a small oven and all the utensils and ingredients they would need to make the candies we had on our list for the day. In total there were twelve stations, but because I was alone, I was relieved that the class wasn't full.

I had an identical station in front of me and a white board behind me, where Maeva had kindly transcribed the three recipes we would be making.

The interactive cooking classroom had been a splurge on my part. It put me overbudget for the factory, but I felt it was necessary. It was a value-added service that other candy and food factories in Holmes County did not offer. I was always looking for ways to set us apart.

I smiled. "Thank you all for coming. I'm so grateful that you were willing to come back after the tragedy earlier in the week. Today, we will start with making truffles. I know you all were sorely disappointed that you were unable to do that before. What we are going to do first is make the truffle shells so they can harden in the freezer while we make the fillings, and—"

Jenny raised her hand and waved it in the air. I found her action disconcerting, and I was suddenly transported back to elementary school. However, this time I was the teacher, not the student.

"Um, Jenny?" I asked.

"Aren't you going to tell us what happened to that boy who died? Is it true he was behind all the robberies in Harvest over the last month?"

The other members of the class shifted uncomfortably on their stools.

"I don't know what that has to do with making truffles," I said.

"His death disturbed our class earlier in the week and we have a right to know," she said haughtily.

"The Sheriff Department is on the case. That's all I can say."

"You know more than that," Jenny said. "Everyone in the village knows you stick your nose into murder."

I frowned and moved behind my station. "I think we should get to work. This class is only two hours long, and there are many candies to be made."

"I don't like to be ignored," Jenny said. "I am only asking because I want what was taken from me back."

"What do you mean?"

"The Amish aren't the only ones who are being burglarized in this village. My home was broken into nine months ago, and all my mother and grandmother's jewelry was stolen. Some of it was worth quite a lot, but it's the sentimental loss that breaks my heart."

The jewelry I'd seen in Zeph's basement apartment immediately came to mind.

"You think Zeph stole it?" I asked.

She nodded. "I know he did, and I want it back."

"I suggest you talk to Aiden about it," I said. I didn't want to say any more. I didn't know for certain that the jewelry I'd seen was Jenny's, and I didn't want to tarnish Zeph's reputation any more than it already was.

I cleared my throat. "Now, let's get back to making candy." I forced a smile on my face. "It's why we are here, right?"

The other ladies in the class nodded and seemed relieved by the change of topic. Jenny scowled but didn't protest my suggestion.

"The first thing we are going to do is grease our plastic truffle molds so that when the chocolate is ready, we can pour it right in. When it comes to making candy, the key is to have everything ready in advance because many of the candymaking steps require such delicacy and precision." I picked up the stick of butter on my station. "We will be using butter to grease the molds today, but you can use margarine, baking spray, or whatever you might have."

"When we are making these on our own, can we use vegetable oil to grease the mold? I have that at home," Jenny said.

I got the women started on melting their chocolate in order to make the chocolate shell of their truffles. While they concentrated on stirring their chocolate, I texted Aiden and told him about Jenny's jewelry.

Where is she? the text came back.

She's here at the candy factory taking a class.

I'll swing by when the class is over. What time will that be?

I told him and tucked the phone in my jeans pocket. When I looked up again, I saw Jenny wasn't watching her chocolate; she was watching me.

CHAPTER TWENTY-NINE

I must have been losing my mind to think for one second that the president of the Harvest Garden Club had killed a young Amish man because he *might* have stolen her grandmother's jewelry.

Two hours later, while the women packed up all the candy they had made in class, I had all but convinced myself that my assumption about Jenny was not only ridiculous but dead wrong.

At least I thought so until Aiden walked into the classroom in full uniform with his cop face on. Then, my doubts resurfaced.

I have to admit, when Aiden entered the room, my heart skipped a beat. His thick blond hair was brushed back from his forehead in a wave and he had a slight hint of stubble on his face. He was a very handsome man, and my heart ached at the fact that I had barely spent more than a few minutes with him all week. All of those lost minutes had been because of Zeph's murder.

When things were quiet in the county, Aiden and I were able to spend quite a bit of time together. If I had to work late at the factory or candy shop, he would typically come keep me company. However, when there was a murder investigation in progress, there was no telling when I would see him next. Unfortunately, I knew this would also be the case when we married. It was just something that I would have to accept if I wanted to be with someone in law enforcement.

There were hushed whispers as Aiden looked around the room. I heard one woman tell her neighbor, "He is so good-looking. If I was just thirty years younger . . ."

The two women giggled.

The only person who didn't seem pleased at Aiden's arrival was Jenny. She tucked her candies into the canvas cooler bag she had brought with her to the class. She really was a person who thought of everything and was good with details. "Bailey King, did you call your fiancé to come talk to me? I was going to go to the station on my own."

Aiden dropped his cop look and smiled. "Good afternoon, ladies! I hope I'm not too late to be your taste tester."

The women in the room giggled, and the tension dissipated.

He turned to Jenny. "Bailey did tell me about the break-in at your home. Did you file a report?"

"I did, but the sheriff at the time thought it of no importance."

This did not surprise me. The old sheriff would do anything he could to avoid investigating a crime. He would even go so far as to arrest the wrong person to close a case quickly.

"Well, I'm the sheriff now, and I would love to chat with you about it." He glanced at me. "Bailey, can we use your office?"

I nodded and handed him my keys. Aiden and Jenny left the classroom, and I was dying to go with them. I wanted to hear what Jenny had to say about her break-in and whether she would make any hints that she might have been the one who'd been up on that roof with Zeph.

Reluctantly, I stayed in the classroom and answered the women's questions, then helped my staff clean up the candymaking stations when the class was finally finished. I was just putting the last of the dishes in the dishwasher by the sink when Aiden returned.

Maeva, who had been helping me clean, picked up the last of the candy molds and fled the room.

Aiden watched her go. "Is she afraid of me or something?"

I shook my head. "I don't think she wants to be mixed up in this murder mess."

He sighed. "Sometimes I wish you felt the same way."

I perched on my teaching stool. "Is Jenny gone?"

He nodded. "She just left."

"And?" I asked expectantly.

"She's not the killer, if that was what you were thinking."

"I wasn't . . . much."

He chuckled and grabbed one of the student's stools. He pulled the stool close to mine and sat.

"I spoke with the other women in the class and they were able to confirm that Jenny was with them the entire time the day Zeph died. I don't see how she could have done anything."

I let out a sigh of relief. Jenny could be a tad annoying, but I really didn't want her to be the killer.

"And the jewelry that was stolen from her? Was it what we found in Zeph's apartment?"

He nodded. "She described the jewelry perfectly. It was stolen from her home. When the case is closed, we should be able to return it to her. She was relieved that we have it now and it is still intact. From what she described, we have all the pieces she lost."

"That is good news. What was an Amish man going to do with jewelry?" I asked.

"Most likely he was going to fence it for cash."

"And do what with the cash, give it away?"

Aiden wrinkled his brow. "That's not what usually happens in these cases."

"It just might have happened in this one if Zeph had more time." I went on to tell him about my Amish Robin Hood theory and what the women at the Double Stitch quilting group had told me.

"That is interesting, but why did he switch and start stealing from the Amish community?"

"That's the question, and I believe the answer will lead us to how and why he died," I said.

When I left the factory at closing time, I was exhausted. It had been another long day at the Candyworks, but every time I saw a child enter the lobby and her face light up at the sight of all the candy and the giant Christmas tree, I knew it was worth it.

I walked across the square and saw that the Candy Land Experience was as big a hit as ever. I checked all the candy stations and found them all to be full. Maami's gingerbread fudge Christmas trees were out on display. My staff had been doing a great job filling the stations. Even so, I couldn't help but miss Lida and wonder how she was doing. Her brother's private service that day must have been extremely difficult for her.

Before I went into Swissmen Sweets, I walked to the cheese shop. As it was after four, the "Closed" sign was on the door and the door was locked. However, I could see Martha Ann moving around the front room, closing the cooler tops on all her cheese displays for the night.

I knocked on the glass, and Martha Ann jumped. She placed a hand to her chest.

"It's just me," I said with a wave.

She came over to the door. One hand was still pressed hard to her chest as she opened the door with the other hand. "Bailey King, you scared me near to death. What are you doing out there in the cold, peeking in my windows?" She stepped back to let me in the shop.

The shop was warmer than the outside but still kept at a cool temperature to preserve the cheese.

"I'm so sorry I scared you," I said, removing my grandmother's mittens but leaving my coat zipped. "I just wanted to see how you're feeling."

"I'm much better. Thankfully, I just had a terrible headache after knocking my head. It could have been worse. But as you can see, I'm still quite jumpy from the home invasion."

"Anyone would be. I'm happy that you're all right."

"*Danki*. I am just so shaken up by all of it. I have never had anything like this happen to me before. I should have been more vigilant when I heard other Amish businesses in Harvest were being robbed. I just have been so busy getting my business up and running after I bought this place, and I didn't pay much attention at all to the news about the break-ins. Honestly, the first time I really took notice was when it was announced in church that someone broke into the Yoders' home. I don't know how anyone could be daring enough to steal from the bishop, much less his wife."

"You didn't do anything wrong. I have been the same way, but the break-in at your place is way too close for comfort. I'm living with my grandmother over the candy shop until Aiden is able to arrest whoever is behind these crimes."

"That is *gut* to hear. I hate the thought of Clara home alone during this."

"I know you answered these questions dozens of times, but I was wondering if you could indulge me."

She frowned. "All right."

"What can you tell me about that night? What made you come downstairs after you went to bed?"

She blushed. "I don't have any plumbing upstairs. It is an attic that I converted into a bedroom and living space. I came down because I needed to use the bathroom. I was coming out of the bathroom and heard a click and a creak. I recognized the sounds automatically because I had heard them hundreds of times before, with the front door opening. Someone had come into the shop." She licked her lips. "I was in complete shock at the sound. I froze. I couldn't run away or go see who was there. I just stood there."

"What did the person look like?" I asked.

"I never saw them," she said. "At least not very well. I just heard them as they moved around the shop."

"What did you hear exactly?"

"The floorboard creaking. The noise was like gun-shots in the room. Each creak sounded like an ice pick on metal. The noise snapped me out of my stupor, and I turned to run upstairs. I tripped and fell. When I fell, I hit my forehead on the wooden step. I remember the pain and then nothing until I came to and called the po-lice on the shop phone."

"Before you said you didn't see the person well. What did you mean by that?" I asked.

"I saw a shadow, and I'm not even sure of that. It could have been a trick of the light."

"Why do you say that?"

"Because the shadow was small, and I thought I saw the outline of a skirt." She looked me directly in the eye. "The shadow I saw was of a woman."

CHAPTER THIRTY

A woman? All this time, I'd assumed the person behind the home and business invasion was a man.

"Did you tell the deputies that? That the person in the shop was a woman?"

"I did," she whispered. "I just can't believe a woman would do this, and she was wearing a long skirt. I feel confident in saying that. I have to think that she is Amish. I can't believe a woman from my community would do such a thing."

It was hard for me to believe, too, but it wasn't out of the question. Women were just as capable of breaking the law and of stealing as men. Even so, home invasion was more of a male crime, at least statistically.

I left the cheese shop more confused than ever. The only female who came to mind as a possible suspect was Lida Lantz. That was just too hard to believe. Lida adored her brother and was a rule follower. She would not break into a building the night after her beloved brother was killed. Would she?

Thinking of her brother Zeph reminded me that she had another brother I wanted to track down. Malachi Lantz had been disconnected from the family for years, so it was a stretch to think he could be involved in all this. Even so, I had to find out for sure. The question was how I was going to locate him.

I turned to something that none of my Amish friends would have thought of: the internet.

I did a quick search in my phone's browser for "Malachi Lantz and Holmes County, Ohio." A dozen search results came up. However, the very first one was exactly what I was looking for: Lantz Rentals, owner Malachi Lantz.

I clicked on the link and found that Lantz Rentals was the premier, at least according to the website, wedding rental service in Holmes County. It was the place to find everything from tents to silverware for a wedding or another big event.

Something about the fact that Malachi owned a wedding rental place made me feel uneasy. I told myself it was ridiculous. Yes, I was getting married in the next year, but it was just a coincidence he had a wedding-related business.

While all the businesses in Harvest closed at four thirty, the Lantz Rentals website told me that they were open until seven and I could find their office and warehouses on Route 39, not far from downtown Millersburg.

Before heading to Millersburg, I popped into Swissmen Sweets to tell my grandmother what I was up to. However, when I went into the candy shop, she wasn't there.

There was a note on the worktable in the shop kitchen that said she was having dinner at the inn with my parents. She invited me to join them.

I had no intention of going to that dinner. I knew it would just be more wedding talk. I couldn't even think of the wedding until I knew what had happened to Zeph. I also knew it wasn't a conversation that I could avoid forever. My mother and Juliet would make sure I didn't.

With my grandmother occupied with my parents, I had time to search for Malachi Lantz. I had no idea what I'd say to him when I reached his business, but I had to find out if he'd had any connection with his younger brother before Zeph died.

I locked up the candy shop again and was making my way to my car, which I had parked at the factory. After the game piece incident, I'd parked in front of the market under a streetlamp, so everyone going in and out of the market could see it. I wasn't taking any more chances at getting scared out of my wits.

"Bailey! Bailey!" called a high-pitched voice with a faint southern drawl. There could only be one person in Harvest who sounded like that.

I turned to see Juliet hurrying toward me. Jethro was tucked under her arm. Even before she said a word, I knew where this conversation was going.

"Bailey," Juliet said, out of breath as she stopped in front of me. "I'm so glad I caught you."

"You want me to pigsit," I said.

"Oh, would you? How amazing it is that you seem to know what I need all the time."

It wasn't amazing. It was predictable. Juliet always

needed me to take care of her pig. There was no mystery in that.

"The children of the church are doing their Christmas program tonight. It's going to be a packed house, and I just can't have Jethro running around in the midst of it all. So will you—"

I held out my arms. "I'll watch him for you."

She handed over the pig. "You are just the dream daughter-in-law, and you and Aiden aren't even married yet." She glanced back at the church. The parking lot was already beginning to fill up with carloads of children in Christmas costumes. "I have to get back, but—" She licked her lips. "I just want to make sure that you and I are all right after this morning."

Jethro shivered, so I unzipped my parka and tucked him inside. He sighed happily against my chest. He was frustratingly adorable.

I patted the pig on the top of his head to comfort him. Maybe it was to comfort me, too. "You mean Hampton, the wedding planner."

"Yes, I didn't even know about him until the night before, and your mother promised me that she would tell you before our meeting."

"She didn't," I said.

"I know, and I feel badly about that."

"Do you really think I need a wedding planner?" I asked. "Your wedding was very large and you didn't use one."

She shifted back and forth on her high-heeled boots. Even in the winter, Juliet was in dresses and heels. At the moment, she wore a long wool coat over a red-and-white polka-dotted dress. I was going to ask her someday where she got all the polka-dotted clothes. I didn't see nearly as many polka dots in clothing stores as she wore on an everyday basis.

She pressed her hands together as if in prayer. "It's what your mother wants. You have to remember that you are her only child."

"I just don't want my parents to waste their money," I said. "And I'm not sure that Hampton and I have the same style, to be honest. I was hoping for something simple."

"I have to say I was surprised at her choice, too," Juliet said. "He's not from the village. When we have events here, we like to use locals."

"Where is he from?"

She shrugged. "Don't know, but if he was from the village, Reverend Brook would know him. He knows everyone who lives here. The reverend said that he had never seen him before."

She glanced behind herself again at the church and jumped. "Oh! I really have to run now. I see the choir director's car pulling into the lot." She hurried away from the square, wiggling her fingers at me as she went. "Thank you for taking care of our Jethro!"

I looked down at the little oinker tucked into my parka like a pig in a blanket. *Our* Jethro? He really should be mine by this point.

CHAPTER THIRTY-ONE

From what I could tell, the wedding and party rental business was good. Malachi Lantz's company had a large compound on the south side of Millersburg. The five buildings, which consisted of four warehouses and a small office building, were set eight hundred feet off the road in a picturesque field blanketed with snow.

There were several cars in the gravel parking lot, and no Amish buggies. To me, that seemed strange. There always was an Amish buggy or two around anywhere I went in the county.

I parked the car, and Jethro looked at me with anticipation.

I sighed. "You can go with me, but you have to be on your very best behavior. I mean it. No shenanigans!"

He lifted up his snout into the air as if he was offended that I might think he would be anything other than a model pig.

I made sure I had Jethro's leash in my parka pocket

before I got out of the car. I then scooped up the pig and tucked him into my parka.

He sighed happily. If I wasn't careful, he was going to become used to this five-star treatment.

I went to the office building first. I stepped inside and found myself in an empty reception room.

A door at the back of the room stood open. It must have led to the inner offices.

"This isn't my fault," a man said.

"If it's not your fault, then whose is it? This could destroy my business. You promised me that it would work. It has to work."

"It will. You're just nervous."

"You made a mistake and it will cost me everything."

"I never make mistakes." There was anger in the voice.

For most people, this would be the cue for them to turn around and leave, but not for me. My curiosity got the better of me, and I inched toward the open door. In doing so, I bumped into a coffee table, and it made a screeching sound across the tile floor.

"What's that?" one of the voices asked.

I bolted back to the front door of the office, opened it, and spun around, as if I was just coming inside as the two men entered the reception room from the back.

One of those men I had never seen before, but the other I knew. It was Hampton the wedding planner.

Hampton's eyes bugged out of his head when he saw me, but a second later his face cleared. "Bailey, what a lovely surprise. Did your mother tell you I'd be here today?"

"No, actually I was just popping in because our conversation earlier at the café finally has me thinking about my wedding." I didn't even convince myself with that lie.

He clapped his hands. "That is wonderful to hear! I'm sure your mother in particular will be happy to know it."

I smiled. "I found this place online, and I guess two minds think alike."

"Two great minds." Hampton beamed, as if I had just told him he was my new best friend.

The second man, who was in his twenties, clean-shaven, and wearing a red flannel shirt and faded jeans, cleared his throat.

"Oh, you will have to excuse me," Hampton said. "Bailey, your showing up here surprised me so much that I forgot my manners. This is Malachi; he's the owner of the rental place."

Malachi held out his hand to me, and I shook it. His grip was firm, dry, and brief.

"Hampton has just been telling me about your wedding. It sounds like it will be the event of the year in Harvest," Malachi said. "Charming little town."

"Don't tell our community planner, Margot Rawlings, that. She will want to plan something bigger and better than my wedding for sure."

He smiled. "I have worked with Margot before on rentals. Your secret is safe with me."

"I must say I am so happy that I found this place," Hampton chimed in. "Margot was the one who put me onto it. She seems to know everything about everything in the county."

"Just about," I agreed.

"I didn't know what I was going to do when it came to renting everything we'll need for your wedding. Finding Malachi is a godsend," Hampton added. Sweat gathered on his forehead, and he wiped it away with the back of his hand.

I frowned. Hampton was nervous. Could it be because he suspected I had overheard their argument? He made it sound as if he had just met Malachi, but the conversation I'd overheard just moments ago seemed to imply they had a much longer working relationship.

"Well, it's fortuitous that you're here, Bailey. I was just telling my friend about your wedding. I want to make sure he has all the tents, tables, and chairs we are going to need. It's going to be a wedding to put Amish Country on the map for destination weddings."

Malachi frowned. "Amish Country is already one the most popular destination wedding locations in Ohio. I wouldn't have a business without it."

"Yes, yes," Hampton said. "But we are thinking bigger than Ohio. We're thinking nationally, even internationally, if we can convince some of the local hotels to raise their standards." He smiled to take the bite out of his words. "Why don't we all take a seat and we can show Bailey some options while she's here?"

Malachi's frown deepened, as if he wasn't so keen on the idea, but then he gestured to a grouping of armchairs in one corner of the room. There was a table near the chairs with four binders on it.

Before I sat down, I unzipped my parka, and Jethro's head popped out.

"There is a pig in your coat!" Malachi cried.

I made a face. "Sorry. Is it all right that he's here? I'm pigsitting."

"Of course it's all right," Hampton said. "Jethro is going to be one of the main features of your wedding. Bringing him here was a wonderful idea. We have to make sure the décor we select goes well with the pig." He waved his hand. "It all has to flow together."

That was a sentiment I'd never thought I would hear.

I removed Jethro from my parka and set him on my lap. "He's my future mother-in-law's pig," I said for Malachi's benefit. "There is an event at her church this evening, and the pig would be in the way."

Hampton smiled at Jethro. "How could he ever be in the way? He's so precious."

Jethro looked up at Hampton with a smile on this face. The little bacon bundle was great at eating up compliments.

"Do you want to get married inside the church?" Malachi asked.

"I don't know. Aiden and I haven't talked about where the wedding will be, other than in Harvest."

"An outside wedding on the square would be beautiful," Hampton said.

"Aiden's mother and Reverend Brook had their reception on the square and it was very nice."

At least, it was nice until Jethro had a run-in with the wedding cake. I didn't say that, though. There was no reason to give the wedding planner nightmares. If he hung around Harvest long enough, he would become well aware of what Jethro was capable of on his own.

Hampton picked up one of the binders and began to

flip through it. "I want to show you the chairs and tables that Malachi and I were speaking of just before you arrived."

As he flipped through the photographs in the binder, I took the opportunity to ask some of the questions that were my real reason for being there. I cleared my throat. "Malachi, your company is called Lantz Rentals."

He stared at me. "Yes."

"Are you any relation to Lida and Zeph Lantz? Lida works for me at the candy factory," I said, using the present tense because I was still holding out hope that she would come back to the factory in a few days, or even in a few weeks.

"They are my sister and brother, but you already knew that, didn't you?" He narrowed his eyes.

Hampton looked up from the binder. "What's this?"

"My brother and sister worked for her at her factory," Malachi said. "And my brother recently died in an accident because of her negligence." He stood up. "Because of that, I don't think I can be involved in this wedding. It would be too difficult for me to see you so happy when I know you are responsible for my only brother's death."

My heart sank. I didn't know how I'd expected Malachi to react when I mentioned Zeph and Lida, but it certainly hadn't been like this.

Hampton laughed nervously. "It was a terrible accident. Malachi, let's not overreact. Bailey's wedding is months and months from now. You may feel different then."

Malachi gaped at him. "I will feel different about my brother's death? You have some nerve to say that."

Hampton cowered. "I didn't mean to cause any offense." He licked his lips. "Accidents do happen, unfortunately. I am so sorry about your brother."

"But I'm not sure it was an accident," Malachi said, and then looked at me. "That's why you are here, right? You want to prove that it wasn't an accident."

"I came here about my wedding," I insisted.

Malachi narrowed his eyes into tiny slits. "We both know that's not true."

Hampton closed the binder. "Maybe we should look at chairs and tables another day. Your parents still haven't been able to settle on a budget. It's foolish to pick out anything without a proper budget." He set the binder back on the table.

Malachi stood up. "I agree, and now I think it's time for you both to leave." He turned to Hampton. "I don't think we have much more to talk about here."

I stood as well. "Did you go to the funeral?" I asked.

He glared at me with green eyes that were the same color as Lida's. "You know I didn't. I'm not welcome around my Amish family. That's fine with me. I have made a good life for myself without them. I have had no communication with anyone in my family for years."

"Has the sheriff come to speak to you at all?" I asked.

Malachi narrowed his eyes. "Why would he? And why would you ask when you are here to talk about your wedding?"

I ignored his question and wished that I had simply been honest about the reason I'd come. "You're right. It is possible that Zeph's death wasn't an accident."

Hampton laughed nervously. "Bailey, I really think we should go."

I tucked Jethro back into my parka. He snuggled down while I zipped it up.

"If my brother's death wasn't an accident," Malachi said, "then it's because his transgressions finally caught up with him. That should be all the answer you need."

It wasn't, but it was all I would receive from him on that day.

CHAPTER THIRTY-TWO

Hampton walked me to my car. "I hope you're not upset that your mother hired me."

I set Jethro in the passenger seat and turned to face him. "I know she did what she thought was best." It was the most diplomatic answer I could come up with.

"I'm sorry about all the troubles you are having at your business with this young man's death. I should have made the connection that Malachi might be related. Honestly, it never occurred to me that he might be. It seems to me many of the last names repeat over and over again in this county. Yoder, Troyer, and Miller."

"You're not from this area," I said. "How would you know?"

"I appreciate your understanding, and even though you weren't the one to hire me, I hope that we can work closely together on this wedding. Your mother and mother-in-law have opinions as to what should be done, but as the bride, you have the final say."

"Thank you. Maybe we can chat after the holidays. I'm just not in the right mindset to plan right now. This is a busy time of year for my business."

"Of course," he said.

I thanked him and walked around the back of my car to the driver's side. I was just about to climb in when he said, "You don't always have to be the hero, you know. You don't have to do everything on your own."

I nodded, and wondered if he was speaking of more than just my upcoming wedding.

Before I left Millersburg, I swung through a fast-food drive-in for coffee because I was dead tired. Jethro perked up when I placed the order, so I got a small order of fries for the pig as well. I needed the coffee because I knew I had a long night of work ahead of me. With Zeph's death, my parents' arrival, work, and all the wedding talk, I just wanted to curl up and go to sleep.

The coffee wasn't great, but it was just what I needed to perk myself up for the thirty-minute drive back to Harvest. Jethro loved the fries. He had no complaints; except he would have preferred a large order.

When I was out of Millersburg proper, the road opened up into wide expanses of snow-covered rolling hills. It was not snowing that night, but it was very cold. The temperature on my dashboard hovered at ten.

I was looking forward to getting back to the candy shop and enjoying some of my grandmother's tea while I worked.

I was driving alone along the country road when a set of headlights appeared out of nowhere in my rear-view mirror. The driver behind me had his high beams on. I angled the mirror to fight the glare.

To my left there was a passing lane, so I slowed down, hoping to encourage the car behind me to pass. The car slowed down, too.

There was no traffic and plenty of room to get around me. There was no reason the other driver needed to ride my tail like this.

Beads of sweat formed on my brow, and I gripped the steering wheel. *Don't stress*, I told myself. The car behind me wasn't doing anything wrong.

It didn't matter how many times I told myself that. I was on edge.

I glanced at Jethro. He was asleep on his side with a single French fry hanging out of his mouth. At least one of us was at peace.

A sign came into view that said I was entering the outskirts of Harvest. Farms and houses grew closer together. The car was still behind me, but with the nearness of home, I began to relax. The guy behind me was simply a jerk. It was annoying but nothing to get too worked up about. I would be in town in five minutes.

Just when I began to relax, the car behind me gunned its engine and rammed into my bumper.

I jerked forward but was held in place by my seat belt. Jethro didn't fall from his seat, but he rolled to the edge, and the French fry that had been hanging from his mouth fell to the floor. He whimpered.

I gripped the steering wheel just as the car behind me rammed me again. I looked in my mirrors, trying to see the person behind the wheel, but the high beams blinded me.

I reached for my phone to call for help, and then suddenly the car turned off and disappeared down a side street. I was too flustered to make out any detail other than that it was a silver sedan. I couldn't read the make or model, or the license plate.

Normally, I would have parked my car at the factory, where it was out of the way, and walked to the candy shop, but that wasn't what I planned to do tonight.

I parked right in front of the shop, scooped up Jethro, and ran inside Swissmen Sweets. It wasn't until I closed and locked the door behind us that I allowed myself to take a breath.

I don't know how long I stood in the shop's front room hugging the pig to my chest. Jethro began to wiggle in my arms, which brought me back to the present.

I set the pig on the wide plank floor, and in a matter of seconds, Puff and Nutmeg hopped and strolled over, respectively, to check on their friend. It appeared the determined little oinker had been through a lot because all three of them returned to Nutmeg's cat bed and squeezed themselves inside. Most of Puff, who was by far the largest of the trio, hung out over the side of the cat bed.

I lifted my phone to my ear, and Aiden answered on the first ring.

"Aiden?" My voice betrayed me by shaking.

"Where are you?"

"The candy shop."

"Are you okay?"

"I am now."

He must have heard the fear in my voice.

"I'm not far away. I'll be there in ten minutes."

By the time Aiden made it to the candy shop, I was in the kitchen making a pot of tea. I needed something to do with my hands, and my grandmother always made tea when she was upset. If it worked for her, it should work for me as well. If she had been there, she would have made the tea for me, and set a plate of fudge in front of me. In Maami's opinion, there was very little that couldn't be fixed with fudge.

I removed the kettle from the stovetop and filled the teapot. I had just set the lid back on the teapot to steep when I heard Aiden's knock on the front door.

I went through the swinging kitchen door into the main room. Nutmeg, Puff, and Jethro all sat in a line waiting for me to let Aiden inside.

I opened the door and he enveloped me in a great big hug. "I see you have the whole crew here for support."

I squeezed him one more time and then let go. "They like to keep an eye on me."

"I'm glad someone does. I haven't been doing a very good job of it lately."

"You've been preoccupied," I said.

"That's no excuse. You're going to be my wife. You have to be my number one priority."

I appreciated Aiden's sentiment, but I also knew that he was the sheriff, and I would have to share him with the whole county. It was what I signed up for when I agreed to marry him. It didn't make it any easier, but at least I knew what I was getting.

He followed me into the kitchen. "I see you are taking after your grandmother and making tea."

"It's the best way I know of coping." I smiled at him

and removed two plain white teacups from the cupboard.

"Are you going to tell me what happened to your car?" Aiden asked as I set a full teacup in front of him.

I winced. "Is it bad?"

"Did you back into something?"

I perched on one of the stools and told him about my drive back to the village from Millersburg that evening.

"Why didn't you mention that on the phone?"

"You didn't give me a chance. You said you were headed here and hung up."

"Bailey, this is serious. You could have been killed." Aiden's face grew pale, and he removed his phone from his pocket. "I have to report this, and I will get a deputy out here to take pictures and scrape your bumper for any paint samples." He stood up and left the kitchen.

Through the kitchen's swinging door, I could hear him talking on the phone. I couldn't hear the words because he spoke in a low voice—on purpose, I was sure—but he sounded upset.

I wrapped my hands around my teacup. He was upset, and rightfully so. How would I feel if someone tried to hurt him and he didn't tell me? In his line of work, it would happen far more often, but I still wanted to know every time. That was part of being married or, in our case, almost married.

Aiden came back into the kitchen.

"I can heat up your tea if it's too cold now."

"It's fine," he said.

I winced. He might as well have just come out and said he was mad at me.

"I'm sorry I didn't tell you over the phone," I said. "I was frazzled, but the car is the reason I called you."

"Tell me everything from start to finish. You were driving back to the village. Where were you coming from?"

"I went to Millersburg today to talk to Zeph's brother Malachi."

Aiden made a face. "Bailey."

"I only wanted to talk to him to see when he last saw Zeph."

"You could have asked me that. I already spoke to him. Didn't you think I would?"

I looked down into my tea. "Yes, I expected that you would, but would you have told me what you learned?"

"I would have if I knew it would stop you from going there." He sat on the other stool at the prep table.

"Do you think Malachi is involved?"

"I have no reason to, but I can't rule anything out at this point."

"I wasn't the only one at Malachi's warehouse."

"Let me guess—Jethro was with you."

"He was, now that you mention it, but that's not that I meant. The wedding planner was there."

He furrowed his brow. "The one your mom hired?"

"Yep," I said. "Malachi is a wedding vendor, and we just so happened to be there at the same time."

He frowned, as if he wasn't buying it. I had to admit that it sounded a little far-fetched even to my own ears.

"Here's the weird part: When I got there, the two of them were fighting about money."

Aiden's frown deepened. "It could be nothing, but I'll have Deputy Little check it out. We are going to leave no stone unturned in this case."

"Thank you. Zeph was troubled, but the more I learn about him, the more certain I am that he had a good heart."

"I could see that. Giving money that he stole to people in need could be viewed as noble, but we can't forget that stealing is still illegal no matter the motive." His phone buzzed on the table.

Aiden picked up the phone and looked at it. "Deputy Little is here to gather evidence from your car. I should go out and meet him."

I followed him out of the kitchen and grabbed my parka from the coat-tree by the door.

He glanced over his shoulder. "Bailey, you don't have to come out here. It's cold."

"I want to see what you find, too," I said.

He sighed and held the door for me. At least he knew there was no point in arguing.

CHAPTER THIRTY-THREE

Deputy Little had a spotlight shining on the back of my car. The light was glaring and attracted the attention of the last few groups who were finishing their game of Candy Land on the square. It also got the attention of Melchior the camel, who glared at the light. It must have disturbed his beauty rest.

"I hope you have good insurance," Deputy Little said. "The back of your car will need some bodywork, and that doesn't come cheap."

I grimaced.

He straightened up. "I will give you the police report when it's done. You will need that for insurance."

"Thanks." I shoved my hands into the pockets of my coat. Despite the cold, I couldn't bring myself to put on my grandmother's bulky mittens.

"Did you get any paint transfer?" Aiden asked.

Deputy Little held up an evidence envelope. "Right here. Looks like it's silver."

"The car that rammed me was a silver sedan."

"Do you remember any other details?"

I shook my head. "He had his high beams on."

Deputy Little zipped the envelope into the inside pocket of his winter coat. "I'll get this to the lab right away to see if we can narrow down the type of car. Silver sedans are pretty common."

Aiden nodded, and I thanked Deputy Little. "Tell Charlotte that I'm sorry to pull you away from home."

"Are you kidding? As soon as I told Charlotte that the call involved you, she practically pushed me out of the house. She wanted to come, too, but I convinced her to stay home. She's going to have a lot of questions for you."

I was sure she would. Her first question would be why I hadn't taken her with me when I spoke to Malachi Lantz. Charlotte hated to be left out of these sorts of things.

Deputy Little got back into his car and drove away just as Juliet and Maami began to cross the street.

"Bailey, what has happened?" my grandmother asked in concern.

I sighed. I had wanted very much not to let my grandmother know what had happened to my car. In fact, I hoped to move the car before she saw it. I didn't want her to worry any more than she already did about me.

Juliet pressed a hand to her chest. "Is Jethro okay? Oh, no! It's my baby, isn't it? What has happened? You can tell me." Tears gathered in her eyes.

"Mom," Aiden put in, "Jethro is fine. He's inside the candy shop curled up in bed with Nutmeg and Puff."

"Oh!" Juliet's face flushed with color. "I'm so relieved."

Aiden shook his head.

"Are you here to pick up Jethro?" I asked and held the candy shop door open for Maami and Juliet.

Juliet nodded as she walked inside the shop. "Yes, and to walk Clara home. We had a lovely dinner at the inn with your parents, Bailey. It's such a shame that you and Aiden couldn't have been there. Your mother has so many wonderful ideas for the wedding."

I bet she did. I guessed that I wouldn't like a single one of those ideas, and my mother would go forward with them anyway. I really needed to grow a backbone and ask her to let Hampton go. From what I could tell, having a wedding planner was going to be more work for me than not having one.

"Lillian is a wonderful cook," Maami said as she removed her coat and hung it on the coat-tree. "Her food is so much more delicate than most Amish cooking."

I was grateful for the change of subject away from the wedding.

"Did she grow up in a district where they cook differently?" I asked.

Maami shook her head. "She told me she has been checking books out of the library and learning to cook lots of different types of food so she can share a variety of dishes at her tea garden. It was quite fascinating to hear her plans for the garden and the teahouse, but she says it won't happen now."

"Because of the money that was stolen," I said.

She nodded. "*Ya,* that's right. How did you know?"

"She told me about the robbery the day Mom and Dad checked in at the inn. How is she? I'm sorry I haven't been able to get back to the inn to check on her."

"She's shaken up, as anyone would be." My grandmother folded her mittens and tucked them into the pocket of her coat. "I believe she'll feel better when the robberies come to an end. We all will. We should not have to live in fear like this, especially at Christmas. I cannot stop thinking of Martha Ann at the cheese shop. I am so grateful that she was not more seriously hurt."

Her mention of Martha Ann reminded me that she'd seen a woman in her cheese shop the night of the break in. A woman. How could I have forgotten that?

"As for Lillian and her tea garden, I'd like to speak to you about that. I think we could start some kind of partnership. . . ." I trailed off when I saw the look on Maami's face.

"I want to help her; I do," my grandmother said. "Her little boy, Adrien, is so darling, and I know it must be so hard for her to run a business without a husband or any other family. However, I don't want us to spread ourselves too thin."

I nodded. That was a fair statement. I was a big-ideas person, and because of that, I have overextended myself at times.

"You have a big heart." Maami patted my arm. "Now, it is time for me to go off to bed. Good night, Juliet."

Juliet said good night in turn.

When my grandmother was out of sight, Juliet gazed down at Jethro and his friends and said, "He looks so peaceful. I don't know how I can take him when he is so happy."

"He'll be all right." I removed my coat and hung it on the tree. Then, I walked over to the cat bed.

"Wait, before you bother him, I would like to talk to you."

I froze in the air with my hand hovering over Jethro's back like a raptor ready to strike. The pig was sound asleep and didn't even notice.

"We can sit down for a bit and talk. I think Aiden will be outside for a little while yet."

At night we set the chairs upside down on top of the tables. I pulled down two from the dinette table closest to the door.

Juliet sat and folded her hands on the tabletop.

"Would you like a cup of tea? Candy? We have plenty of candy." I forced a laugh because Juliet looked serious, and I wasn't used to her looking so. Most of the time, Aiden's mother went through life with a cheery look on her face. She was perpetually happy. Seeing her worried was concerning.

"You are so sweet, but I'm fine. It's late, and I don't plan to stay too long." She took a breath. "Bailey, I don't want you to be upset with your mother about this wedding talk."

I didn't say anything. I didn't know what to say.

"Your mother and I are just excited about it." She took a deep breath. "And I don't want you to be angry at your mother about hiring Hampton. I gave him her name."

I dropped my hands to the table. "You hired Hampton."

She blushed. "No, I am a pastor's wife. The reverend

and I don't have that kind of money. If we did, we would wholeheartedly spend it on you and Aiden."

"But my parents do have money."

She touched my arm. "I never asked your mother to hire him. I just mentioned I had met him on our last call."

"Your last call? The two of you have been talking on the phone?"

"Yes, we speak every few weeks. We are practically family."

"And you talk about the wedding."

Juliet sighed. "Yes, we do talk about the wedding, among other topics."

I folded my arms. "How did the wedding planner come up? Did you go looking for one?"

"Oh heavens, no. It never crossed my mind that we might need a wedding planner until he walked through the church doors."

"Hampton Longly came to the church?" I asked. Now I was completely confused.

"Yes. He was in the village and came to the church. It was a few weeks ago, right after Thanksgiving, I think. He said he was a wedding planner in Columbus and wanted to expand his business to focus on destination weddings in Amish Country. He was driving around the county looking for wedding locations and saw the church. You know how picturesque it is, positioned on the Harvest Square. He rightfully thought it was a perfect wedding location. He wanted to discuss renting the church for nonchurch member weddings.

"Reverend Brook wasn't there at the time, but I took down his information." She didn't meet my eyes. "When

I did, I happened to mention that my son was about to be married and you all were having trouble planning the wedding. I explained to him how busy you were with your business and your candymaking show." She smiled. "Do you know, he was very familiar with *Bailey's Amish Sweets*? He was just shocked that you live right here in Harvest and will be marrying my son!"

I frowned. I bet he was. And I wanted to say we weren't having trouble planning the wedding. We hadn't tried to plan it yet. There was a big difference, but I didn't think that would make her feel any better about the wedding in general. Maybe it would make her feel worse; maybe she would assume Aiden and I didn't care about it. Nothing could be farther from the truth. We cared too much about it, I thought, and only wanted to start the planning process when there was a "good time," but I'd come to realize that there would never be a "good time." I would always be busy with my business and the show, and Aiden would always have the Sheriff Department to administer and another case to solve. Maybe it was time we just did it.

"He said he had vendors in the county that he'd worked with before, and he would be willing to give us a discount because your wedding could be covered by the media," she said.

"I really don't think the media will be involved in my wedding."

"Are you kidding? You have one of the most beloved shows on Gourmet Television."

I changed the subject. "Did he mention the names of any vendors he was working with in Holmes County?"

She shook her head. "I should have gotten a list, but I bet your mother did. She is just so organized."

That was the understatement of the century. My mother was überorganized. She always had been and always would be. In any case, I guessed one of those vendors who worked with Hampton was Malachi Lantz and his rental company.

My head was spinning. It seemed as if everything was interconnected—my wedding, Zeph, Lida, Hampton, the Candy Land Experience, Malachi, and maybe even Melchior—but I didn't know how. I couldn't make sense of how it all fit together.

She reached across the table and squeezed my hand. "I am telling you this because I know you have been upset with your mother ever since you learned about Hampton. I just want you to know she wasn't wholly to blame. I wanted to share my part in it."

I squeezed her hand back. "I appreciate your telling me, I really do. I need to talk to my mom and clear the air. I will start working on the wedding as soon as Christmas is over, I promise, but Hampton is just not the right fit for me."

"I'm sure she will understand."

I stopped myself from laughing because I didn't think my mother would be nearly as understanding as Juliet believed she would be.

I squeezed her hand again. "Thank you for telling me. I need to have a heart-to-heart with my parents about this."

She stood up and hoisted Jethro onto her shoulder. "I think that is a very good idea. They have missed you.

Your mother mentioned that she's barely seen you since they have been in town."

I knew this was true, and guilt washed over me. My parents had come all this way and I had spent very little time with them thanks to being preoccupied by the factory, the Candy Land Experience, and Zeph's death, which was looking more and more like murder.

CHAPTER THIRTY-FOUR

I had another horrible night's sleep, and I couldn't blame it on sleeping at the creaking candy shop any longer. There was just too much on my mind, so instead of trying to talk myself into sleep, I got up with the intention of getting some work done. I wanted to see how the factory was doing with all our Christmas orders.

There were no outlets upstairs and my laptop battery was dead, so I had no choice but to work in the candy shop kitchen, where my computer could be plugged into the wall.

I pulled on a sweatshirt over my pajamas and looked out the window. From where I stood on the second floor of the candy shop, I could see the entire square.

The holiday lights were on all over the square in the live nativity and Candy Land game board. It was almost like looking at the square at midday. However, there were pockets of shadow where the light didn't reach.

Tomorrow evening would be the Christmas parade. It was always the last Saturday before Christmas. The Candy Land Experience would run up to the day after Christmas. When that was over, all the decorations, livestock, and red and green candles would be packed away for another year. I loved Christmas, but I was looking forward to the holiday coming to an end. I was ready to start a new year and a new chapter in my life as Aiden's wife. My talk with Juliet had made me excited about the future.

I opened the window and the cold blasted me in the face as flakes of snow flew into my eyes. I sneezed.

Nutmeg jumped off the bed and walked over to the window. For her part, Puff remained in the cat bed on the floor that I had brought up for the two of them to sleep in. Puff wasn't getting up this early unless there was broccoli or lettuce involved.

Nutmeg jumped on the windowsill.

I wrapped my arm around him. "Careful. There's no screen. You don't want to fall out, do you?"

He sniffed. Nutmeg hated to be told what to do. He was the alpha when it came to the little mismatched gang of Jethro, Puff, and himself.

I was about to tell Nutmeg just what I thought of his attitude when an earsplitting scream broke into the night. I set the cat on the floor and slammed the window shut. I knew that if Aiden was at the sheriff's office in Holmesville, he wouldn't reach Harvest for another twenty minutes, and that was if he sped here with sirens on. Whoever had screamed didn't have twenty minutes.

Maami peeked her head into my room. Her long

white hair fell down her back. "Bailey, what has happened? Did you have a nightmare?"

I yanked on a pair of jeans. "It wasn't me. That scream came from the square. I think someone might be hurt. I'm going to go check it out."

"I'll go with you." She turned.

I stopped her. "No!" I cried. "Call Aiden, and please stay here in case he comes to the shop first."

She nodded. "All right, I will go downstairs and call him now." She vanished through the door, and I finished getting dressed.

She was already on the phone when I got downstairs with Nutmeg on my heels. I threw on my heavy parka, hat, and boots. Thankfully the parka was long and went down to my knees. It was freezing outside.

I made sure the front door was locked behind me when I went outside. Keeping my grandmother safe was my first priority.

I ran onto the square. During the daytime, the Candy Land game looked so endearing and fun, but now it appeared sinister. With all the decorations and game pieces set up around the square, there were countless places to hide, and the glow from the twinkle lights all over the game board created oddly shaped shadows that weren't normally there.

I hesitated. Aiden would be there soon. Perhaps it would be best to wait for him. Just as I had that thought, another scream broke through the night.

I ran in the direction of the cries and spotted a figure in black.

"Please. Please. Don't hurt me. I'll get you your share."

"That's what Zeph told me, and look what happened to him," a man snarled.

"We just need a little more time. It won't take long. It's Christmas."

"I know it's Christmas," the man's voice said. "That's why I have been so kind to you so far, but I have to say that my kindness and my patience are running out. I need what is owed to me. I helped you and now you need to help me."

"Just three more days. That's all I ask. I'll have it to you in three more days!"

"Fine. Christmas Eve is your last chance. Don't forget that."

The figure in black ran away, but I was certain it was a young woman. I saw the swish of her skirt in the twinkle lights.

I took another step in the direction the voices had come from. I didn't see anyone, so I ran to the gazebo that had been converted into a castle for the game. I circled the gazebo. No one was there. Where was the man I'd heard and who was he?

I came around the back of the gazebo and jumped when I found Abel Esh sitting on the steps, drinking a can of soda.

"Bailey King. You always seem to turn up," he said, and then sipped his drink.

"What are you doing here?"

He straightened and walked over to me. "I should be asking you the same thing. You have no reason to be on the square at night. You don't even work at the candy shop anymore since you got that big fancy factory."

"That's not true," I snapped, feeling irritated that I had let him get the better of me. "And you haven't worked in the pretzel shop for years. You leave all the work to Esther. So if I don't have a reason to be here, neither do you."

He snorted. "Esther likes to be a martyr. I let her do the work so she can keep that title. I believe it's the kindest thing to do."

"Who were you talking to just now?" I asked.

"I'm only out for a walk in the snow," he said. "There's nothing wrong with that."

"Did you hear a scream?"

"What scream?" He smiled.

"I heard a woman scream twice. I came out here looking for her to see if she needed help, but she ran away. I didn't get a chance to talk to her."

He smirked. "I think a lot of people run away when they see you coming. You see that I never do." He winked at me.

My stomach turned at his expression.

There were no sirens, but we were alerted to Aiden's arrival when a set of headlights illuminated the gazebo.

Melchior, who had been sleeping in the makeshift stable, raised his head and spat on the ground. The three sheep that slept in the stable with him didn't stir. They were snuggled up close together, so much so that I couldn't tell where one sheep ended and another began.

Abel looked at Melchior in disgust. "I don't know why they bring that creature back year after year. It's disgusting."

Aiden's flashlight scanned back and forth over the ground. "Bailey?"

"Over here," I called. "At the gazebo."

"That's my cue to leave. I wouldn't want to make the sheriff jealous if he found us alone in the dark," Abel said and started to walk away.

I lunged forward and caught him by the sleeve of his coat. "Not so fast. You're not going anywhere until you speak to Aiden."

Aiden shone his flashlight in our eyes, and Abel held up his hands to cover his face.

"Put that flashlight down," Abel snapped. "You're blinding us."

I let go of Abel's sleeve to cover my own face.

The light dropped, and I blinked a few times as I saw dots dance in my eyes.

"What are you doing here, Esh?" Aiden asked. His voice was harsh. It was likely because he had arrested Abel a few times and even sent him to prison once. He was a criminal, but as of yet, he hadn't physically hurt anyone or done anything so horrible that it made incarceration stick.

If he had anything to do with Zeph Lantz's death, that might change things, though I couldn't imagine him climbing onto the Candyworks' roof just to push the teenager off. Abel was far more likely to pay someone to do his dirty work for him than do it himself.

He was just too smart to be involved in a murder. When it came to crime, he walked the line between those that would get a slap on the back of the hand and those that could have him locked up for good.

I had thought that when he went to prison, it would be for good, but I had been proven wrong when he was released so quickly.

"I'm on a walk," Abel said with a sneer. "There is nothing illegal about that. I've already told this to your future wife. The two of you are so untrusting, you deserve each other. You will spend the rest of your lives jealous of the other one's movements. That's not any way to live."

"We're not untrusting of each other," I said. "We just don't trust you."

Abel snorted.

Aiden looked at me. "Clara said that a woman screamed, and you were out here looking for the person." He grimaced as he said the last part.

I nodded. "And Abel, who was just casually walking around the square when it happened, claims he didn't hear it."

"You don't know what I heard," Abel snapped.

"Stop playing games, Abel, and just come out with it," Aiden said.

He narrowed his eyes at Aiden, but much to my surprise, he spoke up. "I did hear the scream. I was at the pretzel shop and came out to see what was going on."

"Why did you lie to me about hearing the screams?" I asked.

He grinned. "I was only teasing."

That was a lie, too, I was sure of it.

"Did you find the woman? Did you speak to her?" I asked.

He scowled at me. "Are you telling this story or am I?"

I waved at him to continue.

He folded his arms. "I don't know who the woman was. When I found where she was standing, her back was to me. However, she was Amish. She was in Amish dress and wore a bonnet."

"And the man?" I asked.

He looked me in the eye. "I don't know who it was. He was wearing a winter hat and dark clothing. I couldn't tell if he was Amish or *Englisch*. I would think *Englisch* because they cause the most trouble in the county."

He said that last part to annoy me, so I was very careful not to react.

Aiden and I watched as Abel walked away. As he'd said, he wasn't in any trouble for walking on a public square, even in the wee hours of the morning.

"The urge to arrest him and take him in for more questioning is almost overwhelming," Aiden said.

"I would arrest him if I could."

"Are you all right?" Aiden asked.

I nodded. "I think so. We should head back to the shop and assure Maami that we are okay. She will be worried. She hasn't admitted it, but all these break-ins around the village have been very upsetting to her, especially in the cheese shop because it is right next door. I'm frightened, too. I hate leaving her alone in Swissmen Sweets for even a few hours."

He fell into step with me. "We are doing our very best to solve this crime."

"I know you are."

"I wish I could say that it will be all over by Christmas, but I can't promise that. We are just a few days away, and it seems as if we run into one dead end after another."

We crossed Main Street and I stood under the gas lamppost outside the candy shop. My eyes were on the pretzel shop, which was locked up and dark. My assumption was that Abel had not gone back there, and to be honest, I didn't believe he was just out for a walk. Abel was known to lie, and I was suspicious of anything he might say. What was he doing out on the square in the middle of night? Nothing that he should be doing, I would guess.

"Do you think what happened tonight is tied to Zeph's death?" I asked Aiden.

"I have no proof, but it feels like all of it is tied to Zeph's death. We know the robberies have to be, because he was involved in the breaking and entering. I have to believe whoever rammed your car is implicated in Zeph's death, too, and putting the game piece in the back of your car. We can't forget that. You are being warned over and over to stay away from the case."

I made a face. Thankfully, it was too dark for him to see it.

"But the screams you heard tonight—I don't know." He stopped in front of the candy shop door. "But my gut says 'yes,' and I trust my gut. My gut also tells me that you are in danger, and that terrifies me." He touched my face with his bare hand. His fingers felt like ice. "I can't lose you. Please, be careful."

"I will be for you."

He kissed me good night.

CHAPTER THIRTY-FIVE

The next morning, I got up as usual and made candies with Maami. I drank coffee and thought over what I was going to say to my parents that morning, because I could no longer put off talking to them about the wedding. I had avoided the topic for far too long.

When Emily arrived at eight in the morning, I said my goodbyes to her and Maami and headed out the door. Outside, the square and Candy Land Experience sparkled with twinkle lights and laughing children. The parade was that evening, but there were already lawn chairs peppering the side of the road as people staked out their places for the best view of Melchior and the Holy Family. Looking around, I never would have guessed there was a frightened woman on the square the night before. Harvest just did not look like a place where that kind of thing happened, but I knew very well that it had.

I would usually go straight to the factory, but I

called Charlotte that morning and asked her to open for me so that I could spend some time with my parents. As always, Charlotte immediately understood, and I was grateful for once that she didn't ask me the million questions she was brimming with.

I walked to the market and cut across the parking lot toward the inn. Margot stood in the middle of the parking lot giving orders to anyone who happened by. She and Uriah threw hay on the pavement. I supposed that was to get it ready for the animals.

Like a coward, I put up my hood and made a dash for the inn. I would see Margot soon enough at the gingerbread house judging. She could give whatever marching orders she had for me there.

The bell rang over the door, and I stepped inside the inn. It smelled like candle wax, cinnamon, and evergreens. I would have loved to curl up in front of the cozy fire with a cup of tea and a good book, but there would be no free time for me to enjoy a quiet morning like that until after Christmas.

I lowered my coat hood.

Lillian put a hand to her chest. "Oh, Bailey. I didn't see your face under your hood and you startled me."

"I'm so sorry."

"It's quite all right. I'm just a bit jumpy after what has happened."

"I can understand that. I had my hood up because I was trying to get by Margot unnoticed. She's in the parking lot, barking orders about the parade this evening."

"That's hours away," Lillian said.

"She likes to be prepared."

She nodded. Every business owner in Harvest had had a run-in with Margot and her planning a time or two.

"Are you here to see your parents?"

I nodded.

"They are in the breakfast room. I'll be in shortly."

I thanked her and stepped through the doorway.

When I was a chocolatier in New York City, I had been in countless tearooms. In fact, there were three that used JP Chocolates for all their chocolate candy offerings and desserts. I would go there once a week with fresh chocolates and a display piece for their customers to enjoy. The atmosphere was proper, elegant, and a bit stuffy. I was in constant fear of dropping something—a fallen serving tray would have sounded like a gunshot in the quiet space.

But Lillian's breakfast/tearoom was different. It was Plain in the best way possible. The furniture was polished maple, the tablecloths were forest green, and all the dishes were simple and white. Greenery decorated the room for Christmas. It looked like an Amish postcard.

I could easily picture the tea garden that Lillian was working so hard to build. I knew I had told my grandmother that I would stop and think before opening another business. I agreed that we didn't want to do too much at once, but I felt in my bones that an Amish tea garden in Harvest would be an instant success and Lillian was the one to partner with. I reminded myself that I had a wedding to plan, and I had promised just about everyone that I would get to the planning right after Christmas. I had a feeling the day after Christmas, I would be inundated by people asking for the wedding date.

"Bailey, are you daydreaming?" my mother asked.

I blinked. I didn't know how long I had been standing in the breakfast room doorway. I stepped into the room. "I'm sorry. I just have a lot on my mind."

"We have noticed," my mother said with a hint of irritation in her voice.

"This is a pleasant surprise," Dad said. "We haven't seen much of you during our visit."

I sat at one of the empty chairs at their table. "I know that, and I am sorry for it. The weeks leading up to Christmas are some of the busiest in the year. Right after the holiday, things will quiet down. You are staying a few days after Christmas, aren't you?"

"We leave on the twenty-eighth," my mother said. "We have reservations to spend New Year's in Iceland to see the Northern Lights."

I wasn't surprised to hear this in the least.

Lillian came into the breakfast room with a tray that held a teapot, warm scones, and jam. She set them near me on the table.

"Thank you, Lillian. These look delicious. Everything is so lovely. I hope you haven't given up on your idea of a tea garden."

She blushed. "I haven't. It just might take a little more time than I thought."

"Good. It's a wonderful idea."

She went back into the kitchen.

After filling my cup, I said, "I am sorry that I have been so busy. The Candy Land Experience is more work than I expected it to be." I laughed. "I don't know why I thought it to be anything less than hectic. Margot is in charge, after all."

"Margot was like that in school, too," Dad said.

I almost spit out my tea. "You went to school with Margot?"

"She's a few years older than me, but Harvest is small, and all the kids knew one another no matter what grade we were in. Yes, we were in public school at the same time. Most of my schooling was at the one-room Amish schoolhouse, but I went to public school for a few years in lower elementary. She was bossy then. Some things never change."

I supposed that was true, but it still blew my mind that my father and Margot had been in school at the same time. It was impossible for me to imagine Margot as a kid.

"Bailey, have you had a chance to speak to Hampton?" Mom added milk to her tea. "He said that he planned to meet with you before he left the village. There are so many things to talk about."

"That's actually why I'm here. I want to see you guys, of course, but we have to talk about the wedding."

"Finally." Mom pushed away her teacup and took a notepad and pen from her purse on the seat next to her. She was ready to get down to business.

"I didn't meet with Hampton, but I did run into him in Millersburg yesterday."

"Where?" Mom asked.

"It was at a wedding rental place. It's called Lantz Rentals. Does that sound familiar?"

"Yes, it does. It is on a list of wedding vendors in the county that Hampton gave me." She smiled from ear to ear. "I'm happy to hear that you are taking some initiative." My mother positioned her pen over the paper and leaned forward. "Are you telling me that you are starting to plan the wedding? Did you settle on colors?"

"I wasn't there about the wedding but to talk to a family member of one of my factory workers." I didn't think there was any reason to mention the Lantzes or Zeph's death. "It was just a coincidence that Hampton and I were there at the same time, but I did come to a conclusion."

My mother frowned, as if she didn't like the sound of this, and I was sure that she wouldn't.

"I don't want a wedding planner. I want to plan a simple wedding on my own, with your and Juliet's help. I don't want some huge affair. That's not like Aiden and me at all."

My mother sat back in her seat as if she had just been told that her passport had been confiscated. "We can afford to give you a big wedding."

"I know you can, but that's not what I want. A small wedding on the square with cookies and cake after to thank everyone for coming is all we need."

She placed a hand to her chest as if she felt a pang. "Cookies? Cake?"

"Fudge, too," I said. "Maami will want there to be fudge."

My father reached across the table and squeezed my mother's hand.

"You will never get this chance to have a dream wedding again," she said. "I never got a dream wedding. I wish I'd had one. I wanted to give my daughter that experience so you won't have the same regrets."

"We are very different people. Something small is my dream wedding."

She shook her head. "So you want me to fire Hampton?"

"Yes, but I can do it if you're uncomfortable."

Even though she was so visibly upset, I was proud of myself for saying what I really wanted. There were only a few times in my life when I had stood up to my parents like this. The last time was when I went to culinary school to become a chocolatier instead of going to college. They were so upset with me, but I believed that now they would agree it had been the right choice.

Dad patted my mother's hand one more time and sat back in his chair. "Susan, this is Bailey's wedding. If she wants something small, we should honor her wishes. Besides, I don't care for that Hampton fellow. He's a little too much of a blowhard for my taste."

Mom looked at us. "I guess I'm outnumbered, then." She pressed her lips together. "I will call Hampton and tell him." She stood up. "If you will excuse me, I need to go back to the room." She left the breakfast room.

I made a motion as if I was going to stand up and follow her.

My dad touched my arm. "Sit. She just needs a little bit of time. She will be over it in a short while. Besides, when I tell her we can use the money we were going to spend on your wedding to go to Brazil, she will be completely recovered. She's wanted to go there for years."

I settled back in my seat. "I really didn't want to upset her."

"I think, Bailey, if you knew you wanted a small wedding, that is something you should have voiced from the beginning."

"I know. But the wedding seemed so important to her, I kept putting off breaking the bad news."

He set his coffee mug on the table. "You need to be honest with your mother. She's much stronger than you think." He smiled. "She married me, after all."

"Was it hard when you left home?"

It was the first time I had ever asked my father about leaving the Amish community. I had never been brave enough to ask for his perspective before. I knew my mother's, and I knew my grandparents', but I didn't know his.

He was quiet for a long while, and I thought he wasn't going to answer me, but then he said, "It was terribly hard, and I wasn't even baptized into the church. I don't know how those who leave can do it after baptism. At least I was able to maintain a relationship with my Amish parents and friends after I left. If I had been baptized, that would not have been the case."

"I think the young man who fell off the factory roof earlier this week was thinking of leaving the Amish way. He wasn't baptized, but his parents all but cut him off."

Dad shook his head. "That is no way to convince a child to come back. It will cause the opposite. When Amish parents are too stern, it is bound to backfire. I am grateful that my parents were more understanding than that."

"Maami and Daadi were okay with your choice?" I asked.

"Not exactly. They wished I had stayed Amish. But I loved your mom very much and knew she would never be Amish. I had to make a choice. I know how hard that choice was on my parents. I don't think it was until you were born that they completely forgave me for it."

I couldn't imagine my sweet grandparents harboring any resentment toward anyone, much less their son. But my experience with them was much different from his. Just as when I had children someday, their experiences with my parents would be much different from mine.

He frowned. "I don't regret leaving, nor do I regret staying in touch. I wanted to do that for you. They were your only living grandparents. You needed them and they needed you." He paused. "You have had a much different experience with my parents than I did, and that is what I always wanted for you. There are a lot of good things about the Amish, and I wanted you to see those things and to be exposed to them. I have many fond memories of growing up in the candy shop."

"Thank you, Dad, for not cutting them off. Having you, Mom, Maami, and Daadi was just what I needed as a kid."

Tears gathered in the corners of his eyes, and he blinked them away. "It's good to hear that. I know we don't say it as often as we should, but your mom and I are so proud of you."

I felt tears well up in my own eyes, too.

CHAPTER THIRTY-SIX

I left the inn feeling a lot better about my relationship with my parents. We had always had our ups and downs, but to hear that they were proud of me would be enough to sustain me into the New Year. I was also relieved I wouldn't have to see wedding planner Hampton Longly ever again. There was just something about his smarmy demeanor that put me ill at ease.

In the time that I had been at the inn, the manger scene animals, including Melchior the camel, had been relocated to the Market parking lot. Margot and her staff had cordoned off at least a third of the lot for the animals. The traffic cones marked the area, and yellow nylon rope ran from cone to cone. I didn't know how Margot thought cones and rope were going to keep the animals all in one place.

But so far, it was working. The sheep and Melchior had snuggled down on a bed of hay. And to my surprise, I saw Millie's two goats, Phillip and Peter, standing next to a donkey. It seemed that Margot had found a replacement donkey for the one who suddenly went into labor. She was resourceful, if nothing else.

If I were Margot, I would have thought twice before putting Melchior in the same place as Phillip and Peter. The goats had a reputation for trouble; perhaps not as large a reputation as Jethro, but close. In my opinion, she was tempting fate with those three.

Ansel Beachy stood in front of Margot, shaking his finger. Ansel was the owner and manager of Harvest Market. Ansel was a heavyset sixtyish man with a bald head except for the tufts of silver-and-white hair that jutted out from the sides of his head. His Amish beard was the same color and just as bristly as his hair.

"You can't do this," he said to Margot.

I hurried toward the factory, but I wasn't as quick as I should have been because he waved me over. "Bailey! Bailey!"

I sighed. I had a feeling this conversation would not go well for me at all. I was sorely tempted to put the hood up on my coat and make a dash into Swissmen Candyworks. Resigned, I walked over to the pair of them. From what I could tell, neither one of them was enjoying their conversation.

"Bailey," Ansel said as I stood in front of them. "Tell her that we can't have these smelly animals in our parking lot all day."

"Don't you think calling them smelly is a bit rude?" Margot folded her arms, and as she did the knit beret bounced on the top of her curls. As the beret just rested on her head, I didn't have the least idea how it was keeping her warm. "I thought you would behave better than that, Ansel."

"They are smelly! You have a camel. Ask anyone and they will tell you, camels smell."

Margot sniffed. "You're being ridiculous. We need a place for the animals to stay for the day. Bailey already said that it was all right."

They both looked at me expectantly.

I held up my hands as if in surrender. "I said that you all could gather here before the parade. I assumed it would an hour or two, not all day."

Margot folded her arms. "We can't have the animals at the manger scene before the parade starts. They need to march onto the square together. We can't move them from the stable while people are watching. It will take away the wow factor of the parade. It's meant to be a surprise."

"Everyone knows that camel is here. He's been on the square for days," Ansel said.

"You just don't understand the magic of a show," Margot said.

Ansel snorted.

"I know it's frustrating, Ansel, but it's only for one day. I'm sure Margot will have the parking lot cleaned up if they make any kind of mess." I gave Margot a look.

"I would be happy to," she said. I translated that to mean she would have Uriah clean it up.

Ansel shook his finger at Margot again. "You had

better or you're going to lose your discount at my store for being an active community member."

She narrowed her eyes. "You would never."

"Watch me."

It was my turn to step in again to keep the peace. I plastered a smile on my face. "I'm so glad the two of you are here. This is a good time to judge the gingerbread houses at my shop, don't you think?"

"Yes, let's get it over with," Margot said. "I have so much to do before the parade, it's best to cross that off the list."

Margot and Ansel followed me to the candy factory. I couldn't allow myself to be hurt by Margot's words. That was just the way she was.

Inside the factory, I removed my hat and coat as Charlotte approached us.

"Bailey, you're finally here," she said. "How did the conversation go with your parents?"

"It went okay. We won't be working with Hampton the wedding planner any longer."

Her green eyes went wide. "Wow. You told them that. I'm impressed." Charlotte was well aware of my rocky relationship with my parents. She went to take Ansel and Margot's coats.

"I'm ready to go," Margot said. "We have to wrap up this judging quickly. I have to make sure everything is in perfect order for tonight's parade." She nodded at Ansel. "I'm sure this is a busy season for the Market as well."

"It's a very busy season," he agreed.

I grabbed three clipboards from the counter that I'd

had Charlotte prepare. They each had a tally sheet to score the different gingerbread houses and a place for comments.

I handed them each a clipboard. "This is our inaugural year for this event, and we only have six houses to judge. They were all made by candymakers or candy sellers at Swissmen Candyworks. I hope in years to come we can open up this competition to the public. I've been walking by the gingerbread houses all week, and I think you will be surprised and pleased by the work that my staff has done."

Margot read over her clipboard and then looked up. "It says that the judging is blind, but you're a judge. Don't you know who made which house?"

I shook my head. "I have no idea. Maeva was very careful to keep me out of the lobby while the gingerbread houses were set up." I cleared my throat. "I think the judging should go quickly. Give each entry a one-to-five rating in each category. When you're done, just leave the clipboard with Maeva and she will tabulate the scores."

Margot reviewed the score sheet. "These questions are simple enough. I'm impressed. I might have to put you in charge of all the judging events in the village from here on out."

Please, no.

The houses ranged from a gingerbread cabin to a replica of the church on the square. The church was by far the largest gingerbread structure, and I wanted to give it the highest marks. Unfortunately, the steeple was crooked, so that cost the maker a point.

The gingerbread house I found most endearing and intricate was a farm that not only included the house but also an outhouse, a barn, and three Amish buggies complete with horses made of chocolate. The chocolate work was as good as any I had seen in New York City, and the gingerbread pieces were fused together with caramel and precisely cut. Every piece fit snuggly with the rest. The gingerbread farmhouse captured the essence of Amish Country. I gave it high marks.

Maeva stood next to me as I examined the house. "It's beautiful, isn't it?"

"I don't think I could have done it half as well."

"Wait until you hear who the candymaker is," she said.

When the judging was complete, Margot and Ansel impatiently tapped their feet as Maeva tabulated the scores. It only took her a few minutes, but the way the two of them were acting, you would have thought it was a week.

She came back with three ribbons. "We have a clear winner. In third place is the church by Ryan Coblentz." She handed me the ribbon, and I affixed it to Ryan's table. "In second place is the village gazebo by Bella Esher."

I put the second place ribbon on Bella's table.

Maeva took a deep breath. "And finally, the first place winner and the winner of the one thousand dollar prize. It's Lida Lantz for the Amish farmhouse scene!"

My jaw dropped when I heard Lida's name.

How could I have had no idea of Lida's talent? She'd

made no mention of it, but it was clear that she had an eye for design. If only she could come back and work for me, I could teach her how to make the most of her natural talent.

Ansel joined me in front of Lida's farmhouse. He tugged on his silver and white beard. "My word, that is impressive. I do love the church, but this one displays such wonderful craftsmanship. To be honest, I suspected that you were the one who made this."

"It wasn't me. Lida Lantz was the candy artist."

"Lida is a sweet girl," he said. "And apparently a talented one as well."

"Do you know her?"

"Some. Not well. She came to me in the fall and asked me to hire her brother, Zephaniah. I was sorry to say that I couldn't bring myself to do it. Zeph had a reputation for stealing, and I just couldn't have someone like that working in my store. It would unsettle my nerves. Beau said I did the right thing by not hiring him."

Did everyone in Harvest except me know that Zeph had a history of stealing? It seemed that was the case.

Aiden walked into the lobby, and my heart skipped a beat. He was in uniform, and his department-issued bomber jacket fit him perfectly. It wasn't often that he had time to stop in at the Candyworks just to say hello, and I was thrilled to see him. After my conversation with my parents, I was more excited than ever to marry him. Finally, the parental pressure from both my parents and his mom had lifted. We could do it our way.

I started toward him but pulled up short when I saw the serious look on his face. Just then, Deputy Little and another deputy came into the lobby as well.

"Is everything okay?" I asked.

"We found the car that we believe hit you."

I blinked. "Where?"

"A couple of miles from here abandoned on a country road." He lowered his voice. "It's registered to Ansel Beachy."

CHAPTER THIRTY-SEVEN

I blinked at him. "What? That can't be right. Ansel is Amish. He can't have a car. I know that my grandmother's district is more lenient, but Bishop Yoder isn't that lenient."

Margot marched over to us. "Sheriff Brody, I'm glad you're here. I expect that you will have several of your deputies on the square this evening for the parade. It's going to be the biggest one ever, and we need crowd control."

"Deputy Little and Deputy Conner will both be there."

"And what about yourself?" she asked and glanced at me. "I'm sure your fiancée would love to enjoy the parade with you."

Margot was as meddling as my parents.

"It depends on a few things. I would like to watch the parade with Bailey, too, but duty calls."

Margot sniffed. "It seems that is always the case for you two." Her eyes wandered to the two deputies behind Aiden. "What's going on here? Is this some kind of takedown?"

"No," Aiden said. "We would just like to talk to Ansel."

Margot's mouth formed a silent "O."

Ansel walked over to us. "Did I hear my name?"

"Ansel Beachy, can I talk to you?" Aiden asked.

"What's this about?"

"Let's go outside," Aiden said.

"It's cold outside, and I have no interest in freezing my ears off. You can talk to me here or at the Market." He held his coat in his arms and began to put it on.

"Very well. Are you the owner of a 1998 Toyota Camry?"

Ansel blinked at Aiden. "I'm Amish."

"Just answer the question, please."

Sweat gathered on Ansel's upper lip. "How do you know this? It's not an *Englisch* crime to own a car. I don't drive it. It's—it's just a memento of my youth. I should have gotten rid of it years ago, but I couldn't bring myself to do it. I've had the car since I was on *rumspringa*." His face flushed with embarrassment. "I have never driven it since I was baptized. I kept it in the garage behind the Market for years. I know that I shouldn't have it and Bishop Yoder would be so disappointed in me if he knew." He licked his lips. "I just can't bring myself to get rid of it, and it's so old, I can't imagine any *Englischer* wanting it. It's not hurting anything in the garage."

He said all of this as if he was trying to talk himself into believing every word he said, but I heard the doubt there. I wondered how many years Ansel had carried the guilt of owning a car.

"How did you find out?" Ansel asked.

"The car turned up on County Road seven. It was parked on the side of the road in some brush."

Ansel gasped. "Someone stole it."

"If you didn't put it there, that would be my guess," Aiden said.

"Who would do that?" Ansel asked.

"We were hoping that you would have some ideas," Aiden said.

"I have no idea. I haven't been in the garage in ages. It may have been missing for a while."

"Who knows the car is there? Does your wife know?" Aiden asked.

Ansel's face flushed red. "I would never tell my wife about the car. She wouldn't like it at all."

"What about your staff?" Aiden asked.

"Some of my staff knows," he said. "The younger men like to go and tinker with it from time to time. I let them because I don't use it."

"Tinker with it how?"

He swallowed. "It hadn't run in years and years, and he got it running."

"Who is he?" Aiden asked.

"Beau Eicher. He's very good with mechanical things. I'm surprised that he stays Amish. With his love of mechanics, I would have thought that he would lose the faith by now, but love will do that to you."

"Love? Love of what?" I asked.

Aiden glanced at me as if he wished that I hadn't

joined the conversation, but I had to know what Ansel was getting at.

"He is in love with Lida Lantz. Everyone in the community knows that. It's no secret."

It was a secret to me. I'd had no idea. Lida was Zeph's sister, and Beau had been his best friend. I wasn't sure what all that meant, but there was something there.

"Is Beau working today?" Aiden asked. "He might have been the last person to see the car before it was taken from the garage."

"*Ya*, he is at the Market."

Aiden nodded at his deputies. "We need to talk to him."

Ansel, Aiden, and the deputies left the candy factory.

Margot put her hands on her hips. "I hope this doesn't put a damper on my parade, Bailey. If it does, I'm holding you accountable for it."

I ignored her and grabbed my coat from the coat closet near the entrance. I ran out the door and was in the parking lot just as the men entered the Market.

Across the parking lot, Uriah was doing his very best to keep Melchior and the other animals calm. Judging by the way the camel was shaking his head, it wasn't going well. I felt as tense as Melchior at the moment.

Aiden met me at the Market door as if he was expecting me to be there. "Beau isn't here."

"He left?" I asked.

Aiden nodded, and I followed him into the Market. A thin Amish teenager stood in front of the two deputies. His legs were shaking. I guessed this was the first time he had ever been questioned by the police. "Beau left when he saw the sheriff go into the candy factory. He was out gathering up shopping carts. He ran inside and said he had to go home. I asked him what I was supposed to say to Ansel, and he didn't answer me. He just ran out. He was scared."

Aiden looked at Ansel. "I'm going to need Beau's address."

Ansel nodded.

As much as I wanted to go to Beau's home with Aiden, I knew he would never allow that, and my time was better spent at the factory. We were closing early that afternoon, so the staff could attend the parade if they chose.

By three, the factory was all but empty. Maeva carried trays of fudge back to the refrigerators behind the lobby. She looked over her shoulder at me. "Our last tour just ended and no one else has come in for over an hour."

"Have you let Lida know that she won first place in the gingerbread house competition?"

"I told Sabrina to get the message to her. I guessed that you still wanted to give her the prize money, even if she doesn't work for us any longer."

I nodded. "I do. Can I ask you something?"

Maeva set the last tray on the counter. "Sure."

"Did you know that Beau Eicher is sweet on Lida?"

"Oh, sure, I think everyone in the factory knew that. He stopped by just about every day to see her."

"I didn't know. I thought he was here to see Zeph."

She nodded. "Zeph, too, but he blushes any time

Lida's name comes up. With his freckles, it was obvious."

"And how does Lida feel? Did you ask her?"

Maeva nodded. "I did once because she's so young. She's only sixteen. I know a lot of *Englischers* think that Amish kids all get married as teenagers, but that is rarely true anymore. I didn't want her to feel pressured."

"What did she say?"

"That she couldn't even think of being courted at the moment—she was too worried about everything going on at home."

"Like what?"

"Zeph. She was worried about him."

Knowing what had happened to her brother, she'd had reason to be worried.

CHAPTER THIRTY-EIGHT

Aiden called me just before closing to tell me that they hadn't found Beau Eicher yet. He hadn't gone home after he abruptly left work.

"I don't know what is going on with Beau," Aiden said. "We can't be sure that he's involved in this at all, but his behavior is suspicious. If you see him, call me. Also, I would prefer it if you weren't alone in the factory tonight."

"As soon as we close up, I will be heading to Swissmen Sweets. It's open during the parade. Charlotte, Emily, and Maami will need an extra set of hands. We always sell a lot of candies on parade night."

"Good. I love you, Bailey, and I don't want anything to happen to you."

"I love you, too," I said and ended the call.

The factory closed a little early that day, so that everyone could go to the parade if they wished. Maeva offered to stay with me to lock up, but I shooed her

away. I knew she had children at home who were eager
to get good seats at the parade.

Everything checked out at the factory.

I went out the front door and locked it behind me.

"Bailey! Thank heavens I caught you!" Juliet cried.

I nearly jumped out of my skin. I dropped the Candyworks keys and had to scoop them up from the front
walk.

Juliet ran from her car holding Jethro. I knew very
well where this conversation was headed.

"You have to take Jethro. The church ladies are serving refreshments for the people attending the parade
and I just can't have him underfoot."

I waved my hands back and forth in a "no" gesture.
"Juliet, I do love it that you trust me with Jethro so
much. I know how important he is to you, but I
couldn't possibly take him tonight. Swissmen Sweets
is open during the parade. We're going to be slammed."

"That's fine. You can take him to Swissmen Sweets
with you. Just put him upstairs in Clara's apartment
while you're selling candy. He can spend time with
Nutmeg. He will love it." She took a deep breath. "You
just need to be back here at five. He will be riding
Melchior in the parade. I got him a specially made saddle. Thank goodness we live in a county where there
are saddlemakers."

"He's riding the camel?"

I searched my memory of the story of the first
Christmas, and a camel-riding pig didn't come to mind.

"Yes! It will be such a showstopper. He and Melchior have become so close over the last few days. I
find it just adorable." She thrust Jethro into my arms.

It will stop something, I thought.

She ran back to her car. "Thank you!" she cried and drove away.

I looked down at Jethro. "Here we are again."

Across the parking lot, Melchior lifted his head as if he sensed his piggy friend was nearby. I noticed that shepherds and wise men were starting to show up to prepare for the parade. Would it be too bad if I handed Jethro off to them? I didn't know how to put a pig in a camel saddle. I guessed no one else in Harvest knew either.

I was just about to walk over to the parade staging area when I heard a squeak like that of a mouse caught in a trap.

I looked around and saw Lida standing at the opposite corner of the factory from the parade staging area.

"Lida?" I carried Jethro over to her. "Are you okay?"

Her face was snow-white. "I'm fine."

I had never seen anyone less fine in my life.

"What are you doing here? I thought your father said that you weren't allowed to come back."

She swallowed. "He did say that, but Sabrina told me that I won the gingerbread house contest and the money. Can I have it?"

"You want it right now?"

She nodded. "Please. It's very important that I get it today."

"I don't have a thousand dollars in cash," I said. "I can write you a check."

"I need cash. Can you get it?" she asked, looking around the parking lot.

"I need to get over to Swissmen Sweets to help out there. Can I get it to you first thing tomorrow?"

Tears slipped down her cheeks. "That will be too late."

I tucked Jethro under my left arm like a football and wrapped my right arm around her. "Here, let's go into the factory and talk. I'm sure we can get this straightened out."

"We can't. I ruined everything, and Zeph is dead because of it."

I froze. "It's your fault Zeph is dead?"

She nodded. "I pushed too hard."

The word "pushed" made me shiver, as it was likely that Zeph had been pushed off the factory roof. I couldn't keep myself from looking up at the roof where the red Candy Land game piece had once stood.

I took a step forward. "What do you mean?"

She stared at the ground. "Did you recognize my gingerbread house when you judged it?"

I blinked at her abrupt change of subject.

"It's an Amish farmhouse," I said.

"It's *my* Amish house. If you look inside, you will see that we are all there. I made gingerbread figures for all of us: my mother and father, my younger sisters, myself . . . and my two older brothers. We are where we should be. Together. That's all I was trying to do, bring us together. Instead, my foolishness tore us even further apart." Tears ran down her face. "I should have left it alone. I just wanted him to stop."

I took another step toward her. "Lida, what's going on? I want to help you. What did you want to stop?"

She swallowed. "I knew that Zeph was taking things. He always had. In the last few years, he had gotten better about it. He tried so hard to stop completely, but then Malachi said that he would come back home, and it changed everything."

"How did it change everything?"

"Malachi wanted to come back to the Amish way with funds to buy a farm of his own. To prove to our father that he could make something of himself. His business wasn't doing as well as he liked. He was barely making ends meet. He knew Zeph's weakness for taking things. He convinced my brother to steal for him so he would have enough money to come back. Zeph wanted our family together again as much as I did."

"So he agreed?"

She nodded. "But after a while he realized that there didn't seem to be any amount of money that was enough for Malachi. So he gave some of the money to Malachi and . . ."

"And the rest he gave away to those in need."

She nodded.

"I always thought my brother was weak and this is the proof of it," someone said by the dumpster.

Lida and I jumped when Malachi came out of the shadows.

Malachi glared at his sister. "Did you get the money?"

"I—*nee*, she doesn't have it. I can have it tomorrow," Lida said.

And now I knew why she wanted the money so badly. To give it to her brother.

Across the parking lot, the parade staging area was

getting more crowded by the second. Joseph and Mary
had arrived. Mary was helped onto the back of the donkey.

There was help just yards away. All Lida and I had
to do was walk over there and we would be safe.

I touched her arm. "Lida, come with me. We will
talk to your brother later. This isn't a good time. The
parade is about to start."

Malachi laughed. "You're going to go off with an
Englischer. I thought you didn't trust *Englischers*."

Lida straightened her spine. "I don't trust you! You
tricked Zeph. You used him. You knew that he had his
struggles and you used them against him. Then you
killed him for it. I'm ashamed to call you my brother."

Malachi laughed. "You think I killed Zeph? You think
I would kill him before getting the money? You think
I would kill him at all! That's the most ridiculous thing I
have ever heard."

"If you didn't, who did?"

"It wasn't me." Hampton Longly walked across the
parking lot. "But I would very much like my money
now," he said this with a gun in his hand.

It was truly time to get as far away from here as I
could, but I couldn't leave Lida with these two men.
One or both of them had likely killed her brother and
would not hesitate to kill her.

The high school marching band joined the parade
staging area and began to belt out a rendition of "The
Twelve Days of Christmas." I couldn't hear myself
think. No one would hear me call for help.

Over the noise, I shouted, "You two can argue over

who killed Zeph. Lida and I are leaving." I pulled Lida by the arm toward the parade.

"I don't think so," Hampton said as he pointed his gun at us. "You're not going anywhere."

"So you're going to kill three people? For what? Money?" I did my very best to control the shaking in my voice.

I had to get Jethro and Lida out of there. Safety was so close, but I didn't know that Hampton wouldn't fire at us as we ran away. And if he did, he could hit us or someone in the parade. I didn't know if he knew how to shoot. It would be a great risk to take.

Malachi laughed.

"I wouldn't laugh if I were you. I can kill you, too. I want the money you promised me. I gave you an advance so that you could fund your operation, and you said you would make it back tenfold. I've seen none of it. We had a deal."

"I had it until my brother double-crossed me," Malachi said.

"That's your problem, not mine. Maybe if you hadn't killed him, you could have got it."

"I didn't kill him," Malachi said. "I was never on that roof."

"I didn't kill him either," Hampton said. "Do you think I can climb on a roof? I'm a wedding planner and have been one for far too long. I'm tired of working for whining brides and their overbearing mothers. This business is going to send me to an early grave. That money was supposed to be my way out."

"That's your problem, not mine, and I don't have the money."

Slowly, while they argued, I slipped my cell phone from my pocket.

"Stop!" Hampton cried. "If you call for help, I will shoot the girl *and* the pig. I have nothing left to lose. Drop the phone."

I hesitated.

"Drop it." He pointed the gun at Lida.

I dropped the phone in the snow. As I did, I noticed movement behind the dumpster. Someone was there. Malachi and Hampton faced Lida and me, so they couldn't see him. I saw him clearly, and it was Beau Eicher. In the security lights, his freckles were even more pronounced.

"We can't stand here all night," Malachi said.

"What would you have me do?" Hampton asked.

"I have an idea," I said. "You, Malachi, and I can go into the factory, and I will give you what money I have there. At least then you would be leaving with something."

Hampton waved his gun at us. "All right. Let's all go."

I didn't move. "No, first you have to let Lida and Jethro go."

"Who's Jethro?" Malachi asked.

"It's the blasted pig," Hampton snapped. "I can't believe that ridiculous woman thought I would be willing to put a pig in a wedding. I'd be a laughingstock in the wedding planner community."

Jethro wiggled in my arms. I tried to hold on to him, but he fought me.

"Put the pig down," Hampton ordered.

"No, he could get lost."

"You want me to shoot him?" He pointed his gun at Jethro.

I set the pig on the ground. "Run, Jethro!"

His hooves scraped on the pavement, and Hampton let off a shot. No one heard it over the high school band playing "Jingle Bells."

The shot seemed to be the cue that Beau needed. He ran at Hampton and jumped onto his back. Hampton's gun flew out of his hand, but before I could reach it, Malachi picked it up and pointed it at me.

I pushed Lida. "Run to the parade."

She didn't move.

I was about to push her again when Malachi said. "Stop pushing my sister or I will be forced to shoot you."

I glanced over my shoulder and saw Jethro lying on the pavement. I felt all the blood drain from my face. He'd been shot? This couldn't be real.

"Get off me," Hampton said and pushed Beau away.

Malachi waved the gun at them both. "Now I'm in charge. Get up, both of you."

They stumbled to their feet.

"Beau, why don't you tell them the truth?" Malachi asked. "Who killed Zeph?"

"I did," Beau said.

Tears came to Lida's eyes and she shook her head. "*Nee, nee,* it can't be true."

Beau's Adam's apple bobbed up and down. "He asked me to help him get the game piece off the roof, and while we were up there, I took the chance to talk to him. I told him that he had to quit his stealing because he was hurting you. He said that he couldn't quit. I told him he was selfish. He said he was trying to save his family, and I told him that he was destroying it. He was so angry with me that he jumped me. We got in a fight. Somehow—" He swallowed. "Somehow, I got the upper hand and pushed him off me. He fell off the roof. He was already dead when I climbed down the ladder. I didn't know what to do, but I knew I would be in trouble. I tried to cover up our boot prints on the roof, and I—I just went back to work."

Lida was bawling now.

"There, there, Sister, now you know the truth." Malachi pointed the gun at me. "About that money in the factory. Let's go collect it now."

Behind us, there was a scream. "The camel is loose!"

Melchior tore through the marching band, and teenagers ran in all directions. He galloped to Jethro's lifeless form on the icy pavement. Melchior touched his nose to the pig's cheek. When Jethro didn't move, the camel gave an earsplitting cry and ducked his head. He charged at us.

Hampton screamed and jumped into a snowbank. Beau grabbed Lida and pulled her out of the way. Malachi threw his gun in the air and ran. Melchior took that as an invitation to chase the man. They ran around the back of the factory, and Malachi screamed.

Shepherds and wise men ran over to help. Deputy Little was among them, and he found the gun.

I ignored all of them and ran over to Jethro on the pavement. Tears ran down my cheeks as I knelt beside him. "Jethro. I'm so sorry. I'm so sorry. I really love you. Don't be dead. Please."

He lifted his head and wiggled his snout.

I blinked away tears. "You're not dead?" I ran my hands over his little body. There was no gunshot wound. There was no wound at all. "You're not dead? You pretended to be dead? What are you, an opossum?"

He licked the tip of my nose, and I swore I would never complain about pigsitting again.

EPILOGUE

Three days after Christmas, Aiden and I stood outside Swissmen Candyworks saying goodbye to my parents. I was almost sorry to see them go. Almost.

My mother sighed. "I am so disappointed at what happened with Hampton. Who would have guessed that he was a criminal all this time? I never would have imagined he would be involved in a robbery-and-fencing operation. I can see why you have such an aversion to wedding planners, Bailey. I trust you to plan this wedding on your own now." She looked at Aiden. "I'm expecting you to keep her on track."

Aiden held up his hands. "I will do my best."

"I promise that I will have the wedding well in hand by February," I said. "January is a slow month for candy. Charlotte and I will get it handled. I'll send you all the details."

She squinted at me. "You'd better, or I will be shipping in a wedding planner from New York this time."

I shivered, knowing that wasn't an idle threat.

Dad shook Aiden's hand. "It was good to finally spend some time with you, young man. I'll be very proud to call you my son-in-law."

"Thank you, sir." Aiden smiled.

Mom and Dad said their final goodbyes and drove away.

Aiden wrapped his arm around my shoulders, and I smiled up at him. "I was really against the wedding planner idea from the start," I said.

"Well, having the man arrested for armed assault is one way to get rid of him."

"How is Hampton?" I asked.

Aiden shrugged. "Lawyered up. He was released on bond yesterday. Malachi, unfortunately, doesn't have those kinds of resources. He'll be going to jail for his part in the robberies."

I nodded. "And Beau?"

Aiden sighed and dropped his arms to his sides. "It's tough. There is no way to prove that he pushed Zeph off the roof in self-defense. I tend to believe him, but I can't know. I think the DA is going to lower the charge to involuntary manslaughter. He's seventeen and still a minor. At the same time, he can't get off scot-free. He confessed to being the one who put the game piece in your car and ramming the back of your car with Ansel's Camry."

"He was trying to scare me off the case," I said. "I think he was trying to protect me from Malachi and Hampton in his way."

"Yes, but he also could have just come forward and told the truth."

Aiden had a point.

He nodded over his shoulder. "You have a visitor."

I turned to see Lida Lantz standing at the corner of the factory, as if she was trying to decide whether or not to approach.

"Do you mind waiting here?" I asked.

Aiden shook his head, and I walked over to Lida.

She shivered.

"Hi Lida. I have your prize money inside. I would love to give it to you."

She shook her head. "I'd rather you give it to the people my brothers stole from. I know it barely covers their losses, but it would make me feel better."

Seeing her mind was made up, I nodded. "All right. I can do that. I'm sure Aiden knows where it should go. Can I ask you a question?"

She nodded.

"Were you in the cheese shop the night it was robbed?"

She swallowed and nodded. "*Ya.* I knew that Malachi was desperate to make some money after Zeph died, and they had planned to steal from the cheese shop that night. I went there to stop him. I wasn't successful. He was already gone when I got there."

I nodded. It was the last piece of the puzzle. Now it all made sense.

"Is there anything you want to ask me?" I asked.

She shifted back and forth on her feet. "I was wondering if I could have my old job back. My *daed* knows you were trying to help Zeph. He said I can work for you, and I really like it here."

"You can't have your old job back," I said.

"Oh." She hung her head. "I understand."

"You can't have your job as a candy packer back because I'm promoting you to the head of displays in the factory and chocolatier apprentice."

She stared at me. "You are?"

I nodded. "I hope you will take the post. The gingerbread house you made was a true piece of art. You have a talent for candymaking, and I want to teach you what I know."

Tears gathered in her eyes. "I will." She hugged me. "I have to tell my family." She ran off.

Aiden strolled over to me. "Christmas is over. I guess the wedding is up next," he said, grinning. "I mean, I promised your mom that I would keep you on task."

I rubbed the back of my neck. "Can I have one day to catch my breath?"

He squeezed my hand. "We could always elope."

I smiled up at him. "Don't tempt me like that, Sheriff. Don't you dare tempt me."

Maami's Gingerbread Fudge

Ingredients
- 1 cup sweetened condensed milk
- ¾ cup brown sugar
- ¼ cup molasses
- ¼ cup salted butter
- 2 cups white chocolate chips
- 1 teaspoon ground ginger
- ¼ teaspoon ground nutmeg
- ½ teaspoon cinnamon
- ¼ teaspoon ground cloves

Directions
1. Line an 8 x 8-inch square pan with parchment paper.
2. Add condensed milk, brown sugar, butter, and molasses to a saucepan over medium heat. Stir until combined and sugar dissolves.
3. Continue stirring until mixture thickens. Remove from heat and add white chocolate, ginger, nutmeg, cinnamon, and cloves.
4. Stir until mixture is smooth.
5. Pour liquid fudge into prepared square pan.
6. Refrigerate for at least six hours or overnight.
7. Remove from pan and cut into squares.
8. Enjoy!

Keep reading for a special excerpt of a new historical mystery series from Agatha Award–winning author Amanda Flower!

TO SLIP THE BONDS OF EARTH

A Katharine Wright Mystery by Amanda Flower

While not as famous as her older siblings Wilbur and Orville, the celebrated inventors of flight, Katharine Wright is equally inventive—especially when it comes to solving crimes—in *USA Today*–best-selling author Amanda Flower's radiant new historical mystery series inspired by the real sister of the Wright Brothers.

December 1903: While Wilbur and Orville Wright's flying machine is quite literally taking off in Kitty Hawk, North Carolina, with its historic fifty-seven-second flight, their sister, Katharine, is back home in Dayton, Ohio, running the bicycle shop, teaching Latin, and looking after the family. A Latin teacher and suffragette, Katharine is fiercely independent, intellectual, and the only Wright sibling to finish college. But at twenty-nine, she's frustrated by the gender inequality in academia and is looking for a new challenge. She never suspects it will be sleuthing . . .

Returning home to Dayton, Wilbur and Orville accept an invitation to a friend's party. Nervous about leaving their as-yet-unpatented flyer plans unattended, Wilbur decides to bring them to the festivities . . . where they are stolen right out from under his nose. As always, it's Katharine's job to problem-solve—and in this case, crime-solve.

As she sets out to uncover the thief among their circle of friends, Katharine soon gets more than she bargained for: She finds her number one suspect dead with a letter opener lodged in his chest. It seems the patent is the least of her brothers' worries. They have a far more earthbound concern—prison. Now Katharine will have to keep her feet on the ground and put all her skills to work to make sure Wilbur and Orville are free to fly another day.

CHAPTER ONE

How dare Bufford Lyons make such a fool of me at the teachers' meeting this afternoon? As we were coming to the end of the fall semester, I had made a formal request to teach Greek III in the spring. The language was one of my first loves and the reason I took my teaching position, but ever since I had begun teaching at Steele High School, I had been regulated to the introductory classes in languages. First-year Latin was a painful course to teach. Most of the students didn't want to be there and had no interest in learning any language, especially not a dead one.

I had thought with so many years teaching under my belt and the upcoming retirement of Mr. Wellings, the current Greek III teacher, I would be allowed to take on a more demanding course.

"We can't have a woman teaching upperclassmen," Bufford had said when I'd made the formal request in front of the faculty assembly. "The young men in these courses are far too close to Miss Wright's age. They won't take a young woman seriously, and they need to concentrate on their lessons, as our students of Greek are the most likely to go on to college. Steele High School has a reputation to uphold."

I stood up. "I studied Greek at Oberlin College and graduated with top honors in the course. I am more than cap—"

"You are still a *woman*." He said the word as if it was some sort of slur.

I put my hands on my hips. "Should I be pointing out the obvious, that you are an old man?"

The principal, Mr. Mellon, took his mallet and banged the table in front of him. "Miss Wright, please calm yourself."

I balled my hands at my sides. Why was I asked to calm myself, but Bufford wasn't? I knew why—because, as Bufford had pointed out, I was a woman. That was reason enough for them to reprimand me, and that truth set my teeth on edge.

"I do understand your educational background," Mr. Mellon went on. "But the school board has already decided it would be best if the upperclassmen were taught by Mr. Lyons."

Bufford sat back down in his chair with a smug look on his face.

"What?" I asked. "He doesn't know half the Greek I do."

Mr. Mellon held his gavel in his hand, as if he was contemplating rapping it on the table again. "A veteran teacher is best for the course. You are still early in your career."

"You mean a veteran *male* teacher," I corrected.

"Miss Wright," the elderly principal said, "the matter is settled. Now we must move on to other topics of concern."

"Yes, Miss Wright," Bufford said. "You should stick to selling Christmas trees. That's more appropriate for a female teacher." He smiled at me, and his gray mustache twitched, as if he was holding in a laugh.

"Excuse me for caring about the students and wanting them to have access to an arts program while in high school. I am willing to make that extra effort for my students rather than sitting on my laurels and accepting positions I'm unqualified for simply because I am the oldest man in the room."

"Miss Wright," Mr. Mellon exclaimed in shock.

The smile had faded from Bufford's face. I had successfully hit my mark. He'd made me look like a fool, but he was the fool. He couldn't even conjugate in pig Latin.

At the end of the meeting, I stormed from the room. Typically, after school I went home, like the dutiful and obedient daughter and sister I was, but on that day, I was just too spitting mad to face the demands of my family.

It was a crisp December day, and a walk into town was just what I needed. Fresh snow dusted the lampposts and street signs, but it was not yet thick enough to stick to the ground. The shop windows were all done up for Christmas with evergreens, red ribbons, and toy trains.

I let out a sigh. I should be concentrating on my holiday shopping instead of what Bufford Lyons had said. His comment about the school fundraiser steamed me the most. I'd been working for weeks to make sure the Christmas tree sale and carol singing went off without a hitch, and it was set for the holiday break. All the proceeds would be going to the music department.

Even though music wasn't my specialty, I loved listening to it and knew it was an important part of a public education. I was working with the Parent-Teacher Association and association president Lenora Shaw to organize the fundraiser. The PTA was in its infancy, but I recognized what a vital partner it could be in achieving our fundraising goals. When I'd told Principal Mellon of my enthusiasm, he'd appointed me as the teacher liaison. It wasn't until later that I learned he'd chosen me because I was a woman, not because of my support of the group.

Bufford, Principal Mellon, and all the men in that building were the same. They believed I should be grateful I was allowed to be in the same room with them, and completely ignored the fact I had more common sense in my left pinkie than all of them combined.

I had to put the incident at school behind me, if only for a little while. Winter recess would be here soon, and I needed the break as much as my students did. This afternoon I hoped to visit the bookshop and find something new to read to take my mind off the ridiculous school rules I had to abide by as a female teacher. I might find a gift for my father and brothers as well.

A gentleman I recognized from town but could not name tipped his hat to me.

"Good afternoon, Miss Wright. We heard your brothers are at it again. What are they thinking? That they can fly like a bird? It goes against nature. If God wanted us to fly, he would have given us wings."

"Are you suggesting humans should not swim, because we do not have fins?"

He blinked at me, as if my retort was some sort of riddle he couldn't make heads or tails of. "I beg your pardon?"

I adjusted my spectacles on my nose. "If anyone can achieve flight in our lifetime, it will be my brothers Wilbur and Orville Wright."

"Two boys from Dayton?" he snorted. "That is as likely as Old Saint Nick walking down the street."

I lifted my chin. "Well, I suggest you make up for being on his naughty list, because I heard he is out on a stroll, checking off names." With that, I marched away.

I left him there and headed into the bookshop and browsed for a long while. There was nothing like books to put my mind at ease.

"Katie, I didn't see you there," a kind voice said. "You were so hunched over that book. What is it?"

I held up the tome in my hands to show my old school friend Agnes Osborne. "A history of Rome."

Agnes snorted. "I should have known you would be engrossed in something of that sort."

I smiled. "My interests have not changed, Ag."

"You're nothing if not consistent." She tugged on a lock of hair that had fallen from its hairpin. "Have you heard from your brothers? I would be interested to know how they are getting on in North Carolina."

"They write, of course, though not as often as I would like," I replied. "They write more often to Father than they do to me, but they seem to be getting on fine. They said they are very close to heavier-than-air powered flight."

She cocked her head. "Haven't they said that before?"

"A time or two," I admitted.

"Why aren't they happy with the bicycle shop? Why isn't that enough for them? Would they not be happier to settle down and marry? Don't they want children?"

I shook my head and said nothing. These were questions I received often in regard to my brothers, and I had tired of answering them after so many years. I was grateful when Agnes changed the subject.

"Will you be at the Shaws' party this Saturday?" she asked with sparkling blue eyes.

"I plan to go as long as Father doesn't need me. Lenora Shaw is hosting and inviting everyone on the Steele PTA."

"I heard of lot of young men will be coming home to see their families for Christmas and they'll be at the party. You know the Shaws' party is the real start of the holiday season in Dayton. This will be the first time I have had an opportunity to go."

"The presence of young men is of no concern to me. I'm far too busy with my teaching, caring for Father, and minding my brothers' bicycle shop to have time for such things."

She clicked her tongue. "You need to have a life of your own. You are too wrapped up in others' lives. Haven't you ever cared for a man who wasn't a family member? Have you thought about being in love?"

My friend gave a little swoon at the very idea, but

Agnes Osborne had been dreaming of love since we were in pigtails. I knew this because I had heard about it ad nauseum for the past twenty years.

I pressed my lips together. When I was in college, I had briefly been engaged. My family never knew about it, and I didn't love the man. It just seemed getting engaged was what senior men did, and as a sophomore, I'd gone along with the proposal. Thankfully, both of us had realized our foolishness before it was too late or before I made the mistake of telling Father or my brothers. They would never have forgiven me had I married. However, there had been another man, whom I'd cared for deeply. Unfortunately, he was now married to someone else.

I said none of this to Ag and was thankful she'd never visited me at Oberlin College, where I had attended school, so she knew nothing of either man. No one in Dayton knew of them. I looked at the small watch pin attached to the lapel of my coat. "I should be heading home. Father will be wondering where I have been so long."

"I hope I didn't upset you, Katie," Agnes said with a frown. "That wasn't my intention."

"I know." I smiled at her. "But I would appreciate it if you would not bring the idea of romance up again."

She didn't give me an answer one way or another as we said our goodbyes.

Taking the Roman history I had purchased at the shop, I made my way home to number 7 Hawthorn Street. The white house with green shutters came into view. I noted that some of the greenery and red bows I had wrapped around the posts on the wide front porch had come loose. I would need to fix those before I entered the house. Ever since my mother had died when I was fifteen, I had been determined to keep a nice home for my father and brothers. That went for both the inside and the outside. Everything had to be just so.

I stepped onto the wide porch and set my satchel on the white rocker, but before I could even pick up the first bow, the front door flew open.

"Miss Wright, you're home!" exclaimed Carrie Kayler, our seventeen-year-old maid. She wore her dark hair in a bun at the back of her head, and her attire consisted of a simple gray dress with a white apron. Her hazel eyes were the size of dinner plates.

"Carrie, what is wrong? Is Father all right?" Fear clawed at my chest. Had my father fallen ill?

"I'm fine," my father said in his booming bishop's voice. He stood in the foyer, holding a telegram. He kept looking down at it.

A new fear overtook me. Had something happened to my brothers? "Are the boys all right?"

He handed the Western Union telegram to me. What I read took my breath away.

SUCCESS FOUR FLIGHTS THURSDAY MORNING ALL AGAINST TWENTY ONE MILE WIND STARTED FROM LEVEL WITH ENGINE POWER ALONE AVERAGE SPEED THROUGH AIR THIRTY ONE MILES LONGEST 57 SECONDS INFORM PRESS HOME CHRISTMAS. OREVELLE WRIGHT.

The paper fell from my hands. It seemed that everything in the world was about to change.

CHAPTER TWO

I stood on the front porch and stared at the telegram. I read it again. This time much more slowly. Then I held it in the air and cried, "They did it!"

I had known from the start that Wilbur and Orville would fly, and now I had the proof in my hands.

"Katharine," Father said. "Don't make such a spectacle of yourself."

As the bishop of the Church of the United Brethren in Christ, Old Constitution, my father was very much of the belief that our family must set an example. We did everything correctly and properly. Loud outbursts of delight were not condoned, but that didn't stop me in the least.

"This is the most wonderful news, and most welcome after such a dreadful day."

"Dreadful day? What has happened, daughter?" Father asked.

"It doesn't matter now. We have to celebrate. Does Lorin know?"

Lorin was one of my older brothers. He lived with his wife and children just a few blocks away.

The bishop shook his head. "You are the first person I have told."

"Rightly so," I said with all the confidence in the world. I should be the second to know after Father. Orville, Wilbur, and I were exceptionally close as siblings. Lorin, who was older, stood outside our triumvirate, and our eldest brother, Reuchlin, lived in Missouri, too far away to be part of our inner circle. "I'll go to Lorin now. Orville instructed us to tell the press. Lorin would be the best one to do that."

"It's growing late," the bishop said. "We can tell him in the morning. He will be tired after work and sitting down with his family for dinner."

I wrinkled my forehead. "You expect me to keep this bottled up all night? My head might burst if I do so."

Father shook his head. "Katie, you are too emotional at times. Everything doesn't have to be addressed the moment you learn of it. Let the reality settle before you act."

"Lorin deserves to know right away. Think of how he would feel if news of this got out before we told him. He would be beside himself."

My father shook his head. "I see your mind is made up and there is nothing that I can say to change it. Go take the telegram to Lorin, but be careful with it. I don't want it to get lost. Wilbur and Orville have solved the problem of human flight. I wish to keep this telegram as a memento."

With that pronouncement, Father went back into the house.

I turned to Carrie. "Hold off on dinner until I come back. If Father complains, give him a little something to tide him over until I return. Today is a day of celebration!"

Carrie rubbed her arms, as if to fight off the cold. "Now that the boys have conquered flight, I wonder if this will be the end of their tinkering. We have spent too many days tripping over bits of their flying machines scattered about the house."

"It won't be the end. It's just the beginning." I folded the telegram and tucked it into my coat pocket. I secured the button on the pocket to make sure it didn't fall out. I knew very well how valuable this piece of paper was. It was proof of a new era.

Lorin, his wife, Nette, and their four children would be as excited to hear the news as I was. I was sure of it. As I hurried down Hawthorn Street, I bumped into Herman Wheeler at the corner. Herman was an old classmate of Wilbur and Orville's. If I remembered correctly, he was now working for the Shaw family at their paper mill. Paper was a big business in Dayton, as five rivers converged in the city. The rivers provided plenty of power for the mills to make paper. At one time, Wilbur and Orville had run their own printing press and published a newspaper too. They still did some printing for faithful clients and for themselves, but when their cycle shop took off with the new bicycle craze, they'd reduced the printing business in size and volume.

Now they had moved on from bicycles to flying machines. My brothers never did anything by halves. If they chose to start a business, they did so with their full hearts and souls and did not stop until they accomplished their goals.

I didn't know where Herman lived, but I knew he wasn't a neighbor, and the Shaws weren't nearby either. The family lived on a grand estate in a much more affluent part of Dayton. I could see no reason at all for Herman to be on the corner of West Fourth and Hawthorn, but there he was.

"Miss Wright," Herman said formally, with the slightest bow. "I'm so sorry. I just about knocked you over."

That was a bit of an exaggeration, but I didn't correct him. I wasn't a delicate flower by any stretch. My father liked to say I wasn't too big or too small. I wasn't too pretty or too plain either. I was in the middle in every way. When I was younger, there had been times when I'd lamented—if only to myself—my unremarkable appearance, but now, as an adult, I found it served me well. Those who had been lulled by the relative dullness of my looks had been disarmed by the sharpness of my wit.

Herman was just an inch or two taller than I and painfully thin. If the December wind gusts picked up, there was a very good chance he'd blow over just like the first test glider my brothers had built for Kitty Hawk.

"It's quite all right," I said after a beat.

"You seem to be in a great rush. May I ask where you are off to in such a hurry?" He smiled at me, and I noticed for the first time how his two front teeth overlapped each other. It was a defect that would not be seen from afar, but close up, I found myself staring at it.

I took two large steps back. "This is my street, which is reason enough for me to be walking on it at any pace I should like," I said rather sharply. "I have every reason to be here. It's a crisp evening, and the cold air is refreshing. It would make much more sense for me to ask you what *you* are doing here, as you don't live in this neighborhood."

He forced a laugh. "I forgot how direct you can be. I suppose that comes from living in a house full of men. If your mother had lived long enough to teach you how to behave as a proper lady, you would not be at such a great disadvantage in life."

I balled my hands at my sides. *Disadvantage?* The nerve of this man! I had no disadvantages in life at all. This Neanderthal knew nothing about my mother. She was the one who'd taught Wilbur and Orville to build with their hands. It wasn't our father, who had been too preoccupied with sermons and church politics. And it was she who had taught me to stand on my own two feet. That was a much more valuable lesson than the feminine teachings that Herman thought I lacked by losing my mother so young.

"Perhaps you are in a hurry because of your brothers' success." He smiled.

"What do you mean?" I asked

"Is it not true that Wilbur and Orville flew?"

I stared at him. How did he know this when I had just heard of it?

"I would love to hear more about their flight if you

have the time. As their sister, I am certain you are privy to many details. I have a great interest in it."

"I do not have the time. If you will excuse me," I said in a clipped tone, "I would like to continue on with my walk alone."

I brushed by him and didn't realize until I was stomping my way down Lorin's street that he never had told me what he was doing in my neighborhood that night. It would be many days before I learned the truth.